In the split-second duration of the demi-dream—it was actually an image more than a dream—the dead man's hand shot up and pointed skyward. At the same time, the man's eyes opened to reveal something horrific and unearthly: solid yellow eyeballs. There were no pupils, as if the eyes had been turned straight around, or as if this creature was not an earthly thing at all. And the corpse's dead lips tightened into a ghastly smile.

Alicia felt her legs move in fright during this half-sleep. Her arms thrashed and her eyes opened.

A few minutes later she was asleep. She slept peacefully for several hours. Outside her window, far above her, the amiable little cloud that had obscured the moon had turned into something much darker. And the moonlight—which was nothing more than the reflection of the sun, after all—was in eclipse to something that most human beings would have found unimaginable.

A. A. McFedries

THE KING
OF THE
SUN

BANTAM BOOKS

New York Toronto London Sydney Auckland

THE KING OF THE SUN

A Bantam Spectra Book / February 2001

ISBN 0-553-58147-3

Published simultaneously in the United States and Canada

Bantam Books are published by Bantam Books, a division of Random House, Inc. Its trademark, consisting of the words "Bantam
Books" and the portrayal of a rooster, is Registered in U.S. Patent
and Trademark Office and in other countries. Marca Registrada.
Bantam Books, 1540 Broadway, New York, New York 10036.

PRINTED IN THE UNITED STATES OF AMERICA

OPM   10   9   8   7   6   5   4   3   2   1

To Patricia,
my favorite traveler
through time and space,
with infinite love

Now I am ready to tell how bodies are
    changed
Into different bodies.

—Ovid, *Metamorphoses*
    translated by Ted Hughes

CHAPTER 1

Detective Sergeant Alicia Aldrich, one month into her new assignment in the homicide division of the California Highway Patrol, was spending a late Sunday afternoon in May with her sister's family when the beeper on her belt intruded. Janet, Alicia's niece, was turning nine and the family was in the midst of a birthday party. An urgent alert to call in to the dispatcher at the San Bernardino County State Police headquarters was not what Alicia needed.

Alicia's gaze shifted from Janet's happy expression to the face of her sister, Linda, and that of Linda's husband, James. Linda was two years her junior and the closest person in the world to her. Alicia's hand slipped to the beeper at her belt and silenced it.

She had wanted her current job—sought it out, in fact. But whatever the message was today, she wished it would go away. She and Linda had worked hard to prepare for this day. The national crime statistics be damned, Alicia mused: she was as busy as any woman in law enforcement had any right to be.

Homeboy gang wars, crazies in the Mojave Desert, head-banging lunatics who lived up in the San Gabriel Mountains, organized crime hits, jilted ex-spouses insane with jealousy, and latter-day acid heads possessed by chemicals. There was no end to the inspiration for carnage.

Alicia's mind drifted from the party and the anxious faces of four little girls: her niece and three of her girl-friends. Several minutes passed and the party continued. Then the beeper chirped again. Exasperated, conceding defeat, Alicia snarled at it.

Janet laughed. The other children watched in antici-pation.

Linda grimaced.

James rolled his eyes.

The roll had an I-told-you-so quality to it. James was a mid-level marketing manager for a Japanese car com-pany that had recently plunked down their national-sales headquarters in Orange County.

James didn't receive weekend work calls and he didn't understand why a woman—his wife's sister, in particu-lar—would want a job that included them, much less a job that included endless weekend tours and rotating round-the-clock shifts. James was a piggy on such issues. He didn't understand why a woman—again, Alicia in particular—would want to be a police officer, either.

"Sorry," Alicia finally said. "I need to use the phone."

"You know where it is. From the last time you were here," James said.

Linda shot her husband a glance.

"Who's calling you?" Janet asked.

"Someone at the police station," Alicia said. "They might have a problem."

" 'Might'?" James said.

"Might," Alicia said firmly, her irritation showing.

"Do they ever call you just to tell you that they don't

have a problem?" James said. He smiled mildly, proud of his wit.

"Shut up, Jim," Linda said.

"Don't tell me to shut up. It's my house," James answered.

The children smirked.

"Use the phone in the kitchen, Ali," Linda said.

"Does it mean a bad guy did something awful?" one of Janet's friends asked.

"Maybe," said Alicia, touching the girl's shoulder gently.

Alicia looked at the family gathered around her. "Hey, look," she suggested. "Let's cut the cake before I phone anyone. That way, if I have to leave . . ."

James picked up the cake knife. "Who wants to do the honors?" he asked. By asking, he was about to appoint himself.

"Aunt Alicia!" Janet blurted. "She knows all about knives!"

James's hand stopped on its way to the cake. He raised an eyebrow and handed the knife—stock first—to Alicia.

"Maybe Daddy wants to cut your cake," Linda said to her daughter.

"No, no. I insist," James said, forcing the cutlery on Alicia. "Alicia knows all about knives, right? So she can carve the cake."

With a final second of hesitation, Alicia accepted the utensil.

Her sister and brother-in-law had been right, of course. She *did* see more carving equipment in the course of an average day than most women. And usually it wasn't in a happy context. Truth was, when she normally encountered a knife in a domestic context, there were usually bloodstains on the floors and walls.

Alicia took the cake knife in her hand. She looked at her niece. The blade gleamed in the California sunshine streaming through the window. She saw blades this large more often at crime scenes and on coroners' reports: she had already been corrupted by her career so much that this was instinctively where her thoughts traveled.

Alicia flipped the knife gently in the air. It spun once and she deftly caught it by the handle. "So I get to cut?" Alicia asked.

Janet gave her a little shrug. "You *have* to!" she insisted. "A knife is dangerous, and you're the policeman in the house."

"Police*woman*," Alicia corrected. "Or 'police officer.'"

"*Detective!*" James said, his tone prickly.

"Even at her age, she knows you're more familiar with knives and various blades than the rest of us," her sister offered.

"That's right!" Janet said. She folded her arms insistently and smiled.

Linda started to laugh. She gave her sister a wink.

"Good logic," Alicia answered the little girl.

James looked bored.

His eyes drifted to the television in the next room—its sound turned down—that showed a squadron of stock cars racing around a dirt track. Alicia followed his eyes and was for a moment reminded of a similar track she once visited where a driver had murdered his girlfriend and stuffed her—minus her hands and head—into the trunk of just such a car.

Alicia remembered that the vehicle had a purple chassis and black doors—purple and black, the color of a bruise—and when she had pried open the trunk there was the stench of butchery and death.

Her mind flashed back to the present.

Happy birthday.

It disturbed her that her mind kept flashing forward and back so indiscriminately. Recently, with no control over where her thoughts would take her, her stream of consciousness had been misbehaving, leaping from one unpleasant thing to another, as if little frightening windows had been opening up then slamming shut in her head. It had grown much worse in the past few weeks. So far, she chalked it up to the pressures of her new job and the serious injury she had sustained about a year earlier on her previous tour.

She wished the flashes would stop. She didn't want the words "job-related psychological counseling" anywhere in her file.

"Okay," Alicia finally said. "Time to chop up Mr. Cake."

Janet laughed ghoulishly.

Chop him up. As soon as Alicia had made the remark, she regretted it. Over the course of her law-enforcement career, she had seen too many real chop-ups.

The blade of the cake knife was just starting to cut through the top layer of icing when the beeper interrupted again.

"Aaah," Alicia said. "Damn!"

She considered ignoring the message completely. But she relented. She cut the cake swiftly, served the entire table, and made some small talk. Then she repaired to the kitchen where, over the joyful din of the small party in the dining room, she called in to California Highway Patrol headquarters in San Bernardino.

"Alicia Aldrich," she mumbled into the handset. "You paged me?"

Her own words echoed in her ears. To herself, she sounded hesitant and rusty. What was going on here? Was she already burned out and expecting herself to fail? There was no response on the other end. So what was this?

She cleared her throat immediately and said her name more forcefully a second time. "Alicia here!" she snapped.

On the other end of the line, she heard the voice of a woman named Helen Warren. Helen was a freakishly tall pear-shaped woman with a wide face and dark narrow eyes. She was also the county 911 dispatcher.

Helen, all seventy-five inches of her, worked behind bulletproof glass in a small office on the outskirts of San Bernardino, often in an extra-large L.A. Kings hockey jersey—the old purple and gold one with DIONNE on the back—and a pair of pressed indigo blue jeans, a man's size with a very expansive waist. Like many of the truly unusual people in Southern California, she was a transplant from the East Coast, in her case Deer Lake, New Jersey.

This call was exactly what Alicia would have described in advance if someone had asked her today to specify exactly what she did not want. A dead body had been found out in the high desert between Lancaster and Palmdale. The discovery had been within the jurisdiction of Section Five. Alicia's department.

White male. Middle-aged. Dead as a broiled mackerel. Probably a casual dump job from the previous evening.

"So, I'm not on duty," Alicia said. "What about Bill Lattimer? He's catching today."

"He's working a fatal road-rage assault just off the 105 West," Helen said cheerfully. "Out near Santa Anita. Some guy leaving the racetrack flipped a finger to a carload of Cambodian gang members."

"Great. How about Jerry Myerson?"

"Assisting a local plainclothes team on a store robbery in Alhambra."

She sighed. "Mike Racineau?" she asked, citing the third and final other member of the department who might be called ahead of her on a homicide. "Or shouldn't I ask?"

"Can't find him."

"What do you mean, you 'can't find him'?"

"Can't find him," Helen repeated.

"He's supposed to have a beeper. I have a beeper, why doesn't Racineau?"

"Ask him when you see him. He also has a new girl-friend. Maybe he turned off his beeper."

Then why didn't I turn off mine? she wondered.

Wondered, but did not say.

Instead, a few profanities boiled up. But as she looked at her sister, her niece, and the other children, the words remained uncomfortably in her throat. She could let them rip in the car, she reasoned, as she turned and looked away from the birthday party.

"I'll be there shortly," she said into the phone. She put the handset down and turned back to Linda and her family. Their expressions had already fallen from the ceiling to the floor.

"Sorry," Alicia said. "Let's do presents. Then I need to go out for a few hours."

Silence. Then Janet spoke. "Do you have to?" she asked.

"I have to, honey," she answer. "Try to understand."

"That's four Sundays in a row," Janet said.

"There are a lot of bad guys out there," Alicia said. "I guess I have to catch one."

"Are you going to be on television?" Janet asked.

"I hope not. Time for presents," Alicia said. She picked up the one she had brought and handed it to her niece. Janet set it aside.

"If you have to go, will you stop back later, Aunt Alicia?" Janet asked. There was a wavering tremble to her lower lip.

"I promise," Alicia said. "Now, let's open your presents."

"I want to show you this," Janet said. She produced a box. It was long and black.

Linda smiled. "Janet's been bugging me for this for a year. She says she wants to take a better look at the sky."

Janet grinned.

"The sky?" Alicia asked.

"There are people up in the sky," Janet announced.

"Yeah. Right," her father intoned.

" 'People'?" Alicia asked. She smiled. She winked to Janet's mother. Meanwhile, Janet opened the box. She pulled out a long black telescope with aluminum trim.

"Janet's been having all these dreams about spacemen and space travel," Linda announced steadily. "Kings of this. Kings of that. So she wants a telescope to look for these people."

"That's not a bad thing," Alicia said. "Dreams. Imaginations." She paused. "Maybe you'll catch a glimpse of an angel sometime. Not a bad thing at all."

"It's a good thing," Janet said with emphasis.

Good. In a remote silvery corner of Alicia's mind, the word had a funny distant resonance. *A Good thing.*

"A God thing?" James muttered, making a joke of it.

"Aren't the two the same?" Linda shot back.

"Usually," James said. "Not always."

Meanwhile, Janet had extended the telescope for as far as it would stretch.

"Can we take a look?" Janet asked her aunt.

"At the sky? Now?"

"Yes."

"You won't see much in the daytime, honey," Alicia said. "You have to wait till nighttime."

The girl pouted.

"The sun is too bright. You can't see the stars yet," Alicia attempted.

"Then we'll look at the sun."

"Sweetie, it's much too bright," Alicia said. "It would

hurt your eyes. You never look directly at the sun. Bad things can happen from that."

Janet paused. "Then let's just look at the sky," she insisted.

Alicia shrugged. She let Janet lead her outside with the telescope. The afternoon was fading into evening, yet the sky remained bright, particularly along the horizon where the sun was sitting.

Janet scanned the sky with the telescope. The girl smiled.

"See anyone?" Alicia asked. She placed a hand on her niece's shoulder.

"Not yet."

"Let me look. Maybe I'll find someone," Alicia said.

Janet handed the telescope to her aunt. Alicia squinted one eye shut, then peered through the lens with the other.

The sky brightened where she scanned. Her line of vision neared the sun as she swept the horizon.

Then suddenly there was a flash in the sky. There was something out there so stunningly bright that it made Alicia's eye blink shut and stay shut. Her head snapped back and her brain throbbed.

It was like being punched. Or poked in the eye.

She had seen a brilliant yellow flash. A minisun. A brilliant yellow glowing disc embedded in her brain. Almost a strobe-light effect from a hole in the sky.

"Wow," she said.

"Auntie . . . ?" Janet asked.

Alicia still reeled. Her eyes blinked but couldn't remain open. They hurt too badly.

She settled onto the ground.

"Auntie . . . Auntie . . . Auntie . . . ?"

The girlish, childish voice persisted. "What was it?" Janet asked. "What happened?"

Alicia braced herself, a bare knee on the grass. "Something in the sky," she said. "I don't know what it was. I don't know what I saw."

But she knew how bright it had been. And it had jangled something very deep in her brain. As Alicia blinked and took her niece's hand, she knew something strange had happened. Something that defied reasonable explanation.

Her eyes returned to normal, little blue dots dancing everywhere, bizarre visions in her mind. A nearly comprehensible vision of a humanlike form stepping out of sunlight.

Maybe. She wasn't sure.

"Auntie . . . ?"

"I'm all right," Alicia said softly. "I don't know what happened, but I'm all right."

Janet stared at her questioningly.

"Hey. Got to get moving," Alicia said. "Work to do. Bad guys to catch."

The little girl forced a smile, then spoke.

"See? There are people out there," she said softly.

Alicia pretended she hadn't heard.

Fifteen minutes later, Alicia was in her Jeep starting the engine when she felt something funny.

In the center of her forehead, almost like a pinprick, she felt a little tiny pain, as if something small and invisible had landed on her forehead and was now boring into her skull. It manifested itself so suddenly and so intensely that Alicia let go of her keys with a little gasp and moved her hand to her forehead to address the discomfort.

She swiped at the spot.

But then the surface pain was gone and a headache followed, one that spread out from the center and then sat in the middle of her brain.

Again, she figured it was tension. Tension, and maybe some anger over how the new job was going. She pulled out of her sister's driveway and onto the main road. Two stoplights later, she turned for Route 10A, which would take her out into the desert and the watershed event of her life.

Alicia had started her law-enforcement career on the Long Beach, California, police department. She had spent six tough years there and had ultimately moved to Los Angeles and partnered with a senior detective named Ed Van Allen, with whom she'd worked on the celebrated "Cemetery of Angels" case.

The latter had been the most bizarre case of her life so far, an affair with hints of the occult and overtones of the supernatural. The case had focused around the San Angelo Cemetery in Los Angeles, the disinterred tomb of a silent film actor named Billy Carlton, and a pair of children missing from a family that had recently moved to southern California from Connecticut.

Alicia still thought of the investigation as *her* "Cemetery of Angels" case, although she had been secondary on it to Van Allen. The case had been resolved and a criminal had found a bizarre form of justice, though in many ways the case had posed more questions than Alicia could ever have hoped to have answered in her lifetime.

Detective Alicia Aldrich was one of the new generation of detectives.

Female, obviously. Frizzy dark hair. A free spirit who had grown up in Van Nuys and had quizzed well as a recruit. Spent a couple of good years as an undercover narc in Long Beach. She was five eight and had a nice figure. She was a bright young woman, and there was something about her that made drug dealers want to impress her. Made them want to brag to her in their clumsy attempts at seduction. She'd put handcuffs on so many big shots that she had outgrown Long Beach and applied to join the LAPD.

She had quizzed well again and the City of Los Angeles had hired her. She did four years on a beat, then aced the detective's exam. She hated the concept of partners, preferring the Lone Ranger route. The veteran Van Allen was an equally free spirit. So they chose to work together officially, which meant they were actually partners, although they didn't work together much at all, except to bounce ideas off each other. They complemented each other nicely. She played yin to his yang, Alicia reasoned, or was it the other way?

The politics of the job had gotten to her, however, not long after the resolution of the Cemetery of Angels case. The incessant shuffling of bosses, the unending reorganization of the Los Angeles County Detective Bureau, and the daily frustrations of a sometimes thankless job had all worn her down emotionally.

Then there had been all the bad publicity that had tainted the job. The Rodney King case. The bungling of evidence in the Simpson/Goldman murder case and the associated Mark Fuhrman controversy. Who could have criticized her for desiring to disassociate herself from the dispiriting aspects of the job?

Then she had gotten it into her head that, as an accomplished homicide detective, she could range farther and have more autonomy if she transferred to the California Highway Patrol, the state's version of the state police.

Transfers from one force to another were never routine, but for the second time in her career, she managed it. No one in the history of Golden State law enforcement had ever done more than two transfers. But the California Highway Patrol was under a court order to hire more females for their detective squads, so allowances could be made on seniority.

So, despite the fact that the patrol was fighting the new directives every inch of the way, Alicia had seized the opportunity and switched forces earlier that year.

None of that meant, of course, that she was *welcome* in her new assignment. In her first month with CHP, she found herself in an entire brigade of men who seemed to be waiting for her to fail. Fact was, they couldn't wait. If they could speed her failure along, so much the better.

Alicia was already an unhappy woman as she walked through the soft sand of the desert less than an hour and a half later. She was now in a location two hundred yards off State Highway 14 and a world away from the domestic tranquility out of which she had been plucked.

A chill was upon her as the wind kicked up. No matter how hot this area got during the day—and it had been getting *plenty* hot all over Southern California recently—the temperatures would plummet in the late afternoon. The winds would stir up the sand and whip it across the flats, putting some people in mind of a hostile alien landscape.

She continued to walk. About a hundred paces in front of her there was a uniformed CHP guy and a pair of uniformed men from the local Lancaster precinct house. They were standing near something lying on the ground, covered by a blanket.

Alicia nodded to the three men who were standing sentry. They stared at her in return.

"Who the hell are you?" the CHP guy asked. His name tag said his name was Pfleuger.

"Alicia Aldrich. CHP." She showed the badge and their surprise registered.

"I didn't know CHP had any women working homicide in the fifth," one of the San Bernardino bulls said.

"They didn't. They do now."

"Is that progress or a step back?" Sands asked.

"A third of the homicide victims in this state are women," Alicia said, "so why not have the occasional woman investigating?"

"Yeah. Sure," said Pfleuger.

"You sound unconvinced."

"I am," he said. "Every female cop I meet is secretly hunting a husband. But that's okay. Why not?"

"You married?" she asked.

"Just got engaged."

"Then how's that any different?"

"I can't tell you, but it is."

The other two cops smirked. Alicia ignored them. "Then deal with it," she said, "and show me what we've got today."

He hesitated. A Lancaster cop named Fletcher took over. "White male. Maybe thirty years old," he said.

"Let's have a look," Alicia answered.

The harness bulls pulled the blanket away and Alicia looked steadily upon the remains of a murdered man.

She had worked homicide in Los Angeles for several years and was no stranger to such scenes. But an unusual queasiness came upon her unexpectedly. It was as if something lurked beneath the surface of what she was seeing. She would remember the feeling—her initiation to this case—for some time to come. A pair of forward-back mental flashes ignited before her like strobe lights.

Alicia was a woman of instincts and impressions, as well as details. She would always look for the little details in any tableau before her. Sometimes the details were subtle. Sometimes they would reach up and slap her in the face.

This one was a slap.

The victim's neck was bent at an impossible angle, like a bird whose neck had been wrung. The head was lying limp and to the side, with bulging eyes, suggesting strangulation.

Oddly, there was also an ample amount of blood on the left side of the neck and throat, evidently from a slash wound. Additionally, the victim looked to be in strong physical shape. So if strangulation was the form of execution, the victim must have been overpowered by someone impressively muscled.

Alicia pulled on a set of prophylactic gloves.

She crouched down to get a good look at the slash mark on the left side of the victim's face, the slash that had drawn all the blood. It was a nonlethal cut, a crude hacking near part of the ear. Alicia gingerly touched the gaping wound.

"What do you see?" Pfleuger asked.

Alicia shrugged. "The earlobe has been hacked off."

"That's a new one, isn't it?" the uniform cop asked.

"First time I've seen it here," Alicia muttered.

"What do you make of it?"

"Could have been a fight, could have been part of the struggle."

Alicia paused.

"Or the victim could have been wearing a five-thousand-dollar ruby ear stud and the killer coveted it. Jesus, who knows? We're in Southern California, right?"

The cops snorted a trio of small laughs. If they were looking at a dump job from Los Angeles or from Interstate 40, anything was possible. They had seen dump jobs in this area that had been hauled all the way from Tennessee and North Carolina. It was only a two-day nonstop red-eye drive if the driver had a good fix of amphetamines and didn't mind a decomposing stiff in his truck or trunk.

"We got coyotes out in this region," Pfleuger offered. "That's a possibility. Maybe a mountain dog chewed the guy a little."

Alicia took a second look. The slash mark reached down into the jawbone.

"Valid idea," she said. "But this guy was hacked with a knife, maybe even a cleaver of some sort."

And moments later, both the robbery and assault theories flew apart, also. The victim's wallet was on him, though all ID had been removed, and there was two hundred dollars in it. Would a killer who had slashed an ear to get an earring not bother to at least check the wallet? Similarly, the victim was clean cut and conservatively dressed—a sartorial characteristic that didn't necessarily jibe with a ruby stud in the ear. And most troubling of all was the trail of blood.

The blood had flowed straight downward from the ear across the flesh on the back of the neck to the sand. None had flowed onto the victim's clothing. And most of the blood was in the sand. Gravity never lied. And here it told Alicia that the slash had been administered after the dead man had been dumped.

But just as the scene told her things, it also raised questions. Not simply, why had the man been murdered, but was this a random attack, or had this man specifically been intended as a victim? And what was the point of the mutilation, the amputation of the earlobe?

Alicia also noticed that the victim's shirt and tie had been loosened. Again, the detective wondered why. The top three buttons of the man's shirt were open and Alicia noticed something yellow and blue underneath.

She pushed aside the cloth of the shirt and saw a tattoo. Then a second one.

"What have you got?" Pfleuger asked.

"Who knows?"

On the left side of the man's upper torso was tattooed a large circle of solid yellow. As Alicia looked further, a solid red circle was also evident a few inches from the larger yellow circle. Alicia looked at the tattoo for a few seconds, then closed the shirt. Who knew what else would be found on the man's body? This was starting to look like a square guy who may have had some unusual private habits.

Alicia stood.

A squad car with two more uniforms had come by to hang out. And because a man was lying there dead, an investigator from the State Board of Health had been notified.

The investigator, a bald double-chinned man named Jack Tinsdale, appeared forty minutes later in a dark green Ford Explorer. He had a Lakers play-off game on the radio and didn't pump the volume down when he stepped from his vehicle.

Tinsdale, unlike Alicia, didn't look as if he had rushed away from his Sunday dinner, or, for that matter, any other recent meal.

The two newly arrived cops, a male and a female, stood nearby and watched curiously, puffing cigarettes, the smoke drifting toward Tinsdale as he crouched by the corpse. Eventually, he stood up and bummed a butt. Tinsdale paused for a smoke, then strolled over to Alicia, who had been walking around the perimeter of the crime scene, looking for anything that might eventually be of help.

"What's your guess?" Tinsdale asked.

"The guy got murdered somewhere else. Then the body got dumped here, where the corpse got mutilated," Alicia said. "I'd say he's been here since last night. Not too much longer than that."

"Yeah, I'd buy that," Tinsdale said.

"Ever look at a crime scene by yourself and arrive at your own conclusions?" Alicia asked.

"Not on Sundays. It takes too much time and nobody gives a shit. Anything else?"

"Ask me again in a few days," Alicia said. "I have a feeling we're going to have to find out some more."

"I'll phone you," Tinsdale said.

Alicia gave him her card.

Already all the dark scenarios were running through Alicia's mind. What was this all about? Various explanations came together, broke apart, and re-formed in her mind with kaleidoscopic brio.

A simple mugging and murder?

A revenge slaying?

A gay thing or something involving a woman?

A coven of devil worshipers who collect earlobes?

Some new sort of Satanic cult?

Or just some frightening new clique of California screwballs, the raw material for New Age nightmares?

Naturally, Alicia reasoned, something like this would have to spring up on her doorstep. Why couldn't this have happened back East in New York or New Jersey, where Alicia secretly felt all this wacko stuff came from? Or why couldn't it have been in San Francisco where—in its sick perpetual-rainy-season sordidness—it could have fit in with the mood of the city?

But, no. It had happened in her town, on her watch. *Why?*

She had a strange feeling of resentment. Southern Cali-

fornia could have been a paradise. Instead, it was a paradise lost, if it had ever been one to start with. Swallowed
up in the flood of sickos and weirdos who came here to
ruin the place.

Now, judging by the mutilation, she might well have
yet one more. And curiously, later on, she remembered
thinking—apropos of nothing—that the sky certainly
had looked beautiful that early evening.

C H A P T E R 3

Alicia did not return to her sister's house till after ten P.M. The young guests were long gone. Janet had been put to bed at nine and James had crawled off to sleep at ten.

Linda brewed a pot of herbal tea when her sister arrived. They sat across from each other on twin sofas in the living room and talked as they sipped.

"You okay?" Linda asked.

Alicia shrugged. "Why wouldn't I be?"

Linda shook her head. "I can't believe what you do, what you expose yourself to. Or why you do it."

"The worst part is, I'd miss it if I *didn't* do it," Alicia answered.

Her career choice had always been considered a quirk in the family. They had a brother who lived in Encino and had gone to law school. Their father had been a banker and their mother a teacher. And yet Alicia had always had this sense of justice, this flaky sense of adventure, this *calling*. But years earlier, when she had applied to the police academy at Long Beach, the whole family had been shocked.

"Was it bad?" Linda asked. "Today? Out in the desert? Is that where you said you were?"

"That's where I was."

"And so?"

"No homicide is good," Alicia answered. She paused. "You don't want to know about it right now. I'll tell you about it in the morning."

"I want to know now," Linda said.

"Why?"

Linda smiled. "I just do. I'm curious."

Alicia sighed.

Linda always wanted to know about the darkest impulses and deeds of human nature—the details of man's inhumanity to man, or the chronicles of man's brutality toward women—even if she feared it. It wasn't something Alicia easily understood about her.

"Linny, I don't know much more than what I saw," Alicia said. "A middle-class white man, maybe about thirty years old. The body was dumped out in the high desert west of Antelope Valley. Crime lab took the body in so I'll know more in a day or two. No ID. Maybe it was a robbery, maybe it wasn't."

Alicia paused. She guessed she could feel the next question coming.

"Sexual angle?" Linda asked.

She had guessed right.

"None that I could see," Alicia answered. "I don't think it was a gay thing. The man had a wedding ring on. Not that the ring precludes a gay angle. Obviously."

"Obviously," Linda agreed.

"And it didn't look like the type of thing a woman would have done. There was a mutilation involved. Part of the victim's ear was slashed off."

Alicia paused.

"I have a bad feeling about it. I don't know why. I had

a headache going out there and a worse headache coming back. Bad vibrations, I guess. I don't know."

She fell silent for several seconds, hoping that her sister would be content with that much.

Outside the living room window a little cloud scudded slowly toward the moon. Alicia waited till it hit, and a certain dreamy restfulness finally settled upon her, easing her headache slightly.

Then she looked back to Linda.

"Did that bizarre little man find you, Ali?" Linda asked.

"What 'bizarre little man'?"

"Didn't you read my note?"

"What note?"

"I tacked a note to the front door so that I wouldn't forget to tell you. You didn't see it?"

"I came in through the garage, if you recall," Alicia said. "Now. What note? And what creepy little man?

"A man came to the door looking for you," Linda said. "He said it was police business."

"Who was he?"

"He had a funny name."

She thought of names from the department. Short men with unusual names.

"Tom Perkins?"

"I know Tom Perkins," she said. "And Perkins isn't a funny name.

"Ron Kleber."

"I know Ron Kleber, too. This wasn't anyone from the department."

"Then who *was* it, Linda?"

"It was not anyone I'd ever seen before or any name I knew," her sister answered. "It sounded as if it were Spanish but was spelled strangely."

Alicia thought for a moment and then rose from the sofa. "Where's the note?" she asked, gathering herself.

"I'm sure it hasn't moved. Want to go take a look or shall I get it for you?"

"I'll go," Alicia said.

Alicia rose to her feet and walked toward the front door.

What a pain in the butt this case already was, Alicia thought to herself. A dead guy in the desert under a glorious evening sky and already the case was unnerving her extended family.

She had missed Janet's birthday party. She was now getting testy with Linda. Maybe it was just the heat, which was already promising to be severe, even this early in the summer.

"Oh, God, what a start for this case!" she mused.

If she were lucky, Alicia reasoned, the case would disappear as quickly as it had arrived. How she wished that she could take the dead man's body, drive it fifty miles up the Golden State Freeway till she was well within Kern County, and dump it again.

Problem hypothetically solved. CHP's Section Six could then worry about it. It would serve them right. They had been dumping stuff in L.A. County for years. Better to keep their own stats low and vacation time intact, not that the transplanted Okies in Bakersfield didn't keep them at least a little busy.

Alicia arrived at the front door and found the note still hanging there. She took it down.

Five-fifteen P.M. Just when all the kids were at the house and the cake and ice cream were being served, this "bizarre little man," as Linda had phrased it, had come trotting to the door.

Seeking Alicia. For what purpose?

Alicia frowned as she read the note. A name, a strange unfamiliar name, had been written on the paper:

SaY MoJo

Alicia stared at the name for several seconds. It added up to a big fat zero for her. It meant nothing.

For that matter, less than nothing.

"Who the hell," she asked herself politely, "*what* the hell, is 'SaY MoJo'?"

Alicia stared at it for several seconds. She set it down on a table and looked at it. Must have been some sort of joke, she decided, good-natured or bad-natured, but it sure didn't make much sense.

She walked back to the living room.

"The name means nothing," Alicia said.

"He said it would," Linda said matter-of-factly.

"It would *what*?" Alicia settled down on the sofa.

"Mean nothing," Linda answered.

"And you didn't ask anything further?"

"No, I *didn't!*" Linda said.

"Maybe he had the wrong house," Alicia suggested.

"Alicia, he asked for you by name," she said, an edge to her sleepy voice now. "And he said the name might not ring a bell immediately. But it would eventually."

Alicia thought about it. "I don't know what that means at all," she said. She pondered it for another half minute. She remembered a line from an old song: "*Get your mojo working . . .*"

She hadn't known what the line meant when it was written, and she didn't know what it meant now.

"Do you?" Alicia finally asked.

"Do I what?" her sister asked.

"Do *you* have any idea what it means?"

"No," Linda answered. "And I don't want to."

Linda finished her tea. "You look really tired, Ali," she said. "Stressed. Why don't you bed down here?"

Alicia protested. But her first order of business the following morning would be to visit the medical examiner in San Bernardino, which was more convenient from her sister's home than her own. So eventually, she accepted.

Linda always kept the guest room made up and ready for a visitor. And Alicia always kept a change of clothing stashed in her sister's home. So within another twenty minutes, Alicia was tucked into a pull-out sofa bed and ready for sleep.

But just before she dropped off, there was one unsettling moment. She felt herself drifting and falling, and for a moment—with uncanny realism—she was back in the desert, shining a light into the dead man's face.

In the split-second duration of the demidream—it was actually an image more than a dream—the dead man's hand shot up and pointed skyward. At the same time, the man's eyes opened to reveal something horrific and unearthly: solid yellow eyeballs. There were no pupils, as if the eyes had been turned straight around. And the corpse's dead lips tightened into a ghastly smile.

Alicia felt her legs move in fright during this half-sleep. Her arms thrashed and her eyes opened. But the guest room was dark and quiet. Distantly, she heard a car pass Linda's home. She listened till she was sure it had kept going.

Then she carefully closed her eyes again, as if to exclude any image that would disquiet her. The strategy almost worked.

Almost.

At the edge of her consciousness, another image appeared. At first it was just a small red light in the middle of a black field. Then the illumination grew more intense until it spread and whitened slightly. She tried to open her eyes again, but couldn't. This image was going to force itself upon her.

Then it clarified. There was a whiteness in the center

of the red light. And from that pale center stepped a small figure. It was human, or at least humanlike, though its head was disproportionately large.

The figure stood as if waiting. Watching. Almost as if it were there to guide Alicia off to sleep, off to another realm of consciousness.

A few minutes later she successfully slept. She dozed peacefully for several hours. Outside her window, far above her, the amiable little cloud that had obscured the moon had turned into something much darker. And the moonlight—which was nothing more than the reflection of the sun, after all—was in eclipse to something that most human beings would have found unimaginable.

C H A P T E R 4

The next morning, Alicia drove to the county CHP head-quarters in San Bernardino for a nine A.M. encounter at the medical examiner's office.

The day again broke unseasonably hot over the county, with steady blasts of warm air rolling across the desert and into the inhabited regions of the Southland. The temperature in San Bernardino would hover in the high eighties by eleven A.M. It was unfair and unnatural that it was so hot so soon into the year.

Photographs of the previous day's murder scene had already been brought, along with evidence from the crime scene. Both were sent to the concrete-and-glass structure that housed the support offices for the county's various rural and suburban police agencies. The building had all the charm of a bad motel and frequently half the efficiency. Somehow, some way, however, the job often got done.

The remains of John Doe—as the dead man was now called—had gone to the lab. The medical examiner was on the first floor in the rear, where trucks could roll in and out with lifeless cargo.

Alicia began her day in the evidence room, examining the deceased's clothing. The murdered man had worn a Brooks Brothers suit. Ready-to-wear. His shirt was white, a Burberry. It could have come from any good men's store around the country. The quality of the man's tie and shoes were upscale, also, suggesting that he had been middle class. Of the clothing items, the suit might be easiest to trace. But Alicia also knew that it was only a matter of time before a missing persons report connected with the deceased.

White middle-class guys in suits might occasionally die lonely deaths. But there were frequently families, employers, and insurance companies left behind, and plenty of lawyers looking to connect the dots between them.

Alicia went to an office computer and scanned recent missing persons reports from Los Angeles and its surrounding suburbs, hoping to get a quick hit on a potential ID. She didn't get one, and a few minutes later presented herself at the office of William "Whitey" Sugarman, M.D., the county medical examiner.

Sugarman, the local slice-and-dice man, was an alumnus of an undistinguished out-of-the-hemisphere medical school. Sugarman's specialty had always been cutting, asking questions, and doing some more cutting.

Surprisingly, as MEs went, he wasn't even bad.

Sugarman *was,* however, frequently irritable and ugly as a horned toad.

He was tall, gaunt, and narrow-faced. He was also an albino, with cream-colored hair, pink eyes, and pasty pinkish skin to match.

The other people in the office often called him "W.S." Sometimes he was known as "Whitey" Sugarman. "W.S." also stood for "White Snake," the albino doctor's behind-his-back nickname. There were reasons that the doctor was sometimes touchy. There were some jokes he had

already heard too many times. The problem was, he
hadn't helped his cause when he first had taken this post
in the 1980s and had been in the habit of playing White
Snake and White Lion CDs on a yellow splatterproof
Sony Walkman.

He claimed he had a wife, and there was even a picture of a very pretty young woman with a shockingly in-
discreet two-piece swimsuit on his desk. And she was
holding the bikini strategically, not wearing it.

Sugarman claimed the doll in the picture was his wife.
But in fifteen years on this job, he had not produced her in
person even once, and the Human Resources Department
had inadvertently divulged that Dr. Sugarman claimed
only a single dependent—himself—on his W-2 tax forms.
So the consensus was that he had been married once, possibly even to the pretty girl in the picture, but that she had
taken off long ago. And no one much blamed her.

Dr. Sugarman had already completed the John Doe autopsy and spent half an hour running through some basics
with Alicia. The remains of the deceased lay semiexposed
on a steel drawer, in a half-unzipped orange body bag.

Alicia listened attentively. Finally, Sugarman finished
the routine stuff. Alicia fished for some of the less important details of the man's physical condition, then pushed
for the doctor's conclusions.

"Anything else jump out at you?" Alicia eventually
asked.

"Jump out?" Sugarman snorted. " 'Leap out' might be
the better way of phrasing it."

Alicia waited. "Yeah?" she asked.

"Ever heard of a chemical called chrolystron?"

"Can't say that I have," she said. She turned the unusual word over in her mind.

"You wouldn't have unless you're into space exploration," Sugarman said. He blinked his pinkish eyes.

"What?"

Sugarman laughed. "You know, you damned cops would do better if you did some reading now and then. There was an article about this stuff in *Scientific American* two months ago."

"I'm still not following you, W.S."

"Chrolystron is a mystery chemical. It's found nowhere on earth in a natural state. Not harmful and not very useful, either. But it comes back to earth via astronauts."

Alicia blinked. She sorted through the ME's words.

"What in hell are you talking about?" she asked.

Sugarman walked to a unit of shelves and ran his index finger through a stack of magazines until he found the right issue of *Scientific American*. He handed it over the body on the metal table.

"Page forty-eight," Sugarman said. "And don't take my magazine away or I'll never see it again. Photocopy the damned article, okay?"

"Okay. Now tell me what you're talking about."

"No one knows where the chemical chrolystron comes from in its pure state. But it's found in the blood of men and women who have voyaged outside Earth's atmosphere. Astronauts."

"So?"

"This guy," said Sugarman, indicating the contents of the half-opened body bag, "had chrolystron in his lungs *and* in his blood."

Alicia blinked. She looked down at the very ordinary face of the dead man. Then she looked back up at the albino.

"So this guy was in space?" Alicia asked. "Is that what you're telling me?"

"Sure looks that way," Sugarman said. "He was out of Earth's orbit. That means 'space,' I guess."

"Come on," Alicia protested. "This guy looks more like a bummed-out insurance salesman than an astronaut."

"I didn't say he was an astronaut. I said it appeared that he has been in space."

"How can *that* be," Alicia asked, "if he wasn't an astronaut?"

Sugarman was piqued.

"You're the detective. So you get to figure it out, okay? But what I know is that your dead guy had chrolystron in his system. That part is irrefutable. A good, hard kick-ass high dose of it, if you want to know, so it wasn't any accident. Listen carefully: chrolystron is the chemical that astronauts bring back from space. And it's not known to exist anywhere in this world."

"Can you get it at labs or anything? Or from working in the aerospace industry?"

"Not to my knowledge." He nodded to the magazine. "Read the damned article, would you?"

"I will, I will. But how could our dead guy get it?"

"Don't know. If not from actually being in space, I don't know."

"Come on, Doc! What's your guess?"

"I guess you don't want to explore the 'abducted by aliens' thing," the doctor said.

"No, I don't!"

"We've got copies of *The Globe* and *The National Enquirer* on the floor of the men's room," Dr. Sugarman continued, his eyes twinkling slightly. "Got an 'inquiring mind'?"

"I have no desire to read those rags," Alicia said. "Come on. Give me a break."

"Well, then I don't have an explanation for what's going on here," Sugarman said, vexed. The ME pondered the point, calmed slightly, then shrugged. "If he weren't dead, I'd suggest that you ask him. Chances are, however, he might not even know himself."

"The astronaut chemical, huh? The space chemical?"

"Read about it," said Sugarman, motioning to the magazine.

"I will," Alicia said.

Alicia looked again at the dead man's face. She wished it could spring to life again, as it had in her gory dream the previous night, if only to answer a few questions. She also looked at the upper torso again, wanting a key detail now more than ever. She focused on the tattoo of the spheres.

"Got any idea what that's all about?" she asked.

"What?"

"The tattoo," Alicia said. "The markings. Yellow and red shaded circles."

Sugarman leaned over and took a second look.

"Looks like a grapefruit and a cherry," Dr. Sugarman said.

Alicia peered for a second more.

"Actually, check that. If it were to scale, it would be a grapefruit and a very orbicular tomato," Sugarman said. A little cadaverish grin crossed his lips.

"Very funny," Alicia said.

"Thank you."

But Sugarman continued to look at the markings. He poked around at the tattoo with the blunt end of a scalpel. He suddenly noticed something of interest.

"Lord," he finally said. "I've never seen *that* before."

"What?"

"And I missed it the first time."

"What?" Alicia asked again.

Sugarman donned a rubber glove and now poked at the skin with his finger. "See the way the ink spread in those tattoos?" he asked. "It didn't flow evenly. It was meeting some posthumous resistance in the flesh."

"So?"

"So I'd say the epidermis was dying when the ink was injected," Sugarman said.

"The man was already dead when he got inked?"

"Yes. I'd say so," Sugarman said with sudden thoughtfulness.

He continued to poke at the tattoo.

"This man had been dead for maybe an hour or two," he continued. "The skin dies very quickly when the heart stops. So he received his tattoo shortly after he died."

"So we got a man we can't identify," Alicia said. "He was tattooed after he was murdered, presumably by his killer or an accomplice. And his lungs contain a chemical that you normally have to leave planet Earth to obtain. That's what you're telling me?"

"Pretty much," said Dr. Sugarman. He took his gloves off and put his hand on the zipper of the bag. "Finished with him?"

"Yes. For now."

"Can I move him along the food chain? Prepare him for identification or burial?"

"Keep him here for a few days if you can. Okay?"

Sugarman sighed. "Okay," he said.

Sugarman zipped up the bag, cozying up the corpse. Another day at the office. Nothing about this seemed at all unusual to him.

"Any chance you're mistaken about any of this?" Alicia asked.

"No."

"And you expect me to believe all this?"

"Alicia?" Sugarman said, as she slid the body back into its drawer. "The evidence in front of you doesn't lie. Your 'bummed-out insurance salesman,' as you thought of him, was tattooed after he was murdered and his body contains chrolystron. You don't have to believe me on the damn tattoo, you can take that to another examiner and get corroboration. But you have to believe the lab reports. That's pure chemical analysis, Alicia. And the chemical analysis says that this guy took some sort of ul-tra-high altitude ride one day. *Real* high, if you know what I'm saying."

"I know what you're saying," Alicia said. "And I know I'm going to have one wonderful time sorting it out."

CHAPTER 5

The message summoning Alicia came from a woman named Stella Bagnoli. She was the assistant to Lieutenant Albert Mott, commanding officer of the Detective Squad, Fifth Division, California Highway Patrol, Southern District—and Alicia's new superior officer.

Stella was an affable woman who sat at a desk outside Lieutenant Mott's office. She had long red hair, green eyes, and an easy smile. On the afternoon when Alicia responded to the invitation, Stella wore a dark green sundress that would have looked more appropriate at the beach. She looked as if she were trying to seduce the entire squad.

She had an easygoing, pleasant demeanor however, and sent Alicia directly in to see the commander.

Lieutenant Mott sat behind his desk in the San Bernardino headquarters. When Alicia entered, he raised his eyes from the CV and the crime scene reports in front of him.

"Take a seat, Alicia," he said.

There was only one. Alicia took it.

She waited as Mott finished reading. She had her own reading material. She had scored a copy of *Scientific American* from the public library across the street and had read the article Dr. Sugarman had referenced.

After two minutes, Mott's gaze traveled upward and he looked at the woman sitting across from him. His eyes assessed her in more ways than she would have liked. She decided to try to keep this visit as professional as possible.

"Well," he finally said, "welcome."

"Thank you," she said.

"First few weeks on the job and you caught a good weird one, huh? An unidentified dump job in the high desert."

Alicia opened her hands slightly, as if to indicate that one homicide was as good or bad as the next. "One never knows where a homicide investigation will go," she said. "Can go nowhere. Can go everywhere."

"Absolutely," Lieutenant Mott said again. "That's why we do what we do, isn't it?"

"That's one reason," Alicia answered.

She wondered where this was going, aside from the fact that Mott had a reputation of always wanting to thoroughly chat up his new charges within a few days of their arrival.

"Was Dr. Sugarman much help?" Mott asked, moving closer to something substantive.

"Some," Alicia answered, "in terms of time of death and cause. He didn't give me anything that I couldn't see for myself at the scene."

Mott made a slight grimace.

"Ever dealt with Dr. Sugarman before?"

"Once," Alicia answered. "When I was on homicide in Long Beach. He ID'ed a runaway girl for us."

"With Whitey, what you see is what you get," Mott allowed pleasantly. "Whitey Sugarman is like that. Sometimes he muddles more than he clarifies. Not that he's incompetent, because he's not. He just has a way of sending you in the wrong direction." Mott paused. "Sometimes," he added by way of qualification. "Not always. But sometimes."

"I'll keep it in mind," Alicia said.

"I have a copy of the ME's report, too," the lieutenant said. "I'll be looking at it as well. I've also got your CV and the crime scene report from the desert."

"So I see."

"You write a thorough report. I appreciate that."

"Thank you."

"I want you to understand from the outset: it's not that you're going to have me looking over your shoulder, Alicia. But everyone newly assigned to this division goes through an unofficial ninety-day probationary period. You're not on probation in the CHP; you're on probation with me. This is my house. I make the rules."

She nodded.

"I like to monitor new detectives. Make sure there are no problems. You might resent it, but sometimes it can be helpful."

She nodded again. "I understand," she said.

"You don't have problems with that?"

She shook her head. "Why would I?"

"Good," he said. "It also allows me to be of assistance to you if you need it."

"I appreciate it," Alicia said.

Mott was forty-two years old, but looked as if he had been around for a decade and a half longer. He had an unabashedly weathered Irish face that was anchored by a crooked nose and topped by a short iron-gray haircut. He was a thick man, with broad shoulders, beefy arms, a large waist, and stocky legs. In warm weather, such as today, he habitually wore a striped tie and a short-sleeved white shirt. The muscles of his arms were thick and tanned. His biceps hung like a pair of six-guns.

All that was apparent to the eye.

But Alicia also knew the background, the life story, the career history, "the book" on her new commander. It was always wise to know the book before transferring into a unit. It could save hassle and heartache. And Alicia liked to be wise.

Unlike many in the police hierarchy in Southern California, which tended to be native, Mott was a transplant, all the way from the East Coast. He had grown up in south Brooklyn, New York. Most of his early experiences with law enforcement had consisted of running afoul of it.

He had been arrested twice by the time he was eighteen. There was no father in his household, and his alcoholic mother couldn't control him. He was actually facing a short jail term in 1976, when a city court judge named Abner Herskowitz intervened.

It wasn't a cell that Al Mott needed, it was some good kick-in-the-ass discipline, Judge Herskowitz theorized. If young Albert joined the military, the judge suggested, charges could be dropped and all arrests could be expunged from the official record. That was *if* the aforesaid Al Mott could stay out of trouble while in the service.

So Mott had a choice. Three years in the military or two in a state prison. Judge Herskowitz gave him five minutes to decide.

Mott opted for the military and—again with the judge's intervention—landed in the U.S. Air Force, a month after receiving stolen property from a Crazy Eddie warehouse in Ozone Park.

The discipline worked.

Going in as a lowly airman recruit, he emerged five years later as a master sergeant. Also in the air force, he had channeled another skill that he had had since his youth. The ability to throw damaging punches.

In the USAF, Mott had been a competitive boxer. He whipped every other pugilist in his class and scored knockouts against army and navy fighters while based in Texas. Later he had been transferred to Korea and had even fought four professional matches in Seoul while on active duty. He won all four.

He then signed for a match in Kyushu in southern Japan against a rising Japanese middleweight who eventually got a title shot. Mott went down in the first minute of the first round. Sayonara boxing.

After an honorable discharge, he returned to America and took up security work in Oakland.

He became a state cop in 1980 and worked Ventura County, Marin County, and San Diego. Mott was a shining example of a bad kid gone good. He had commanded the detectives in this unit in San Bernardino County since 1995.

Lieutenant Mott's eyes flicked down to Alicia's CV. Then, darkly, they rose again, like little ascendant planets. His gaze settled into hers.

"You were shot in the line of duty seventeen months ago with the LAPD," he said.

"That's correct," she answered.

"You're a tough lady," he said.

"I try to be."

"You deserve credit just being back in police work. A lot of men or women would have called it a career right there and taken the disability pension."

"I was only twenty-eight at the time," she said. "I think retirement would have been a little premature."

"Twenty-eight," he said with a laugh. "I'd like to be twenty-eight again."

"Sometimes I would, too," she parried.

"You nearly died," Mott said, leaning back in his swivel chair now, his ham-hock arms folded across each other.

She sighed.

"Technically," she said, "I *did* die. My heart stopped for seven minutes and my brain flat-lined for thirty-five seconds."

"And?"

"And they got it going again."

"The heart, you mean?"

"The heart, the brain, and everything connected."

She neglected to mention her right arm, which she considered half-dead and which was increasingly resistant to obeying commands.

"Defibrillation?" he asked.

"What? My heart?"

"Yes."

"So I'm told. Ask my doctor. I was unconscious."

"It must have been a strange experience."

"*Strange?* Once in a lifetime, I guess you could say."

He sighed and took a second. Alicia felt they had been fencing with words. Mott shared the feeling.

"I don't mean to make light of it," he finally said. "I'm impressed with you. I like your courage. I like your guts."

"I like my job. I like my career."

"And you're up for it?" he angled.

"Up for what?"

"A challenging case. Like this one. John Doe in the Desert."

"I'm up for it," Alicia said.

She smiled. *John Doe in the Desert*.

Lieutenant Mott was noted for such terminology. It was never the John Doe case. Or, say, the Carlos Valdez case. Anything important always came in a colorful wrapper: Harry on the Highway. Michael of Mount Washington. Ellie of El Segundo.

It was Mott's way of putting a handle on things and it greatly amused his troops. He always sounded as if he were doing dedications on a Top 40 AM radio station. Alicia already wanted to add something more formal to the mix.

Charles of the Ritz. St. Martin in the Fields. Lawrence of Arabia.

But today she was stuck with her commanding officer's new terminology: John Doe in the Desert. Their own high plains drifter, dead as a mackerel in mufti from Brooks Brothers and Burberry.

Mott rocked slightly in his chair, arms folded, lips pursed when he wasn't discoursing.

"I'm just concerned that you could be back too soon, Alicia," he said. "I've reviewed your file. You're an excellent detective. You worked with Ed Van Allen over in L.A., didn't you?"

"I did."

"How is Ed?"

"Fine, the last time I spoke to him."

"Ed's been one of my favorite people for years. If you speak with him again, tell him I send my regards."

"Thank you. I will."

From outside Lieutenant Mott's office, just beyond the half-open door, came a beautiful tenor voice raised in song as it passed. Two bars of "Stella by Starlight," then there was laughter all around and apparently Mott's assistant, Stella, was surrounded by admirers.

Mott kept to the issue at hand between him and his guest. He was, after all, almost finished.

"There's psychological stress involved, Alicia, in a near-death experience. I'd rather wait an extra couple of

months to have you on duty than to have you rush back
and then lose you on permanent mental disability. That's
why we're having this conversation today. See where I'm
coming from on this?"

"You're saying that you're afraid I might go bonkers
on you. And your division. And the department."

"So to speak," he said. "It's crossed my mind."

He paused and waited. She smiled.

"I'm fine," she said. "I want to work."

Mott tugged at his wire glasses and finally smiled. "All
right," he said. "You're a professional. You know what
you're doing." He paused. "Did Sugarman give you anything at all?" he asked.

Alicia mentioned the chrolystron in the victim's lungs.
She explained what it was and where it allegedly came
from.

"Chrolystron, huh? Do I have the name right?" Mott
asked.

"You do."

His brow furrowed with irritation. He could barely conceal his displeasure so, mid-sentence, he stopped trying.
"And Sugarman's talking about spaceships? Or rockets?"

"He only said it was in the blood of astronauts who
return from space," Alicia said. "That's all. He didn't say a
rocket landed out there in the desert and he didn't say
the guy fell out of a spaceship."

Mott's hand found a bare spot on the wood of his
desk. "No," he drawled, "but nothing much *would* surprise me out in the high desert. And what happens out
there pales in comparison to some of the stories I hear
from Arizona and New Mexico."

"Uh-huh," Alicia answered.

Mott's right forefinger tapped slightly on the desktop.
"Do yourself a favor. There must be six aerospace plants

within a hundred miles. Why don't you check your victim with them before you go starting an interplanetary war?"

"That's pretty much what I'd planned," Alicia said.

"I like your style," Mott said. "Good luck with it."

She stood.

He thanked her and dismissed her. She gathered her folio and the copy of *Scientific American*. As she moved to the door, her eyes came back to him for a moment.

She found him giving her another inspection that was hardly part of standard police protocol. When she caught him, he flushed slightly and looked back down to the reports on his desk. The moment considerably unsettled her. The last thing she needed was unwanted attention from a superior. She wondered if he had a record of getting too friendly with women in his command and wondered whom she could ask.

She quickly realized that there *weren't* any other female detectives in this squad and—as her cerebral hardware hit overdrive—she wondered immediately if there was significance to that, too. There were conveniences to being in a relationship: in addition to the predictable and steady sex, relationships warded off unwanted romantic approaches from the outside. She wondered how much Mott knew about her private life, whether or not he knew that she didn't have any particular man in her life right now. And she guessed that her file probably touched upon that aspect of her life; the CHP personnel records were legendarily intrusive.

She wished he didn't know anything. But she said nothing further and departed.

Outside the lieutenant's office, a few of the other men of the precinct had prepared a birthday cake for Stella. Pink icing. White flowers. They had lit a half-dozen pale green candles on it.

Stella, unfashionably short skirt and all, was leaning over the cake, holding back her hair, and giving a long bosomy exhalation to blow out the half-dozen tiny flames. The scene brought to mind many conflicting ideas in Alicia's head, but mostly Alicia focused on the birthday angle, and it reminded her anew of the party that she had been pulled away from two days earlier.

That, in turn, underscored the perplexing nature of the man in the desert. She made a deal with herself that she would reread the *Scientific American* article this evening and talk to the aerospace plants the next day. Something inside her, however, was already taut with foreboding.

And strangely enough—ironically enough—Stella's cake was decorated with a sun, moon, and stars.

The following Monday evening, Alicia sat alone in a small new house in the beachside town of Venice, fifteen miles southwest of downtown Los Angeles. She tried to relax.

Relaxation did not come easily these days. Alicia now lived with a mind that was poised to travel through doors and windows that had never been open before.

Tonight, however, she *had* successfully relaxed on a quilted sofa in front of a prized music system.

It was late evening. She had made herself some soup and assembled an array of CDs, from Pearl Jam to Sinatra, eighties Big Hair stadium rock to Ella Fitzgerald. She inserted the CDs and flipped the switch to random. She would go wherever the music took her. She flipped on the music, curled up onto the sofa, and kicked off her shoes. She removed the cap from a bottle of Bud Ice.

A little voice inside her chimed in with the well-known line from a commercial.

Watch out for penguins!

"Yeah, sure," she thought to herself, mildly amused. "With all the other things I have to watch for, I'll be sure to keep an eye out for black-and-white birds from the South Pole."

She sipped her soup.

Well, what else do you think you must watch out for, Alicia? the same inner voice replied.

She stopped for a moment. What was this? A distinctive internal voice that she had never heard before.

"Jesus," she thought. "I'm losing my marbles!"

Maybe, the voice answered. *And maybe you'll lose even more than that!*

She froze. What in hell was this? A dialogue with herself? An inner self? A demonic inner id?

She listened for more.

"Who the hell am I talking to?" she asked aloud.

No answer came. She settled slightly. Meanwhile, Sinatra sang from Rogers and Hammerstein. Two in a row. "Hello Young Lovers" followed by "Younger Than Springtime." So much for random selection on the CD changer. Then "You'll Never Walk Alone." Was an unseen hand affecting the CD player? Was there a message somewhere in the bittersweet ballads?

The late Mr. Sinatra always mellowed Alicia. That big butch tenor voice made her feel romantic, then transported her to the edge of sadness. There was no romance in her life right now, for example. Sinatra's bittersweet ballads about loss caused her to reflect.

Her free hand rummaged through a dish of potato chips.

Alicia's mind drifted.

Her most recent romance had broken up. Then there was the impending second anniversary of her father's death. Both contributed to her increasing loneliness. The looming prospect of her thirtieth birthday also weighed heavily.

Granted, on paper her career was going fine.

She had recently moved to homicide after injury leave for several months early in the year. She had picked up the advancements and promotions that she wanted within her career. Some of the men on the force had problems with the mere existence of a woman as a professional peer, but otherwise her fellow officers, detectives and commanders, respected her. So obviously it was the *personal* situation that troubled her.

The *injury*.

The near-death incident with a local ne'er-do-well named Hernando Cordero that culminated in gunfire the previous year. The incident that the psychiatrist kept trying to help her work past but that she *couldn't* work past. Not completely. Her father had been right when he had warned her about the perils of police work. She *had* almost gotten herself snuffed.

So she opted for the second beer. Over and over the Cordero incident played encores in her mind, like a movie on a single looped reel. It was *always* at the edge of her consciousness. *Groundhog Day* over and over and over.

She tried to shove it away for the evening. But beer brought with it twinges of guilt. The hard stuff and the suds provided solace, but she battled to keep the booze in check. There were state police offices in Sacramento and San Bernardino just looking for frazzled cops like her to furlough and retire before they shot someone for sport. When Alicia retired, she promised herself, she would do it on her own terms. She didn't want to be let out to pasture by deskbound bureaucrats.

She got up from the sofa and straightened her living room and kitchen. She kept a neat, orderly home. It disappointed her that other aspects of her life couldn't fit so appropriately in place.

She went upstairs and settled into bed.

Still, her mind was working.

Lying perfectly still, she finally isolated what was bothering her. It was this deep down, inexpressible sense of *imminence*. Her nerves were stretched taut as drumskins. She had this overwhelming notion that *something was about to happen.*

Something big.

Something horrible.

Something unlike anything that had happened to her before.

She lay in the darkness just before midnight and felt as if she were being enveloped by a major league premonition. She wondered whether this was a creeping sense of mortality. A little pathway through which everyone travels. No wonder the booze helped.

For many minutes, sleep refused to descend. A headache, much like the one that she had suffered Sunday, crept over her. For a moment she could see that small figure stepping out of the sunlight again. Then it vanished, like a mirage, leaving her alone again with her premonitions.

Her shoulder throbbed. The pins-and-needles feeling, the tingling sensation that could become pain or become numbness.

Fitfully, impatiently, she turned in bed. The tingling eased. She wondered how psychosomatic the discomfort was. Was the pain in her mind, or was it like a divining rod, sensing trouble before trouble was even visible?

Alicia? Alicia?

She bolted upright in bed.

What in hell was *this* all about? Some damnable voice was speaking to her from the edge of her consciousness.

It was unlike anything that she had ever experienced before. The voice was so creepy, so clear, palpable, and realistic that it seemed as if it were in the room with her.

She answered it aloud. "What?" she asked.

Alicia, will you listen to me? Will you heed me?

She looked all around the room. She saw nothing strange. She sensed no presence other than her own.

The voice came to her a third time.

Alicia?

"Who the hell are you and what do you want?"

No answer.

She waited several minutes. Nothing further came.

She settled in again. Her right shoulder gave another twinge.

She felt exhausted. But finally sometime after midnight, sleep finally came.

Time passed. The next thing Alicia knew, there was a persistent screaming in the room. She roused herself heavily out of sleep. She felt as if she were emerging from a trance.

What was she listening to? What had she heard?

A human voice?

No: an electronic voice!

Or an electronic noise, actually. Making sounds, not words.

She lifted herself from her semicoma and realized that the screaming was the telephone. It had been ringing incessantly, perhaps for several minutes.

She answered.

"Alicia?"

She hesitated. The voice was familiar.

She finally responded. "Yes?"

"You must have been sleeping soundly."

"Yes."

"Quite a night, huh?"

"Who is this?"

She had no sooner asked, and heard the hesitation that was its response, than she recognized the voice. Her commander, Lieutenant Albert Mott, at San Bernardino headquarters.

"You *were* sleeping pretty soundly, I guess, huh, if you don't recognize *my* voice," the lieutenant answered.

Her professional self kicked into gear. She squinted slightly and her eyes found the morning light beyond her blinds. The morning in Venice seemed abnormally bright. The sun was raging, its light bouncing off the ocean. What time was it?

"I'm all right," she said groggily. In the distant recesses of her brain a dream that she couldn't place receded. She only knew that it hadn't been a good one. It had made her uneasy. Almost frightened.

"What's happening?" she finally asked.

"What's new on John Doe in the Desert?" Mott inquired.

"Not much."

"How's the case going?"

"Pretty shitty," she answered. Her eyes found her clock radio and settled in on the bloodred LED that told the time. "Is that what you phoned me at six oh fucking six A.M. to ask?"

"No. I wanted to know when was the last time you were in Beverly Hills."

"Two weeks ago on the Gardella burglary ring. Why?"

"That's where I am right now. I'll give you an address."

Her ears perked. So did her interest.

"Why? What's up?"

"Well, hell, Alicia," Lieutenant Mott answered. "I'm standing here having coffee. Nice house, great neighborhood. Fresh new morning. And goddamn! There's something here in a body bag you ought to see, vis-à-vis your John Doe in the Desert stiff."

She exhaled a long breath and involuntarily entered the new day.

"I'll be over," she said.

C H A P T E R 7

Alicia skipped her usual four-mile morning run along the beach. She showered and dressed quickly. In a funny way, she welcomed the call to Beverly Hills. It took her mind off the foul dream, as well as the vision she had entertained.

Her hair still damp from the shower, she found her way quickly to Venice Boulevard. The clutter of morning traffic was already beginning, so she flipped her blue priority beacon onto the roof of her Jeep. At the intersection of Lincoln and Venice, local police waved her through. Minutes later, she accessed 405 North. She moved quickly to the car pool lane and hit her accelerator.

Alicia's destination was a three-story house on North Canon Drive in Beverly Hills, four blocks north of Santa Monica Boulevard. It was a handsome property, and when the local real estate people eventually got hold of it again, they would put it on the market for three and a half million dollars. It would have priced out for more, but high-profile crime gives a place bad karma. Bad karma does nothing for resale value.

The house was French Revival, also known as pseudo-Norman, nestled on a well-manicured lot between a Spanish adobe style and a colonial. Across the street lived a woman of fifty who had been a major recording star twenty-five years ago. Errol Flynn had once owned the house two doors away, Fred Astaire had lived three lots in the other direction. Bugsy Segal had been blown away at 810 Linden Drive around the corner.

Three houses down the block, behind a brick fence and second iron fence within the brick, lived the sixty-one-year-old former finance minister of a Middle Eastern fundamentalist monarchy with his third wife, a leggy thirty-year-old blond beauty from Arizona.

There were five local police cars in front of the house to which Alicia had been summoned, along with a phalanx of reporters and photographers. Above, two helicopters from local television stations hovered noisily. No freeway car chase this morning, so North Canon Drive would have the choppers' attention.

Alicia stopped her Jeep beyond the police line. Lieutenant Mott spotted her and guided her past the perimeter set by uniformed officers.

"Jesus, these Beverly Hills detectives are pissed as hell," he said in a low voice. "You know, they don't even *have* a homicide division. It's just detectives, major cases. Whoever is catching gets the case. Now they got a homicide they don't want."

Mott nodded to a pair of Beverly Hills detectives. One was in a dark olive-green suit, the other in sharp navy blue. The taller one was blond, buffed and crisp. The other man was older, with a touch of gray at the temples, which gave him a wiser, more dignified air. He was also smaller and had very broad shoulders.

Alicia glanced around. Every cop she saw looked as if he had a personal trainer.

Mott kept her walking. They passed through the front door of the house. "A man named Sands lived here," the lieutenant said. "Bill Sands. I guess we can call him the late Bill Sands now."

"Wife? Family?"

"No," Mott said. "And when we get upstairs, you'll see why."

They walked through the ground floor. The interior was starkly modern, its architecture at odds with the exterior. The front room was spacious and airy. A vast living room, dramatic art all over the place—sculptures, paintings. Alicia knew enough about art to recognize the artists and the worth. Modigliani and Picasso. A sculpture by Calder. A small Matisse. Major artists, minor works. Big bucks nonetheless.

A tearful woman named Maria sat on a white leather sofa in the living room, talking to the detectives in Spanish. She was chunky with a kindly Mexican face. Maria was the maid, Lieutenant Mott said, and it was she who had found her employer's body. Maria looked about thirty but Alicia guessed she was probably closer to nineteen.

In an adjacent dining room, there was more art.

This time, a vast hyperrealistic mural of an earthrise from the perspective of the moon. And in another side room, Sands had kept a study. No fancy-pants art here, no space-age motif. Instead, a giant silk screen of a pig-tailed Judy Garland dominated a dark green wall.

They came to a spiral staircase with brass fixtures.

"So who lived here?" Alicia asked as they climbed the stairs. "Just Sands?"

"Just Sands," Mott answered.

"What did he do?"

"He made money," said Mott, who was carrying a

notepad. "Something in entertainment. An agent or a producer or something, judging by the dough. Don't know yet. But he owned the place."

"Neighbors have anything to say?" Alicia asked.

"The neighbors are Iranian. Both sides. They don't talk to the police. They don't even talk to each other. I've got a couple of people canvassing the block. A woman across the street said she didn't like Sands. Threw noisy parties with a lot of single men."

The lieutenant rolled his eyes slightly and made a gesture with a limp wrist. At the same time, Alicia eyed the pictures that greeted them on the second-floor landing.

They had entered a Norman Rockwell world. Sands had blown up old family photographs, many of them black-and-white, many in pale color tones. A photographic history of a childhood in what looked like New England. Lots of leafy green trees in the summer, tons of snow in the winter. Prominently displayed was a white middle-class family, 1950s style. A mother, two daughters, and a boy, presumably Sands. There were even class pictures from grade school.

It was a photographic biography of the early part of the man's life. Alicia noticed that there was no father in any of the pictures. She theorized readily that there was always the chance that the father had been the man holding the camera on the family shots.

"One more flight up," Mott said. "Our own stairway to heaven this morning."

The steps were wooden, and creaked as they climbed. The owner of the house had painted them black.

Black changed the mood. There was a pink flamingo whimsically painted on the top step, and on the wall, just before they arrived on the uppermost floor of the home, another portrait of Judy Garland. Unlike the one downstairs, which captured her as a pure young girl, looking much as she had when she had visited Oz, this one showed her older, more haggard. Borderline dissipated.

Kind of twisted, actually.

Judy was wearing a dress far too short for her and her face showed the ravages of chemical abuse. Alicia guessed that it was taken not long before her death. She further wondered what Sands was trying to tell his guests between the ground floor and the third.

They arrived at a third-floor landing. Ahead was the sleeping area, which was already occupied by cops and medical techies.

Death-scene regulars.

Alicia recoiled when she walked into the bedroom.

First there was the stench of carnage, despite the fact that two large windows in the room were wide open. There was blood spattered along the walls, the floor, and across the sheets of an unmade bed. The yellow body bag, occupied, was on the floor. And finally there was the further transformation of the art. The mom 'n' pop 'n' apple pie stuff had given way to something that was only hinted at by the Judy Garland submotif.

One of the cops turned toward the door when Alicia entered. He was a big bear of a man, bald with a trim mustache, black uniform, matching black boots, stormtrooper style. He eyed Alicia and Lieutenant Mott. His nameplate said DAVOOKIAN.

He smirked and addressed the only woman present, Alicia. "Hey! If you like life-size fag-porno pictures, lady," Davookian said, "you've come to the right place. You knew this guy?"

Alicia was too busy taking it all in to immediately answer. "No," she mumbled. "Did you?"

"This is Detective Alicia Aldrich, Cal Highway, Homicide Division," Mott interjected.

"If you like life-size fag-porno pictures, Detective Alicia," the cop corrected himself, "you've come to the right crime scene."

Alicia continued to take it in.

Two walls were completely covered with homoerotica.

On one wall were two handsome young men in leather, kissing each other. One man was white, the other black. Plenty of muscles, all a-ripple. On the opposite wall, a four-foot-long photograph of a naked man, beautifully muscled and proportioned, penis-aroused and sleeping—dreaming?—on a sofa. Above the bed, two rough-trade guys in their twenties were about to have it on with a resisting teenage boy.

"While you're at it," the BevHilz cop added to Alicia, "don't miss the overhead."

She looked up. The ceiling: a full-color poster the size of a bed sheet. Two gay lovers, orally involved, inverted, enthusiastic and intertwined.

Alicia lowered her eyes. Davookian was smirking, waiting for her reaction.

She refused to give it to him.

"I can see why the window's open," she said.

"Why?" Mott asked.

"Air. This place stinks."

"It stinks in more ways than that," Davookian answered. "Fucking wealthy perverts. Probably came home with a fag hustler from Sunset."

"The window was like that when his maid found him," Mott said, prompting Alicia to take a second look at the open window.

"So maybe the killer flew away, huh?" Mott added. "Who the hell knows in Beverly Hills?"

A slight breeze entered the room. From a corner, there was a tinkling. Alicia glanced and spotted a metal mobile—a yellow sun, tennis-ball-size—hanging in the middle with fluted metal reeds strung to its side.

Tinkle, tinkle.

"Show me what you have," Alicia said.

Mott indicated the body bag on the floor.

"Sure. I just want to show you something, then we got to get the deceased out of here."A brigade of black uniforms and dark suits yielded to the lieutenant and the detective. Alicia walked to the body bag without speaking.

"Ready?" Mott asked.

"Ready," Alicia said. She knelt and one of the cops unzipped the bag. Alicia looked down.

Sands's eyes were wide open and his blond head was bent at an impossible angle. He had delicate features. In death, however, his expression was one midway between benevolence and horror. His throat had been carefully cut on the right side, with what looked more like an incision than a slash.

Idly examining the dead man, Alicia pondered the notion of death. What a final blessing, she mused, to die quietly in one's sleep as her father had. She wondered where God was when these things were going on. Why hadn't He interceded?

Mott spoke quietly. "No robbery in evidence. Or at least none that we could find."

"No signs of a break-in?"

"No. The window wasn't forced."

"Yeah?" she asked.

"So look for a personal angle on this," Mott said in a low voice. He scratched his face with his ham fist. "You know how fairies are," he said. "Probably walked his killer through the front door."

Alicia ignored the remark. "Your people dusting his cars for fingerprints?" Alicia asked Davookian.

"Yeah. It's being done."

"Anything the maid could tell us?" she asked Mott.

"Nothing yet. Though you can talk to her, too."

"I still don't see where this connects with my case," Alicia said.

"I'm coming to that," the lieutenant said.

Mott reached to the man's shirt and unbuttoned it.

"Remember, I read your report on John Doe in the Desert," he said. "That tattoo thing caught my fancy. So take a look at this."

With latexed fingers, Mott pushed aside the fabric of the victim's sleeping clothes. On his chest was a tattoo similar to the one borne by the victim in the desert. Seven small dots, one of them blue, plus a larger canary-hued one.

Alicia grimaced. "Okay," she said softly.

Then she bristled.

Next she froze. Something kicked in her chest.

See? came that damnable voice within her. *See? See? See?*

Mott must have guessed that she was emotionally distant. He waited several seconds. No response from her.

"What?" she whispered aloud.

See! the voice exclaimed in gladness.

"Hmm?" she asked, almost from within a minitrance.

". . . all right? Alicia?" She turned and saw Mott close to her, his brow furrowed, looking at her. "Alicia, hey? You all right?"

"Oh. Yeah," she answered.

"You looked like you blacked out. Where the hell did you go?"

"Just thinking," she said. She gave her head a quick shake. She noticed that the other cops in the room, all men, exchanged a glance. "So. Okay. What else?" she asked.

What else!

She steadied herself. But involuntarily, Alicia again tuned out the room she was standing in. The mysterious voice grabbed her attention, like a pair of hands on her arm, like a face thrust in front of her. It recited a line of doggerel, nursery-rhyme style:

Apple-dapply, Little Brown Mouse,
Goes to the cupboard in somebody's house;
In that fine cupboard finds everything nice
A quick violent death for human race mice.

She hurtled back to the present. Lieutenant Mott was expounding again. ". . . looking pretty damned familiar," said Mott, bringing Alicia back to the details before them. "Same as the desert. A mutilation."

Mott fully unzipped the bag and motioned to the victim's right foot. The man's small toe had been severed.

A missing toe. A small scar. This time, no blood.

"Okay?" Mott asked.

"Okay," she said.

Mott gave a nod to his staff. A cop zipped the bag again.

Alicia stood. There was something very cold in Alicia's own blood. Her back felt as if some unspeakable pressure were bearing down upon it. Her injured shoulder throbbed. She was suddenly aware of the heat of the day again, flowing in the open window as the sun climbed in the California sky.

Alicia raised her eyes to the photographs. Sands, the dead man, was also the man pictured naked on the coach on the opposite wall. And the sofa in the photograph was the leather one downstairs. Further, she noticed as she raised her eyes to the ceiling, Sands was one of the two lovers in the overhead scene.

Alicia shifted her weight as the medical technicians hoisted the body onto a gurney. Outside a boxy ambulance arrived. It was the size and shape of a Pacific Bell repair van. She could see it through one of the open windows.

For a moment, another irritating flashback. Alicia saw

herself at the death scene in the desert. There was a similarly eerie feeling in the air. Alicia was navigating in large part on feelings these days.

Then Alicia thought she saw a small figure standing in the shadows near the vehicle. For some reason, it reminded her horribly of the dream she had escaped earlier when Mott had phoned.

Her heartbeat quickened. Then the figure turned.

No. Not me.

The man's face was not what Alicia had expected. It was a Los Angeles cop. And on closer examination, the man she was watching had considerably more size and girth than the figure in her dream.

"Alicia, *how?*" Mott repeated. Still no response.

Alicia emerged from another minitrance and realized her commander was speaking to her.

"Hey! Are you listening to me or are you on another fucking planet?"

"What?" Alicia asked.

"Any idea how this could be related?"

"Related?"

"You *are* on another planet! I asked you three times."

"You did?"

Mott's expression changed to sympathy. "Alicia, you okay?"

"I'm fine."

"Something going on in your private life?"

She shook her head after a second. "No." It was as bald a lie as she knew how to tell. Her head was as scrambled as Sands's sex life. And her hesitation left Mott unconvinced.

"If you need to take more time off, you can, you know," he said.

"I know."

"The department shrink is available. You know that, right?"

"I know that," she said. Another awkward pause passed between them.

"So you agree that this has parallels to the John Doe in the Desert case?" Lieutenant Mott said.

"Obviously, yes."

"Any idea *how* it connects?"

"No," she answered. Her mind was teeming. A universe of conflicting emotions.

Mott flipped closed his notebook.

"I already talked to Captain McGraw this morning," Mott said. "I can assign you some help. I know you like to work alone, but I can assign one or two other detectives to work with you if you want."

"I don't want anyone else. Not yet."

Mott was silent for a few seconds.

"In a short time, that might be a luxury we can't afford," he said. "I'll indulge you for now. I know you're effective working alone. That was always your way of doing things in L.A. and Long Beach. But if we get another one of these . . . ?"

"No promises," Alicia said.

"I understand," Mott shrugged. "But the Beverly Hills department is going to be working on it, too. This one, at least."

She nodded again, grudgingly.

Actually, as she learned when she went back downstairs, the BevHilz cops had already started working on it. For starters, they had learned that Sands had been a programming executive at one of the three big broadcast networks.

"Family Entertainment Division," one of the BevHilz cops told her.

"Somehow," Alicia mused to herself, "it figures."

Nothing surprised her anymore. Nothing at all. But now the problem was to tie it all together.

That evening, back in her office, she was given something else to try to factor in. A man named Richard Hyde appeared at CHP headquarters in response to the publicity surrounding the body that had been found in the desert. Hyde was a long-haul trucker who normally drove cross-country, Wilmington, North Carolina, to San Francisco. On this past Sunday, however, Hyde had been completing a shorter job, Phoenix to Bakersfield. His drive had taken him across 14 North.

"That's when I saw them," Hyde said. "When I was driving past that stretch of high desert near Palmdale. I seen lights."

"Lights?" she asked. "What sort?"

Hyde had rough edges, both to his person and his story. His eyes drifted as he talked to Alicia, down from her eyes to her breasts. The interstate truckers could be a piggish crew, she knew. But they were often fine witnesses to the highways of the southwest.

"That's what I couldn't tell," he said. "Strange lights."

He said it must have been between eleven-thirty and

midnight. Hyde was always looking out for places where he could stop if he started feeling tired and didn't want to hop himself up with pharmaceuticals any further. Lights usually meant that other truckers had stopped.

"So I seen this one big bright light out in a stretch of the desert," he said. "And I couldn't figure out what kinda truck or vehicle it was. See, it was all one large light and it was way off the road."

Alicia folded her arms and listened.

"I figured it might have been some dudes having a right good time. You know, ma'am? Taking care of business?" He paused. "Know what I mean? Getting laid."

"Yeah. Getting laid," she repeated. From somewhere a little twinge of loneliness shivered through her. "But we didn't find any tire tracks to or from the position where the body was dropped."

"Yeah?" said Hyde. He smirked.

"But let's say that a big wind came up and wiped away all traces of tire tracks," she suggested. "What do you remember about the lights? What sort of truck do you think it could have been?"

"That's what don't make no sense," he said.

"Why?"

"It was some sort of aircraft. Chopper or something. Maybe something military," the trucker said. His eyes narrowed.

"Why?"

"It rose and took off," he said. "Flew away like a bat outta hell. I was watching it in my truck mirror. Watched till it was just a little yellow dot in the sky."

"So you think the body was dumped by air, Mr. Hyde?"

"Don't you?" he answered.

She answered cautiously. "We're still investigating." And a little voice inside her invoked the chrolystron factor at the same time.

"Well, investigate what aircraft were in the area around that time and maybe you can make an arrest," he said, sounding pleased.

"Thanks," Alicia said. "We'll work that angle."

Hyde went on his way.

Alicia worked that angle exactly. The angle, however, led nowhere. Plenty of air traffic in that area on Saturday night, she learned, but nothing that had officially touched down in the desert.

And there were questions about the identity of some of the craft, also. The thing was, low altitude was Indian territory out there—Piper Comanches and Cherokees making nighttime runs from Mexico into Southern California. The pilots were latter-day cowboys, smuggling drugs and undocumented Central Americans into the Golden State.

Nothing, in other words, out of the ordinary. And nothing that shed any light on John Doe in the Desert.

Alicia closed her books for the day, left her office at 11:20 P.M., and went home. She was asleep without the help of beer within five minutes of the moment her head hit the pillow.

Asleep, but not to stay.

CHAPTER 9

A night not soon to forget: a black spooky four A.M.

Alicia entered the elusive land midway between wakefulness and sleep. It was the hour of the wolf, the darkest middle hours of the California night.

She tossed fitfully in her bed. The night outside her home was quiet. The last thing she had seen when she looked out the window was a beautiful clear sky.

A starry sky. Millions of galaxies out there. Billions of planets.

And there you are on the small wet blue rock!

So why was a tranquil sleep proving elusive?

She was safe in her house, wasn't she? But what was forming inside her was not something that solid walls could exclude. What was bothering her was coming from somewhere else.

A nightmare.

Every mother's worst nightmare. Her only child dead.

She hurtled through a horror that she had never experienced before. A vision was coming together in her subconscious mind, and she didn't like it. She knew it was going to be unsettling.

Frightening.

She rolled again in bed.

She could hear herself thinking: she'd flashed into her own future this time. Alicia saw her firstborn daughter in her coffin. The loveliest and most beautiful daughter in creation—lying dead in a long white satin dress.

"Oh, God," Alicia thought with a tremor. Her eyes were open in the darkness of her bedroom. It was a four A.M. world and not a pleasant one.

Dead as dead can be on this planet!

"Now where did *that* come from?" she wondered. Something, someone, was whispering evil in her ear in the middle of the night, pouring venom into her dreams.

A power too strong for you to understand is now watching you, Alicia.

She sat up in bed. The room was dark and still. Spooky still. *Too* still.

Ah! Wonderful! We've made contact!

"Who in God's name are you?" she asked.

The King of the Sun.

"What?"

I'm the King of the Sun.

"What sort of gibberish is that?" she whispered aloud.

You can sense me! You know I'm here! Well, that's fine!

"Go away!" Alicia said. "Leave me alone! Go!"

She tried to settle back into the warmth and comfort of her bed. But she couldn't.

The voice was so clear that it made her think a pair of lips hovered near her ear. The imaginary creatures that inhabit the night and the land of half-sane, half-rational dreams were all here.

A blast of cold air hit her. Cold as a frozen lake in the

San Gabriel Mountains. Cold as a granite mausoleum on a winter morning.

Your daughter will die very young, Alicia.

"I don't have a daughter yet! I'm not married!

That's because you're a slut! You sleep with a man but can't keep him.

"Go away!"

Slept with Adam, but couldn't land him.

"I have no child!"

Someday you will.

"Leave me alone!"

Never had Alicia so questioned her sanity. What was this? A dialogue with her self-esteem? Or lack of it? She had taken six lovers in her life. Not a high number, she reasoned, by anyone's standards. Now from where was this damnable self-flagellation coming?

Six, huh?

"Jesus! Someone's reading my thoughts and responding!"

Yes!

"Not possible!" she breathed aloud.

It's happening. And your daughter will die very young if you don't obey me!

Alicia's eyes went wide with fury. What in hell was this? A line of hot sweat ran across her brow in thin little beads. Her vision settled into the near darkness and—

Hey! Want to see me? Got the nerve, Alicia! I'm right here!

She thought something moved in her bedroom.

"Oh, God! It's not possible. Oh, please God, no, not possible!"

She managed to dismiss it. Her eyes were wide as saucers. Then something glimmered in the darkness. A little reddish-silver glimmer.

"Jesus!" she thought in stark fear. "Something is moving! There is someone in here!"

Her heart pounded like a kettle drum.

Her hand punched at the lamp on the night table beside her. She fumbled with the switch and the room was flooded with the stark, intrusive light of a seventy-five watt bulb.

Everything was still.

She looked around. Nothing there except familiar objects. The usual dressers, the drawn shades. The clothing she had left out.

She exhaled a long breath. She allowed the moment to settle, and her nerves with it. Her heart still felt like a fish flapping in her chest. As her fear subsided, she felt silly.

She shook her head. The fear was still within her, a little menacing blue pilot light that wouldn't extinguish. Her shoulder stung as if someone invisible had just squeezed it.

Me.

Her mantra: "There's no one here. There's no one here. There's no one here."

Me.

"No one."

Me. I just have to step through what you would call an invisible window.

Alicia sat for several minutes without moving, trying to dismiss the uneasy echo and half-sense gibberish of a dream. Or what seemed like one. And yet, there had been something about that "dream" that disturbed her more than anything she had previously experienced.

It was as if this particular nightmare—this particular horror—had her name on it.

Several minutes passed. Then, with an inexplicable cold draft, another thought came to her. It was accusatory and personal, like an unwelcome footstep elsewhere in the house.

This dream is yours, Alicia. It's just for you.

She shuddered. Was she carrying on a psychotic dialogue with herself? Or was this originating from somewhere else?

Yes. You're right. It is!

"Yes, *what*? It is *what*?" she answered aloud.

No answer. But she had the worst damned feeling that there was a presence in the room. Something that she deeply feared.

Remember the invisible window.

But then Alicia told herself she was being silly. She tried to dismiss these night terrors. She looked around again and saw nothing out of the ordinary.

She listened for that strange inner voice to see if it would come to her again. It didn't. She breathed a little better, thinking she had dismissed it.

She closed her eyes for another grasp at sleep.

Sleep did not come easily. And it was not peaceful.

This time, she felt the terror advancing on her. The sensation reminded her of a stormy day at a waterfront cottage her parents had owned up at Lake Arrowhead when she was a little girl. The lake was many miles long and on hot summer afternoons she could see storm clouds rolling toward her, presaged by an extreme drop in the temperature.

She had felt a cold draft again just when she'd started to enter this realm of sleep, as if storm clouds were advancing. Then she felt herself on her back and staring up into a blue sky. But the storm clouds overtook the blue and the heavens raged. Then it was night and she was staring up into the firmament.

Billions of stars. A big fat canary-yellow moon. It should have been a beautiful image. Instead, it was deeply disturbing.

Good, good, good! Search the infernal night sky! Perhaps you can locate the planet from which I came!

Alicia could hear herself talking in her sleep. Her own voice, plaintive, frightened. "Damn! Who *are* you?"

Monarch of the grandest star!

"What!"

Le Roi du Soleil.

"What?"

The King of the Sun!

"Again?"

Oh, yes, my darling!

Then the nighttime heavens clouded over. Another storm approached until Alicia abruptly experienced the sensation of tumbling. She was drifting downward into the scarier nether regions of sleep.

Floating, flying, flailing.

Free-falling through reality. Hurtling through time and space.

Or into another reality. Faster and faster.

And then she felt a shock. She twisted in her bed, but her eyes were locked shut. No escape, no exit.

Hey! It's the same dream, Alicia. Thanks for coming back!

She was at a funeral again. Under a clear azure sky, there was a little girl in an open casket. The girl bore the name Julia, the name Alicia had always favored for the daughter she wished to have someday.

Julia was all dressed up to be buried.

"Good-bye, Mom," said Julia's corpse.

"Good-bye, Julia," said her mother.

An open coffin.

A gabfest between the dead and the living. Gradually, in Alicia's dream, people came into view around her. Everyone was crying. People she loved. Her family. Her mother and father. Her grandparents were there, too. Both had died years earlier. They turned to Alicia with yellow eyes and smiled.

"Hello, Ali. Grampa and I came back just for Julia's funeral," her grandmother said.

Alicia shook in her bed. So nice of her grandparents to make the trip.

"From where?" Alicia wondered.

The voice whispered and rasped. Intense. As if someone were standing over her as she slept.

From the other side of the universe. That's where the dead go, you know, Alicia.

Someone laughed. A horrible sound, like laughter from an old horror movie, but very real.

Three strange young men turned toward her. They looked like three high school boys whom Alicia had known many years earlier. Then she realized that's who they were. Three boys who had died in a drunken car wreck in 1990. The name of one of them was Sam.

Sam had been Alicia's first lover. Prom night of senior year.

Sam turned toward her. "Of course we're dead," he said.

"Everybody is dead on the cold planet where we live," said one of the others.

"Do you remember what it felt like when I was inside you?" Sam asked. "How come you never married?"

"Why shouldn't you be dead, too?" another added. "You got shot, didn't you?"

"Alicia almost came to join us but turned back," Sam said. "Too bad. I could have fucked her again."

Then Sam pointed to his head and indicated where it had been broken open in the car crash. His brains spilled forward.

The other boys laughed. Alicia shrieked in her sleep. The boys faded and were gone. Alicia turned back to the small coffin. She wanted badly to escape this vision.

Oh, but it's not just a nightmare, Alicia. Remember, all stories are true!

In the dream, Alicia couldn't move, and she couldn't move in her bed, either. And she realized that she was looking at herself estranged from her own body. She was at Julia's funeral, and suddenly she was seeing it through the eyes of others.

Then just as suddenly, the dream was over. Alicia was lying in her dark bedroom with her heart thumping wildly.

In the stillness of the night, she waited. She was so shaken that she was afraid to move. Finally, she rose from the bed. She had to leave her bedroom just to escape the oppressing atmosphere.

She quietly put on a light in the second-floor hallway. She found her way downstairs and turned on a light in the living room.

She sat down on the sofa, very conscious of the quiet of the night that surrounded her.

Alicia felt another deep surge of fear. It didn't flow or wash over her. It was much more violent and it ripped through her. At the same time, she felt something cold pass beside her, as if someone had opened a window to an eastern winter.

The coldness danced around her, then vanished. She looked away. "This is crazy," she whispered. "I don't believe in such things."

A response came seconds later:

You will.

"Never," she said, whispering again, after too long a pause.

Soon, replied the silky rasping voice that had now taken residence within her. *Very soon, Alicia. Very, very soon.*

She sat in fear in her living room, unable to move, unwilling even to attempt to return to sleep.

Then her eyes went wide with terror. She gazed across her living room and a shape seemed to take form in front of her, as if a small silvery cloud had entered her home. She looked at it, dumbstruck, unable to move.

The light in the room was different now, something she had never experienced. It was reddish. And the atmospheric pressure in the room dropped, as with the advent of a storm.

She was unable to move her eyes. The small cloud took shape, the image like the red light in her mind's eye. But this was real.

And bigger.

It formed a nearly human shape. A small body with arms and legs, maybe about five and a half feet in height. No distinct features or face, and amorphous arms.

Then the vision fell apart again, only to re-form. Alicia felt as if she were on the fringe of sanity. But something within her clicked on: her police officer's instincts, her heightened powers of observation.

Whatever the phenomenon was, she wanted to see it.

To understand it.

And you will, Alicia.

There was a foul smell in the room, and a vision of the dead man in the desert flashed before her. Then there were a series of flashbacks—in small micromoments that had no measurement in earthly time—and she saw herself as a much younger woman in a medical examiner's office in Long Beach, seeing her first dismembered corpse. Then she saw herself again as a horrified rookie on that same Long Beach force, looking into an oceanside Dumpster in the shadow of the *Queen Mary* on a beautiful cloudless day in Southern California, and gawking at the nude dismembered remains of a sixteen-year-old girl, gagging at the putrid odor. And then she was back in that horrible dream again, seeing the funeral for a daughter that she had not yet conceived, nor even met the man with whom she would conceive her. Then Alicia's consciousness spiraled again and lurched backward into time present and there was—

A man standing in front of her!

He had materialized out of the misty, cloudy condensation that had formed in front of her. First he had looked like the steam that emanates from dry ice and then he took human form.

He was stocky and pudgy, with a face that was not quite human, though there were definite human features. There was something wrong with his eyes, but Alicia could not tell what.

Something about him was just off.

She looked at the intruder as if she were watching Death himself. She thought to reach for her service pistol. Just as quickly, she knew the act would be useless.

Then she was strangely calm. Stunned, like a small animal before a snake or a predatory cat, just before it was to be devoured.

She felt very vulnerable, both in terms of her physical safety and her sexuality. Something female ached inside her and went on a momentary rampage. As if this man could see through her and was enjoying her sexually right here, violently against her wishes.

"What do you want?" she heard herself say.

A thin smile crossed his lips.

You'll know soon.

Then he faded and was gone.

No physical trace was left behind.

She didn't move. Hours passed like minutes. The only sound she could hear was the thundering of her own heart. The next thing that she was aware of was the light in the east beyond her home.

The sky was brightening with the new dawn, driving away the darkness, dismissing a night that had been unlike any other. And with the dawn came the grandest of all stars.

The sun.

CHAPTER 10

Two hours later, Alicia walked on the edge of the Pacific Ocean in Venice, her feet bare, her running shoes slung over her shoulder.

She had successfully taken her morning workout, a four-mile run along the edge of the ocean. Twenty-seven minutes, slightly faster than normal.

The morning air invigorated her. She felt good for the first time since the John Doe body had been found in the high desert north of Palmdale. The exercise had even helped her dispel the unsettling dream she had suffered hours earlier.

She glanced at her watch. Quarter past seven. She was not due at work for another hour and a quarter. She trekked across the beach to where she had parked her Jeep.

Sometimes on these morning workouts she felt like a girl again instead of a grown woman with a professional career in law enforcement and a service revolver stashed away in the glove compartment of her Jeep.

A sweatshirt and shorts. Bare feet. The ocean.

The early hours past dawn brought back memories every time, usually those of past romances.

She remembered a day years earlier. A hiking vacation in Mexico with a young man named Adam.

They had climbed a set of steep crumbling steps on a hillside in Baja. As they reached the crest they had a view of both the countryside and the ocean. They climbed higher and came to some ruins from the Iztecqui tribe, ruins that looked like large piles of sun-bleached bones, except for a collapsed stone wall here and there, a broken crumbled tower and walls that were now rubble, an ancient dwelling or village left exposed to rot in the scorching Mexican sun.

The ruins—seen from a distance, viewed from a certain angle—formed distinct geometric patterns, squares within rectangles within squares, patterns that the ancients had pointed toward the heavens as a signal for visitors or gods who would descend from the sky. Once this place had had a purpose; it had housed humanity and a small primitive society.

But no more.

Rows of palm trees marked ancient overgrown pathways. There was no hint of a breeze. When they were at the summit of the hillside, and very much alone in a private place, Adam drew her to him, holding her so tightly that she had trouble breathing.

"Adam, for God's sake," she had said, half laughing, half protesting. "Later, okay? Not here, not now."

"Why not? There's no one around."

Part of her coursed with excitement. Part shook with horror.

He kissed her again, across the back of her neck from behind, and leaned around her, one hand working on lifting the back of her skirt, the other hand moving gently up her abdomen. Her breasts were bare beneath a flimsy T-shirt.

His kiss was salty.

Exciting. Good.

"Adam, no!" she breathed again.

She felt his hand arrive at its destination. At the same time she felt him get hard.

"We can do it quickly," he said. "Right here. On top of the world."

He held her firmly by the hips. One of his legs was wrapped around one of hers. Perhaps half a mile away, down below the hill, a man fished from a small boat. As Alicia fought off her lover, she wondered who the man was. Could he have had the remotest inkling that an American man and women, battling their desire to tryst, were watching him?

She managed to pull away. She heard Adam sigh.

"It's too hot," she said.

He sighed again. "Too hot," he finally agreed.

She took his hand in consolation.

"I'll take a picture of you," he said.

On the summit of the hill, he shot a beautiful photograph, one that stayed in her heart and on her dresser for years. In it, she was forever a pretty girl in her early twenties, with light brown hair and very dark sunglasses, wearing a skirt that seemed to have no more width than three strips of bacon, side by side.

In the picture, her warm, cryptic smile is that of a young woman who had just fought off a handsome persistent lover, but who knows she will eagerly gave in to him when he tries again later in the afternoon. Her legs are long, sleek and lean.

This morning on the beach in Venice, the squawking of a pair of seagulls overhead jolted her back to reality. She stopped at her Jeep and grabbed a towel. She mopped her face and dried the sweat from her arms. The ocean breeze cooled the sweat on her legs.

She grabbed a few dollars from the compartment between the front seats and walked to a small bakery across the street. After buying tea and a croissant, she walked back to her car and slid into the driver's seat. Her memories were abruptly sabotaged by other concerns and concepts.

Her recent nightmares. Chrolystron. A still-unidentified tattooed body dumped and abandoned in the desert. And linked to a case in Beverly Hills.

And that funny voice that seemed to be addressing her.

Alicia sat in her car at the edge of the beachside, looking out over the Pacific Ocean, trying to find sense where there didn't seem to be any. The car door was open. One long bare leg stuck out, exposed, cooling in the breeze.

What was bothering her was not just this case, she conceded, but also the tangle of emotions that had erupted since she had become involved with it. Her mind was a mess. At the far edge of her consciousness she sensed some little warning mechanism that was sending her thoughts about the emotional frailties of police officers who return to work too quickly after traumatic injuries.

One recent evening—it was the evening before her niece's birthday party, the night before she had been called to the desert to view the first body—she had been home alone bathing and had been convinced that someone was watching her. And yet she knew that she was alone in her house and she knew that every significant window shade had been lowered. It was as if, she recalled, there had been another window that she didn't know about or had forgotten.

She sighed and sipped the tea. She didn't think that she had gone back to work too soon. What good would sitting out on disability do her? And for that matter, was she as loco as she felt?

El Polo Loco. La Vida Loca. La policewoman loca, also.

Abruptly the tea tasted strange. It almost made her gag.

Green tea with honey and ginseng. Now what was wrong with *that*? She had been drinking this brew for years.

The voice returned.

Nothing's wrong, Alicia. Just wanted your attention.

She cringed.

She whispered aloud. "My attention for what?"

We meet today! the voice answered in triumph.

She spoke much louder. "We do *what*?" she demanded.

There was no answer. Then she jumped slightly, startled.

Outside her Jeep there was movement. The thought ripped through her that it was the owner of the voice. She turned, spilling a few drops of tea, one hand reaching for her weapon.

But the movement was nothing more than two teenage boys. They were looking at her, a pretty thirtyish woman sitting in a car alone talking aloud.

They both wore Dodgers caps. She smiled at them.

They stared for another few seconds as they passed, then turned away. One boy's eyes had been on her legs and body. The boy said something to the other and they both laughed. Alicia assumed the comment was lewd and she was the object of it. She felt a surge of indignation.

People had resented her before. People had been angry with her and had violently confronted her. But no one had ever laughed. She wasn't pleased. She thought back to some advice her mother had urged upon her years ago.

"One day you'll wake up," her mother had said, "you'll

be a middle-aged lady and no one will take you seriously any more. People listen, they nod, they're polite. But they just plain ignore you, and the next thing you know you're an *old* lady and no one has any use for you, except maybe your own children if you're lucky. And that's God's truth. So have your fun while you're young."

What had she meant by that? Find a nice man and get laid a lot? She hadn't done that, either.

Alicia watched the boys stroll down to the beach. She felt an unfair dislike for them and their youth, sixteen, seventeen years old, as they were. She wondered if she had looked good to them from the distance, then seemed too old when they drew close. She had an urge to give them a hassle on general principles, something she had always sworn as a cop that she would never do.

Maybe she would go see if they had any booze or pot. Then they wouldn't snicker up their adolescent sleeves, would they? Hey, empty their pockets and who knew what she might find.

She let her indignation subside. What was going on with her? she wondered. John Doe in the Desert was warping her personality. So was the presence of that damned intrusive voice.

Try to relax, she told herself. Try very hard, diligently. She flicked on the car radio. She found an oldies station from Pasadena, and Smoky Robinson, every silky note of him, filled the car. She thought of her partner Ed Van Allen, who was zeroing in on fifty—or had he zeroed past?—and who listened to the same station. Ed remembered all those songs when they were new.

She smiled. She let go of her anger and thought back to her dead man with the chrolystron in his blood.

"Okay. So he's a space traveler. Or was," she said.

Very good, Alicia. You are starting to understand. Yes, he was a space traveler.

The voice was so dead-on realistic that it startled her.
And you could be, too.
She looked around. No one close. No one near.
"Could be *what?* Understand *what?*" she demanded aloud. "What could I be and what the hell am I supposed to understand?"
But the voice clicked off, almost like a radio from which the batteries had been suddenly yanked. Not one syllable more.
Alicia broke into a light sweat. Deep down, she recognized the source.
It was fear.
Anxiety.
The realization that she was facing a strange window upon the unknown, and a small menacing hand was slowly lifting the shade.
Something like an acid flash was upon her. She was suddenly overcome by a vision of stars. She blinked to resist it. It gave her a headache the size of an aircraft carrier.
Then it was suddenly gone.
Her attention jumped to something at the near edge of the water. Something small and animated with a lot of color, about fifty yards in front of her. She reached for a pair of binoculars that she kept in her Jeep and raised them to her eyes.
A bizarre California scene.
Two parrots fought with a seagull over a piece of food. Each year, hundreds of parrots were smuggled into California for resale. Many of them escaped, then staked out adversarial positions against local wildlife for a place in the ecological chain.
Alicia watched the dispute. The seagull was bigger but the parrots were scrappier. She found herself rooting for the home team: the gull.

Alicia leaned back in her Jeep and placed her hands on the steering wheel. The police radio under her dashboard crackled intermittently. In her rear-view mirror she watched a man in a suit unlock a Lexus and climb into the driver's seat.

She guessed the driver was about sixty. The car was metallic blue and gleaming. On its rear window was a red, white, and blue Grateful Dead sticker and on its license plate holder was the logo of a dealer in Santa Monica.

Details gave away so much. Deadheads had more than a touch of gray these days and they had more than a touch of cash, too. They were also moving farther up into exurbia where half a million bucks could buy something more than the cheapest house on the block.

The Lexus pulled away, taking with it the specter of an aging millionaire ex-hippie. A vision of her John Doe appeared again in her mind, replacing that of Bob Weir and the late Jerry Garcia.

What was it about this case that Alicia couldn't stay away from? she wondered. What was the feeling within her that was tugging at her subconscious?

The chrolystron?

That's just the beginning of it.

As she searched the knowable details about her tattooed John Doe, she felt herself hungry for any connection of facts, however oblique, that would draw a detail or two into focus. But she had nothing. She barely had a context for John Doe's death.

Worse, she found the front part of her mind at odds with the back. Her eyes had settled upon Santa Monica Bay before her and she was watching something else unfold by its shore.

The two boys who had walked past her car now stood on the edge of the bay skimming shells across the water.

Their voices were animated. She could hear them all the way from their spot at the edge of the water. Alicia used her binoculars to watch and count—five, six skips—before the shells sank.

Alicia watched the boys for several minutes.

Suddenly there was a call on her police radio for any available assistance. Accident on State Highway 10 toward the 4th Street exit in Santa Monica. A three-car slammer with a lot of blood. The officer on the scene needed immediate assistance.

"Well, why not?" she said to herself.

Sweatshirt and shorts not withstanding, she still had her weapon and her shield. She had a commitment to her job and a sense of duty, too. She flipped the beacon onto the roof of her car and pulled out of her parking place.

She never arrived in Santa Monica.

C H A P T E R   1 1

Alicia was driving past an In-N-Out Burger in Venice when something pulled her attention from the road. She saw a small elfin figure, a man who stood about five and a half feet high.

Her heart kicked. She recognized him from the previous day. It was the man, or the human form, that had materialized and disappeared within her home.

She was certain!

She hit the brake hard and cut into the parking lot, where she pulled the Jeep to a stop and stared. She couldn't believe it!

If she had imagined a physical presence in her house, this was the man she had imagined.

She kept her engine running while she unlocked her glove compartment and withdrew her weapon. Alicia knew danger when she sensed it.

The little man stood next to the cab of a green pickup truck and put the key in the lock. He wore dark glasses and was dressed in a pair of tan trousers and a denim jacket over a black T-shirt. At his neck was a gold chain with a small yellow disc hanging like a medallion.

Alicia stepped out of her Jeep.

She had an extra sweatshirt in the Jeep. It was heavier than the one she already wore, but she pulled it on, carefully stuffing her weapon into a pocket. The sun upon her suddenly felt intensely warm. She started to sweat again.

She walked toward the little man, stopping ten feet away.

She watched him carefully and kept a wary eye on the man's hands. She placed her hand on her weapon.

The hair rose at the back of her neck. Bumps rippled up and down her arms.

"Hello," Alicia said.

The little man turned and glowered at her. Then he turned away. He didn't speak.

"Hello," Alicia said again.

Alicia reached for her shield and held it aloft. "California Highway Patrol. I'm Detective Alicia—"

"I don't care who you are," the man said softly.

His voice sounded like a heavy body being dragged through sand. And strangely, at the farthest fringes of her own consciousness, she thought she sensed some sort of high-pitched whining.

"We know each other from somewhere, don't we?" Alicia asked.

"I don't think so. Not yet, anyway."

"We've met before," she insisted.

"Only if I say we have," the man said.

She hesitated.

Then the little man looked her way again through his dark glasses. It was only a glance, but it contained a universe of contempt. Alicia felt something strange, something oppressive and dangerous when she was within his line of vision. Then the man turned and spit on the pavement near Alicia's sneakers.

She let it pass.

She was too busy looking for details.

The man's hands and arms did not seem quite right. They looked too fleshy, as if he were a complete stranger to any sort of exercise. There was a bizarre ageless quality about him. As she studied him, her mind trying to rapidly assess information and draw conclusions, she could barely decide the most basic things.

Was he very young or very old?

Neither!

He was somewhere between twenty and seventy, she decided. She had never seen anything like it. Within her head began the dull pounding of a headache.

"Why don't you go away?" the man asked her. "I haven't done anything. I don't know why you're bothering me."

"I feel as if I know you," she said. "Do I or don't I?"

He remained quiet.

He unlocked the cab and opened the truck door. "A little of both," he said. "You know me, but you don't."

"So in what way *do* I know you?" she asked.

A sly smile creased his face.

Something strange about that, too. Not quite human, she would remember thinking. Not quite of this world.

"It's California and you're a cop," he said. "You assume things."

It made no sense to her. Her headache was in full flare now, and for some reason she had a flashback to the scene in the desert with the body of John Doe, then a subsequent flash to Janet's party.

Next something even more peculiar, frightening, and astonishing happened.

The man reached to his dark glasses and removed

them. He folded them away and turned. Alicia watched his hands carefully.

Then their eyes locked, Alicia's upon his, and his cold dark eyes upon the policewoman's. Alicia froze. The man sent her a signal that was almost like receiving an electric shock—vibrations unlike any other she had ever picked up from any living human.

She sensed something that she knew contained fear, but was much, much more than that. It was something deeper and darker. There was something very wild and immeasurable within him.

Something here reminded Alicia of the night she was shot, and the sensation of tumbling into that resolute brightness that was her seven-minute death. Her old wounds started to hurt, the spot where the bullet entered her body, and the inside areas through which the projectile had ripped.

Then it was gone.

But Alicia couldn't shake the intense discomfort she felt in this man's presence. She felt vulnerable, as if she would have no way to defend herself if he attacked her.

You won't even be able to resist.

"God Almighty," she found herself thinking. "Where are these thoughts coming from?"

"Otherworldly?" the man said aloud. Or at least she thought he did. "I think the term you want is 'extraterrestrial.' That's what it's called here, isn't it?"

She stared at him. *"What?"* she asked.

"I didn't say anything," he said pleasantly. "Please leave me alone."

He eyed her up and down. She wished she had worn something other than a sweatshirt and shorts. She probably looked like a dumbassed seventeen-year-old girl putting herself on drunken display in a wet T-shirt contest.

"Both now and when you're alone," he said. His voice was now akin to a silky hiss.

"Now and when I'm alone, *what?*" she asked.

"You hear me," he answered very succinctly. "You hear me now and when you're alone, Alicia. Those are *my* thoughts in your head."

Her heart thundered.

"What you need to start doing is obeying me," the small man said engagingly. "That way things will be good for both of us."

"Who are you?" she mumbled.

"Need a name?"

"Don't you have one?"

"Amos Joy," he said.

She repeated it.

"Master it. For I will master you," he said.

"I don't understand what you're talking about," Alicia answered, knowing how feeble she sounded. Her left hand held the stock of the gun in her pocket. The man glanced down to where she held the gun, then he raised his eyes again.

"Going to shoot me?" he asked, his lips twisting into a parody of a smile.

"I think not," he continued. "Fa la la la la."

Alicia groped for something to ask next.

Yet she was suddenly aware that her preparation for this moment had mysteriously disappeared. Something about the presence of this man had thrown her that far off.

The man climbed into the cab of his truck. Alicia wanted to raise a hand to stop him but some instinct told her not to.

The truck's engine turned over with a clank. It gave a long blast of sooty exhaust. The driver started to pull his door shut. Alicia, in a sudden bold move, stepped forward and held the door with an extended left arm.

His eyes fell upon her again. Another smile crossed the little man's face. The man sat in the cab and slowly pulled the door shut with one hand. Alicia was helpless. She felt as if she were trying to stave off a machine. Having barely exerted himself, the man used his other paw to reach to his side and push Alicia away.

Alicia was so stunned, so overwhelmed, by Amos Joy's raw physical strength, that she stood helpless for several seconds.

"I want you to stop," she said.

"I don't know why you're bothering me," he answered.

"What did you mean by 'extraterrestrial'?" she asked.

"I said nothing of the kind."

"Are you sending me messages?" she asked. "Mentally? Are you doing something to me?"

"I think you're crazy," Amos Joy answered. "I don't even believe you're a cop. And if you are, you won't be one for long."

Her adversary gunned the accelerator.

He hit the gas and pulled away. All Alicia could think of as he rode away was how frightened she was, and how much she could use a drink.

CHAPTER 12

After an unproductive day at work, Alicia found that drink several hours later at her home in Venice. She sat in her living room· before a large-screen television. She could have used an episode of one of her favorites. A new *Friends* or a rerun of *Three's Company*. But the set was not on and Alicia was deep in thought.

She had sensed an eerie connection with Amos Joy, and didn't want to admit what it was. All that Alicia could think about since encountering Amos was the night when she had almost died. Or, more accurately, the night when she had died . . . and come back.

Over and over, she replayed the moments when she had been shot and killed and then, through the miracle of wires, tubes, and electric shocks, been brought back to life again.

Dead and then returned to the living. The complete round trip, to eternity and back, all in a few hours.

It had happened on an early morning in Irvine on the previous January tenth. She and her partner, Martin Freeman, were working undercover narcotics, hot on the trail of a Tex-Mex coke dealer named Hernando Cordero.

Alicia and Freeman received a tip that Cordero was holed up in a two-story housing project four blocks south of St. Vincent's Hospital.

Dressed in flak jackets, they responded and requested backups. When they arrived at the address, however, they found a run-down hacienda-style bungalow with an open front door. Within, they saw a cluttered hallway leading to a back room.

They waited.

The night was quiet. No cars, no activity, even in a neighborhood where the business of junk pharmaceuticals usually went on twenty-four seven.

It was two-fifteen A.M.

Alicia volunteered to enter the premises for the first look. Freeman would follow. They had worked on the arrest for two months and were hungry for the collar.

Alicia entered the first floor of the unit.

Nothing happened.

She went quietly up the staircase with her partner behind her. She entered a room at the top of the stairs. It was cluttered. A large mattress, two lamps, and drug paraphernalia. Some motel chairs, orange and blue. If Alicia had five dollars for every cockroach she stepped on, she could have retired wealthy on the spot.

Instead, she nearly died poor. It was hard to tiptoe across a room when one's shoes kept crunching big brown live roaches.

She went into the first room. Nothing. There was a closed closet. She passed the closet and went to a back bedroom. Again, nothing but rubble.

Crunch, crunch.

Her partner stood at the door, weapon ready.

Then everything exploded.

When Alicia entered from the bedroom, Hernando Cordero emerged from the closet, his finger tight on the trigger of a Glock-9.

The first two bullets hit but failed to penetrate Alicia's flak jacket. The force sent her sprawling. The third shot, however, found the upper edge of the right-side arm hole and hit flesh.

The bullet severed an artery and lodged near her heart even before she hit the ground. Her partner, meantime, emptied his own weapon into Hernando Cordero. Three shots while Hernando was standing and another five after he hit the floor.

No one complained.

In the twenty minutes that it took the medics to respond, Alicia lost consciousness and two pints of blood. By the time she was on the operating table in the hospital, her heart had stopped.

Electric shock was applied to her chest.

It was enough voltage to kill a woman if she weren't already dead; more than enough to zap her back to life if she were.

But nothing worked.

The doctors gave up. They were pulling sheets over Alicia's body when David Aldrich, Alicia's younger brother and also a state district attorney, arrived, roused from bed in the middle of the night.

"We lost her," said the doctor. "I'm sorry."

"When?"

"Five minutes ago."

David Aldrich had been a lifeguard for three summers. He had also seen action in the Gulf War and had witnessed miracles before.

"Is she still on the respirator?" David asked.

"We haven't flicked the switch yet, so, yes. Why?"

David again: "How long's the brain been down?"

"Seven minutes," said another ER doctor.

"Seven's a lucky number."

"Not tonight, I'm afraid."

"Try it again, Doc."

"Waste of time and I have other emergency patients."

According to local lore, David Aldrich drew a pistol from an L.A. cop who had also responded. The state troopers present stood by as he pointed it toward the intern.

"Try it again," he said softly. "Now."

Seven minutes turned into eight. But during the eighth minute, the heart fluttered, then started again. Then brain waves perked, too.

Alicia was back. Incredibly, brain function returned completely and unimpaired. Her flesh and internal organs were stitched together. Hernando Cordero had been buried for three weeks by the time Alicia went home.

The department offered her retirement on full disability. She refused. What she wanted was her job. The LAPD gave it to her, but not without six months of rehab, physical and psychiatric.

And therein lay many recent irritations.

Having been shot, killed, and then brought back to life drew attention. For example, a battery of questions from the psychologists. The shrinks. The psychic researchers. The busybodies. The priests.

What did you see while you were dead?

God?

Eternity?

The future?

The past?

Long-lost relatives?

The Simpsons?

On this evening in her home eighteen months later, she spoke aloud to no one. To everyone.

"I'm sorry," she answered, as she had many other times, as well. "I didn't see anything."

And, she might have added, if she had wanted to see long-lost relatives, she would have hit the family picnic in Pasadena each year. But she took a pass on that, too.

What did you feel? Everyone wanted her to feel something different.

Jesus.

Enlightenment.

Liberation from worldly concerns.

A soaring sense of flight.

A "higher state of being," whatever that meant.

She spoke again, the words coming easily but defensively, as they always did on this subject.

"I'm sorry. I saw nothing. I was conscious, but I saw nothing. I felt a certain brightness but I was just *there*."

"Where?" they all asked.

"It was very bright. That's all I know. That's all I remember. Everything was very bright."

"Did you see God?" one psychiatrist from UCLA Medical had asked at a subsequent interview session.

"No," Alicia answered.

The shrink was a small, very pregnant Cambodian woman in a lab coat, a brilliant weirdo from the pysch ward. Her name was Dr. Samrin and she stood two inches shy of five feet. She had a blunt nose that gave her the facial qualities of a midget pig, not to mention the shape. She also had an irritating nasal voice, particularly when she was sniffing around with metaphysical questions.

"Your heart had stopped. No blood was being pumped. So, if you please, that sense of brightness *could* have been from preliminary stages of chemical decomposition of the brain, is it not?"

Alicia had problems with this interview. She felt as if she were hallucinating. Again. The doctor looked as if she were left over from someone's sixties Haight-Ashbury acid trip.

Dr. Samrin pursued the issue.

"Now, all right, if you please, did you notice if this was a yellow brightness or a white brightness?"

"What the hell difference does it make?" asked Alicia.

"White brightness, good. Yellow brightness not so good."

"Why's that?"

"No one know yet."

"I'm getting tired of these questions. They're going nowhere."

"Me, neither. What color? Yellow?"

"I guess. Yes. Yellowish."

"Ah. Did it remind you of anything?"

"What do you mean?"

"The color? The lights? Associations, if you please. Yellow?"

Alicia shrugged. "Cat urine on a white shag carpet."

Dr. Samrin blinked. "I see," she said. "I have cat. I understand."

"Do you?"

"Yes. Have cat. Nice cat. Big fifteen-pound mouser!"

Alicia waited for a moment. "I meant, *do you understand*. And it was a joke."

"Joke! We not here to joke and have fun!" The shrillness of Dr. Samrin's voice raised bumps on Alicia's arms. She took a final look at the pipsqueak shrink, assembled her things, and tried to leave. But Dr. Samrin pursued her down the elevator and into the parking lot.

"Joke? Please? Meaning?" she kept asking, over and over, a pad and pen ready. That had been Alicia's last therapy session.

Tonight, Alicia sighed and her thoughts drifted again. She had never wanted to share her private ruminations with strangers. She missed her father, who died before Alicia could put her life in order. She missed not having a particular man in her life, someone to be there when she came home each day. But she was not the type of woman to share thoughts with shrinks. All the head doctors she had ever met had been in psychoanalysis themselves, and came off to her as humanold versions of Daffy Duck.

So Alicia became intensely introspective. Her hunch was that she was back on this planet for a reason, though there was no way anyone could wrap any science or psychiatry around a theory like that. Whether the reason presented itself now or thirty years in the future remained to be seen.

So she cut a few corners to get back on the force.

No one could tell, but the bullet in her right shoulder had diminished her feeling in her right side, as well as her mobility. A right-handed draw, she was a half-second slower than she used to be. Her shot, as demonstrated at the range, was only eighty percent as accurate. And there were various pains and discomforts that came and went, though there was almost always something.

A tingling numbness, for example, frequently came up out of nowhere in her shoulder and spread down to her arm. A little miniparalysis, which lasted for only a few seconds, followed shortly by an intense pain. Sometimes it deadened all feeling in the fingers of her right hand. The doctors couldn't trace it—nerve damage was elusive like that—but it threatened to keep her off active duty until she stopped admitting that she felt it. And if it didn't go away at all, they would "retire" her on disability.

No way.

She was not going to permit that.

She stopped mentioning the paralysis and refused to admit the pain persisted, telling the surgeons that the symptoms had vanished. And with them went the final hurdle to getting back on active duty. But the incident had left her very much a woman on the edge.

On the edge of giving herself over to heavy drinking.

On the edge of the true terror of having been so close to losing her life.

On the edge of walking into yet another situation that would finish what Hernando Cordero had begun. Sometimes, a violent death seemed to be just one wrong step away, one more doorway that she did not need to walk through.

Nor was it ever far from her thoughts. Not with the pain in her lower arm and shoulder, and not with that damnable moony-yellow brightness that flashed relentlessly back on her.

Not when there was already the heavy whiff of homicide in the air, and the inescapable feeling that more would follow. As she sat in her home and finally guided her thoughts away from the night she died, the strange mood that was upon her began to lift.

She drained her second bottle of beer, then a third, but resisted opening a fourth. And she also resisted making any preliminary conclusions about Amos Joy. She would have to study the little mutt up close again and reconsider what it was that was "wrong" about him.

Today she hadn't even dared to run his name through the national crime computer. But she knew that in the next day or two she would.

For better or worse, she felt herself repelled by the man, then drawn to him, as if her emotions were being somehow manipulated. There was no explanation: this was just one more thing that Alicia was incapable of understanding. She closed her eyes for a moment.

She thought back to that intense brightness that had accompanied her near death. And then a startling revelation was upon her, almost like something coming to her out of hypnosis.

In the midst of the brightness, she saw now, was a small humanoid figure. It was of unnatural shape.

Limbs too long and thin.

Head too damn big to be human!

Eyes too dark.

Grayish skin, the color of a dove, but with a sheen like metal. A hazy red hue outlining the body.

Worse, she had the sense of having seen this figure all along, as if it had been on the edge of her consciousness. Yet she had never been able to admit it was there till now.

"Oh, God! Why, why, *why* is it here *now!*"

In fear, her eyes—the windows to her soul—flashed open.

The room was quiet. Her shoulder ached. The house was warm and stuffy.

She was alone.

A deep surge of depression was upon her.

She wasn't even certain whether she had actually stopped a little man with a truck or whether she had imagined the entire incident. And she felt more lost and confused than at any moment since she had left the hospital.

Sitting at her desk at the state police barracks in San Bernardino, Detective Alicia Aldrich took some time to engage in the never-ending battle against paperwork. But she had also run a request through the national crime computer for anything touching upon a man named Amos Joy. The inquiry had also been cross-referenced to the FBI in Virginia. She had been promised a response by the next day at noon, Pacific time.

Meanwhile, she attempted to sort through a small bin that contained unfinished but still-open cases, most of which she had inherited from an older detective who had retired. It was late on Wednesday evening, a time when she might have been home.

Many of the cases were incidents that she had worked on with the local town police, before she had been pro-moted to homicide.

Irvine. Riverside. Santa Barbara, in particular. In-cluded were numerous housebreakings, car thefts, and store thefts, punctuated by a smaller number of assaults.

There was a series of bank robberies with the same

signatures up and down the west coast, most recently in Fresno, a place with no shortage of such activity. The Feds had become involved there, and hadn't been able to resolve it, either.

They also had airport police involved. The theory: the robbers were jetting into the area, hitting, and flying out. Several different law enforcement agencies in the area were waiting for the robbers to strike again, and make a mistake. Every airport was covered.

She went through her files.

Constant reviewing kept her familiar with each case, even while she dealt with the two tattoo murders. She had spent hours of her own time on many of these investigations. The most aggravating part of police work, aside from the risk of getting killed, was to have doped out a case, to know how it had been perpetrated, sometimes even know who had done it, but remain unable to bring it to closure. Anything that was on her desk and couldn't be closed bothered her. But the world was gloriously imperfect and inexplicable, and gave every indication of remaining so.

Being alive was a bonus, she reminded herself. So why become stressed about some unresolved cases? Besides, she mused further as the hour grew later, unresolved meant unresolved *as yet*.

Most of these dossiers returned to the right-hand corner of her desk. A few, perhaps one in every six, she put into a deeper section of her department's files, one for cases that were likely to remain static forever. Every such case that she released to the department Siberia pained her.

Her arm gave one of those irritating twinges and began to radiate pain.

She shuddered. The barracks were quiet and stuffy. Someone had cut down the air-conditioning. If there had been any windows nearby, she would have opened one.

Then she felt something funny again. She raised her eyes for a moment and a new horror was upon her.

Amos Joy standing there in front of her. Solid and substantial. Without a doubt, he was there.

But then Alicia blinked and the image was gone.

Now Amos *wasn't* standing there, and neither was anyone else.

It was as if Alicia had picked up a split-second flash of something from another reality, or something loitering on the edge of her consciousness.

She stared at the spot before her desk.

Her shoulder gave another painful spasm and she grimaced. The image before her had been so clear and insistent that she had difficulty rejecting it. Yet by all that she had been accustomed to believe, there was no one in front of her.

She was alone.

Or so it appeared.

Gradually, she lowered her eyes.

She looked at the file in front of her. She flicked her line of vision upward again to see if she could re-create the circumstances that had thrown the image of Amos Joy before her.

But she couldn't.

It didn't happen a second time. At least not here.

She breathed deeply and tried to wish away the pain in her shoulder. It wouldn't obey. She reached into her desk for some ibuprofen, and attempted to ignore the pain. She tried to clear away the series of otherworldly images that coalesced within her head. While they failed to take shape completely, she was unable to fully dismiss them, either.

Alicia opened the file on the Fresno burglary ring. She studied everything she had, hoping the routine nuts and bolts of quotidian crime would anchor her in reality.

This failed, too.

She closed the file and looked up at the old-fashioned round wall clock. She noticed that the minute hand had turned the corner past the 6 and the hour hand was inching toward one A.M.

Damn! The clock had stopped!

Something about her current investigation bothered her terribly. Maybe it was the absence of normal logic. Maybe it was the simultaneous appearance of Amos Joy in her life.

Searching solace, looking for a link to the rational world, Alicia turned to her desktop computer, checking for electronic mail.

The usual department garbage. A meeting to discuss pension benefits for officers planning to retire within the calendar year. Notice of a ruling in the California Superior Court on whether asthma or allergies were covered under normal sick time if the employee didn't see a doctor each week. Something about approved security work for officers moonlighting. Someone who had a full-grown bull terrier named Terminator that needed a home. A proposed meeting of Asian-born officers, strangely named the Hiroshima Association, which had to be the smallest affinity group in the department.

Then she noticed, amid the other drek, something that had arrived earlier in the evening, something she had previously missed. It bore Lieutenant Mott's e-mail address, but had been forwarded by him from the Beverly Hills Police Department.

The BevHilz cops had a man who admitted to having been Sands's occasional companion in recent months. The individual's name was Ted Sternfeld and he lived up in Santa Barbara.

Sternfeld had expressed shock when the BevHilz cops came to visit him and informed him of Sands's death, but he had been cooperative. Reading between the lines, Alicia realized that this Ted Sternfeld had a tight alibi for his whereabouts at the time when Sands had been murdered.

The local bulls in Beverly Hills didn't seem to link him to any involvement in the slaying. But if Alicia were interested, he would be available for questioning at his home two mornings hence.

She was interested.

Alicia noted the address and put it in her appointment book.

She was also interested in what followed: the medical examiner's report from the Sands homicide. The slice-and-dice was done in Los Angeles County this time, which meant the scalpel had been wielded by Dr. Chris Constantopolis. Reports from the guttered table were more dependable in the city than the suburbs, possibly because the higher volume brought a greater expertise to the cutting and sawing. Just the type of scientific analysis that Alicia wanted.

Alicia read rapidly through Dr. Constantopolis's report. There was an intriguing addendum.

. . . examiner notes the particle presence of an unusual chemical in serum analysis of the subject. Chemical resembles a derivative of a substance known as chrolystron. (Presence reaffirmed by second independent examiner on 6–6–00; see L.A.C. ME, Case file 00–243, sec c.) Origins of chrolystron and significance here are difficult to ascertain as substance has only been seen previously in highly uniquie [sic] cases, always touching upon members of United States or former Soviet space exploration programs (Ref., also, I.A.C. ME, Case file 97–364/closed) . . .

Presence of said compound chemical is not considered to be in any way an active contributing factor in the mortality of the deceased, William Robert Sands, of North Canon Drive, Beverly Hills, California, 90210 . . .

Subject's death, as noted, was caused by multiple traumatic lacerations and willful external incisions from a keenly sharpened bladed instrument of unknown and previously unseen design. Metallurgic analysis of particles from said instrument proved inconclusive as well. Microscopic metal residue from said instrument of execution proved equally elusive; metallurgic tests did not reveal any identifiable chemical elements . . .

Alicia stared at the screen for several seconds, then pushed herself back from her desk. Dr. Constantopolis's report only unsettled her further.

There was something grossly off kilter somewhere, not in the ME's reports but in the way events were unfolding before her. Even in the infinite capacity of human beings for mayhem or deception, there was usually a skein of logic. But here she couldn't peg it.

Somewhere she sensed something very sinister.

But where?

She wished she had a brew with her. It was against department regulations, sure, but who was going to bitch, especially at this hour of the morning? She could have concealed it in her hand, kept it low near her desk. Plenty of male cops did that.

Hey, there had been a time before Hernando Cordero when she would never have *dreamed* of knocking back a brew on duty. Now she had the urge all the time.

She wished she were leading a normal life. Why couldn't she be spending time at home with a family, like her sister? So her brother-in-law was a dip. But domestic life had its attractions.

She sighed. The details of the two related murder

cases preyed on her mind all the more. Alicia shook her head. There was something before her that she knew she couldn't see.

Something big.

Over the years, she had learned to trust her gut. Everything within her told her that Amos Joy was the linchpin of her investigation. Follow Amos. Find the solution.

Well, yes.

"Ah," she said aloud. "I'm glad you agree."

The two cases plus the coming of Amos Joy, she told herself as her thoughts rambled on, were like a bad dream. Unconnected events resulting in god-awful holy terror.

Like your usual bad dream, Alicia?

"Yes. That, too," she whispered aloud.

In her usual bad dream she was back in that housing project in Irvine, standing there, helpless, as a scumbag drug dealer shot her from ambush . . . then she was falling, listening to the shouts and screaming surrounding the second round of gunshots . . . then she was dead in the hospital . . .

. . . drifting . . . drifting . . . drifting . . .

. . . toward whatever bright light it was that she had sensed when her heart stopped.

But in the dream, she continued to drift. She never came back from the dead. Not until she woke up.

Your usual bad dream?

The question repeated. Then it amplified itself.

Is there some link between what happened to you in Irvine and Amos Joy?

Why *would* there be a connection? How *could* there be?

Because she felt so uncomfortable in Amos Joy's presence? Jesus! Could he manipulate her *past* in addition to her *mind*?

Maybe your problems are coming from beyond your own experience, Alicia. Maybe your problems are unearthly.

"What?" she said aloud.

Have you considered the extraterrestrial, my dear?

The words had popped into her mind straight out of her subconscious. She shivered in fear. She knew the origins.

She clutched her head.

"No, no, no," she said, closing her eyes tightly. "I'm going crazy. He's not in my head! I'm just going crazy!"

The more she posed rational questions, the more other questions suggested themselves. Suddenly all her world was chaos. She prayed for order.

Words came to her on wings. Now like a friendly soothing familiar voice whispering in her ear.

Have you ever considered accepting the extraterrestrial, Alicia?

Her head shot up. She looked for Amos Joy but didn't find him. She spoke aloud now, a conversation with an empty room.

"What?" she asked.

The extraterrestrial!

"Spaceships? People from other planets? I don't believe in it!"

You will have to.

"No!"

Alicia, dearest, you must accept the extraterrestrial. It is your only hope for salvation, for understanding and survival.

"No!" she insisted. "No, no, no! I won't."

She waited for a response.

But all she heard was the quiet walls of the police station late at night. Somewhere distantly she heard a sergeant talking on the telephone and then the crackle of a radio, then, somewhere else, she heard two male cops laughing, probably at an off-color joke.

Nothing else.

Then: *You should listen to the voice within you. It is a much wiser voice than your own, an advanced state of intellectual discourse. This voice will impart great wisdom to you.*

Alicia drew another breath, then pushed herself completely away from her desk. She rubbed her tired eyes and backed off from this line of thought, too.

She closed her eyes. Another image rose from the past.

She was out in the backyard of the home where she had grown up. It was nighttime. Summer. She was with her father and they were looking at the sky. Her father was trying to point out something to her but she couldn't grasp the message.

Consider the extraterrestrial. That is the message.

It was her late father's voice in her mind this time, as if he now had a cameo role in her incipient madness. Her eyes shot open and she looked around. The words had seemed so clear, so distinct. It was almost as if she had heard them audibly rather than in the stressed-out memory chambers of her mind. She studied the vision in her head and tried to determine whether it was actual memory or something that was planting itself within her.

She didn't know.

She looked around uneasily.

She heard her heart pumping.

She was thirsty as a woman in a desert.

She was also overtired, multiply stressed, and slipping into a delusional state, she told herself. That's why her thoughts were becoming irrational.

Two A.M. *Earth time present.*

The clock on the wall had started again. It occurred to her that it had only stopped when the vision of Amos had been there. Now, with him gone, time had unfrozen.

She shuddered. "I'm going crazy," she said aloud to herself. "Completely crazy. Psycho. Bonkers."

She didn't care who heard her now.

Hell. What was any reasonable woman doing at work at two A.M? She had come in at eight A.M. the previous morning. By this time, she should have been home in bed with a husband or a lover.

She recoiled further from these strange ruminations. She reminded herself that she was a woman who dealt with the physical world, the world of tangible empirical proof.

Fingerprints.

DNA tests.

Gunshot wounds.

Times of day.

Clear-eyed, clear-thinking, sane-and-sober witnesses. The answers to her questions were moored in this tangible world, not floating around among the stars. She scolded herself. It was delusional for her to pose questions better left to the astrology columns.

She was *not* ready to start postulating on otherworldly explanations for things. She may have traveled to death and back, but she was a rational woman.

She wasn't going star-hopping.

Foolish little girl!

She wasn't sure who was sending her messages now. Dad. Amos. Or her own troubled mind. "I'm sane," she said aloud. "There is a rational explanation for everything!"

She repeated the words. Here was her mantra for the evening, her morning prayer. Her catechism.

She was a *rational woman* who believed in demonstrable things! But why was it that she hadn't *convinced* herself?

She blew out a long tired breath.

She rose from her desk. Time to go home.

She was due back at work within another seven hours. She sometimes felt as if she were on a treadmill, and the treadmill never stopped moving, day after day. Nor did her feet.

Alicia turned the light off on her desk and departed from the main workroom of state police headquarters. It was two-fifteen A.M. Her eyes were red-rimmed, the lids heavy with fatigue.

A moment later she was in the parking lot.

She felt very warm when she walked to her car. Her shoulder spasmed and jabbed her with pain when she placed her right hand on her car door. During the drive home, she passed a big time-and-temperature display that overlooked the turnpike, a bank logo parked on top of it, the logo with the listing steamboat.

She winced. But not at the image of the ship. The temperature read seventy-nine degrees.

The hot rush of air from Mexico that had crashed northward across southern California had apparently settled in.

She shuddered.

She took it as an early signal of the summer to come and felt more discomfort than usual from that thought. It had been an abnormally warm night in January when she had been shot, she recalled, and was in no mood to chalk such things up to coincidence.

The drive home was uneventful except for one thing.

At one point on a lonely stretch of road, her car hesitated and shuddered. It felt as if something were wrong with the engine, as if she were losing power. She pulled to the side of Interstate 10, and all at once, the vehicle seemed bathed in a strange pulsating light from above.

"Jesus!" she said to herself, putting two and two together. "Oh, Jesus, no!"

Consider the extraterrestrial, Alicia. Consider it now!

For all that she had been on edge before, this scared her even more.

She drew her service weapon, and for a split second actually entertained the notion of shooting herself if she found an unearthly presence above her.

She stepped quickly and aggressively from her vehicle and gazed skyward, pointing the weapon.

She saw the source of the pulsating light.

It was a broken roadside highway light. A five-hundred-watt phosphate bulb was flickering wildly, on the fringe of blowing out.

She breathed easier and got back into her car. She turned the engine on again, then realized what the problem had been. She had been driving with the parking brake on.

And at home a bit later, with the help of a beer or two, she slept peacefully.

CHAPTER 14

Two mornings later, Alicia met Bill Sands's former "friend" at his home in Santa Barbara, a two-hour drive north from Los Angeles.

Alicia entered the property via a long gravel driveway. As she stepped from her Jeep, she was greeted by fresh air, and she heard all around her the restless ticking of wet leaves.

Rain showers had played peekaboo with Santa Barbara County for the last two days, and the most recent precipitation had ended an hour earlier. Strange for, like in Camelot, it normally rained here only after sundown.

But now the sun was apparent and the heat of the day was returning. Alicia found herself reaching for a pair of sunglasses as she stepped out of her Jeep. As she put them on, Ted Sternfeld emerged from the front door of his home to greet his visitor.

Sternfeld was a trim, good-looking man in his mid-thirties. He was about six feet tall with short black hair, seemed low key, and dressed conservatively in tan slacks and a blue shirt. There was something familiar about him, but she could not immediately place it. What she did notice was an air of sadness and edginess that prevailed over both Sternfeld and his home.

The Sternfeld house was a big, expensive Victorian, with a high porch and a roof that lifted above several surrounding treetops. It was a lush piece of property set on two acres.

As Ted Sternfeld led his visitor through the first floor of his home, Alicia spotted many things she expected. An upright piano, littered with musical scores. An oil portrait of an attractive blond woman who must have been nearing thirty. Antiques from the East Coast, combined with a few more curious items from Europe, Africa, and Asia. Booty and souvenirs from many trips, Alicia guessed.

Curiously, there was also what appeared to be a wedding picture in a silver frame on a side table in the living room. It was ajar, as if abandoned suddenly. Alicia wondered if Ted Sternfeld had been looking at it when she had pulled into his driveway.

Sternfeld led Alicia to a sitting area on a back patio. Although the sun was out and bright, the flagstones were still wet from the day's rain. So was the outdoor furniture, so Sternfeld took a moment with a towel to dry off a pair of wooden chairs. Alicia and her host appeared to be alone.

"I'm sorry about your friend, Bill Sands," Alicia said. "I know you're feeling a loss."

"Yes. Thank you. I am." He paused for a second. "I can't tell you what a shock the whole thing is." Another slight pause, and then, "I've never known anyone who was murdered, know what I mean?"

"And hopefully you won't again," Alicia said gently.

Ted Sternfeld gave an assenting tilt to his hands. "The funeral's tomorrow in Thousand Oaks," he said. "I'm planning to attend."

In the forefront of her mind, Alicia found herself reaching for the convenient phrases of comfort. In the back of her mind, she was considering the funeral, and whether or not she should attend.

It was only then, however, that the realization was upon her, the recognition of what had been familiar. Sternfeld was the other man in the homoerotic photographs that she had seen in Sands's bedroom. The realization jarred her. Again, a touch of the surreal; the tranquil suburban squire sitting before her had been rated Triple-X the last time she had seen him.

A moment passed. Alicia had a hunch that Sternfeld sensed exactly what she was thinking. Alicia recovered quickly.

"I think I mentioned on the phone," Alicia said, "I'm working on what may be a related homicide case for my own department. So some of my questions might take a different turn than the ones you've already answered for the Beverly Hills police."

Sternfeld shrugged. "Ask me anything you wish," he said. "I'm as anxious to have the killer found as you are to find him."

"Why do you say 'him'?"

"Just a figure of speech," Sternfeld said. "But statistically, isn't it usually a 'him'?"

Alicia conceded that it was.

Now, as the sun brightened even more, Ted Sternfeld donned sunglasses. Then he seemed to soften. "I'm sorry if I'm seeming cold," he said. "Or jittery. This has all been a nightmare."

Alicia reached for a few more phrases of comfort, then she and her host talked for several minutes about the deceased.

Bill Sands and Ted Sternfeld had known each other for six years, Sternfeld related, and a relationship had blossomed halfway through that time. Sternfeld, a free-lance insurance and risk analyst for several banks and Fortune 500 companies, found his way down to Los Angeles every other week to visit clients. He was in the habit of staying over, often every other Wednesday night.

Sands and Sternfeld found themselves together at those times for drinks, dinners, and often a movie. It was kept discreet. Nothing flamboyant, nothing to shove in to the faces of friends.

But Sternfeld in particular did not want his secret life pursuing him back to Santa Barbara, where he was middle class and straight-respectable. Those pictures in Sands's bedroom had been an abomination to him, he said convincingly, taken from a hidden camera. Sands's idea of amusement, not his. Ted Sternfeld was greatly concerned as to exactly where those portraits were headed next.

"It's not that I didn't love Billy," he said. "But you understand, I'm sure. It's not the type of thing I want flying around."

"There's still some question about who's the trustee of the estate," Alicia said. "Once that's established, maybe you could reach out in that direction. I think it would come under the heading of 'personal property' of the deceased."

"Yes, yes, I know, I know," Sternfeld interjected nervously.

He found a half-dead pack of Lucky Strikes on a glass table by his chair and offered one to Alicia, who declined. He lit up a smoke.

"I've already spoken to my attorney," Sternfeld said. "I think it's moving in the right direction. I should be able to get those pictures back so that I can destroy them. Mercifully."

"If I can help you, I will," Alicia said. "I do sympathize."

She recalled that when she was seventeen she had briefly had a boyfriend named Nick who—on one drunken evening—had taken some topless Polaroid shots of her. She cringed and wondered where those shots were today.

"I appreciate that," Sternfeld said.

Alicia's sympathy broke some ice between them. Sternfeld lapsed into a pleasant memory, recalling how he and Bill had met. It had been half a dozen years earlier in West Hollywood; the two men had bumped into each other one Monday night on Santa Monica Boulevard at a small establishment called 'The TV Boutique.'

"Billy had come in because he was in the TV business. 'TV' meaning 'television,'" Sternfeld said. "The shop had this big sign in the window, with a picture of a beautifully dressed 'woman.' The sign said, 'Let your dreams become reality.' Billy was quite shy back then about who he was. And he honestly hadn't understood what the shop was all about until he was inside.'"

"Sure," Alicia said, still baffled.

"It was a clothing shop. Women's apparel in very large sizes," said Sternfeld. " 'TV' meant 'transvestite.'"

"Oh. Hence, The TV Boutique."

Sternfeld smiled. "Uh-huh. You're a smart lady," he said good-naturedly.

"And *you* were there for . . . ?" Alicia asked.

A wry smile. "Just buying some personal things," Sternfeld said with a wink.

Alicia nodded. Then both smiled. More ice thawed.

"I'm curious about what some of the other pictures in Bill Sands's home suggested, too," Alicia said.

"Which pictures?"

"There was some interesting 'space exploration' stuff."

Sternfeld reacted. Alicia knew she had hit something.

"Oh. *That*," Sternfeld said.

"Did Bill have an interest in flying saucers? Space?"

Sternfeld snuffed out his cigarette and blew out a final stream of thick white carcinogenic smoke. "Too much of an interest," he said.

"Why's that?"

"A few years ago Billy produced this kids' cartoon show. I don't know. Flying saucers and some space alien claptrap. But he got really hooked on the subject."

"Did a lot of reading on it? Background?"

"More than that," said Sternfeld. "Billy got *obsessed*. First he started going to these *Star Trek* conventions. Dragged me along to a couple of them. Well, that was fun for a while. We went to one up in Monterey on a Halloween weekend. 1998 I think it was. I dressed as Data and Billy drag-dressed as Tasha Yar. Oh, he was *beautiful* as Tasha, even if he was the concubine of a Romulan."

Sternfeld sighed again and shook his head, presumably relishing the memory of a gay Halloween bacchanalia.

"Interesting enough, the Trekkie horseshit," he continued. "But then Billy started hanging out with some real nuts."

"Nuts?"

"Saucer nuts. UFO crazies. People who swore they had been abducted. People who said they were from other planets. People who claimed they'd had sex with aliens. And poor delusional Billy was buying into the whole thing. Kept saying things like, 'Maybe these people are really telling the truth.' And, 'Wouldn't it be great to *see* a flying saucer?' 'To go up into space?' 'To be taken aboard a craft?' 'To *meet* a gentleman from another planet?' Jesus fucking Christ, Detective. A gentleman from another planet. This was a programming executive for a major TV network, making two hundred fifty thousand dollars a year. What got into his head?"

"Don't know," Alicia said philosophically. "I'd hesitate to guess."

Sternfeld forged onward.

"I met this one friend of Billy's," Ted Sternfeld recalled. "Emaciated little woman with fire-engine red hair. First time I saw her I thought she was a deranged dwarf. Had eyes round like quarters and, with the hair, could have been the winner of an Annie Lennox look-alike contest. Said she was from the planet 'Clarion' and could 'guide earthling visitors' back there with her."

"Clarion?" Alicia asked. She flipped out a notebook, long overdue, and started writing things down.

"Clarion."

"Never heard of it. Should I have?"

"All the saucer nuts know about it. They claim it's, quote, on the other side of the sun, unquote. So conventional astronomy knows nothing about it."

"Oh," said Alicia, following carefully.

"It's bullshit, of course," said Sternfeld. "I asked a friend who works at the Mount Wilson observatory about Clarion. He gave me a horse laugh. Said there was such a thing as serious ufology and this sure wasn't it. Clarion doesn't exist any more than the Easter Bunny does. That's my point. Billy started hanging out with people who were progressively kooky."

"Have any names?"

"No."

"None?" Alicia pressed. "Not one?"

"No. Sorry."

"You must have heard some names from time to time."

But Sternfeld was shaking his head with emphasis.

"No," he said. "I told him what I thought. I said, 'Billy, come on. Having fun is one thing. Hanging around with crackpots is another.' He said, 'These aren't crackpots, these are my friends. If you don't like them, I won't invite you along.' "

"So what happened?"

Sternfeld reached again for his pack of Luckies. He started another weed, puffed, coughed, and shrugged. "Exactly that," he answered. "I wasn't invited along. I started seeing less of him."

He paused, then continued in a lower voice.

"Look, I'm a financial advisor in the insurance business. I'm a Wharton MBA. This is *not* an industry for free spirits. There's enough of my life that I need to keep quiet about," he said. "The last thing I needed was to be spotted with saucer nuts."

"I understand."

"Some of these people belonged to a sort of informal club. They called it the Amen Society, or the Almond Society. Something like that. Ever heard of it?"

"No," Alicia said. She wrote the name down, giving both spellings.

"That makes two of us," Sternfeld concluded.

"Do you know anything more about it? Who's in? Where they meet? How many members?"

"Billy was closemouth. About that, at least, and you know what? I didn't *want* to know. Can you understand that?"

Alicia nodded. She pondered the larger picture for a moment.

"Think any of these people were dangerous?" she eventually asked. "The 'saucer nuts,' as you call them?"

"*Most* of them, no. *Some* of them . . . ?"

Sternfeld curled his upper lip, then looked away for a second. Far away. Then he came back, an uneasy glimmer in both eyes.

"In all honesty, I never thought any of these saucer folks was dangerous," he said. "But who knows, right?

When somebody's so unbalanced in one aspect of his life, the wheels could fly off the wagon elsewhere, too. Know what I mean?"

Alicia knew. She readied her next question.

"If I told you that there was something strange in Bill's autopsy report, would you be shocked?"

Sternfeld looked confused, then panic-stricken.

"Oh, Christ!" he blurted. "He wasn't HIV positive, was he?"

"No. I'm talking about a chemical in the bloodstream."

"Cocaine? Billy snorted recreationally a little, that's no secret."

"I'm talking about something called chrolystron," Alicia said. "That mean anything to you?"

"No."

In the driveway of Sternfeld's home, a black Mercedes turned in from the road outside, and now, reeking of new wealth, pulled slowly toward a garage, the door to which rose silently by remote control. The car was shiny, big and new, and retailed for two and a half times Alicia's annual CHP salary. Its sunroof open, the gleaming 520E was driven by a blond woman.

"Chrolystron is a chemical found in the blood of people who have been in space," Alicia said. "What if I told you that Bill Sands's toxicology report turned up traces of chrolystron in his system?"

"If you told me that?" Sternfeld asked. "Hypothetically?"

"Yes," Alicia said.

"I'd wonder if you were a real cop. Because it's making you sound as nutty as some of Bill's other 'acquaintances.' "

Alicia smiled. "Then consider it hypothetical. For my own purposes," Alicia said. "But you're going to wonder when I ask you the next question, too," she said.

"What's that?"

"Do you have any tattoos?"

He frowned.

"Tattoos?"

"Bill Sands and a similar victim had a unique tattoo on their upper torso," she said. "Right side, upper breast, below the shoulder."

Sternfeld frowned again.

It occurred suddenly to Alicia that that was almost where the bullet had entered her own body.

"I don't have anything of the sort," Sternfeld said. And, unasked but anxious to please, he unbuttoned his shirt and let Alicia view the tanned but unblemished flesh of his upper body.

"Happy?" he asked.

She smiled, nodded, and folded away her notepad. "Thank you."

"Anything else?" Sternfeld asked.

"Not for now."

As Alicia stood to leave, the blond woman from the car appeared. She was tall, leggy, and California-all-American pretty. She wore a pale blue summer dress. From a child's seat in the rear of the Mercedes, she had retrieved a girl who looked to be about two. The little girl, like Mom, was wearing Calvin Klein.

"It's all right to mention Billy," Sternfeld said softly to Alicia, as the woman approached. "But not the intimate details, please?" For the first time, he actually seemed uneasy about his behavior.

"Of course," Alicia answered. "Discretion is always good."

Sternfeld stood. The blond woman smiled at Alicia.

"This is my wife, Lauren, and my daughter, Jessica," Sternfeld said to Alicia by way of introduction.

"I'm Alicia Aldrich, California Highway Patrol," Alicia said, introducing herself before Ted Sternfeld could.

Lauren seemed alarmed, as would any woman who came home to find her husband talking to a member of the police force.

"Is everything all right?" she asked.

"Just fine," Alicia said.

"The police were interested in talking to some people who knew Billy Sands, honey," Sternfeld said.

"Oh, yes. That poor man you knew down in L.A."

"Terrible thing," Sternfeld said softly.

Lauren shrugged. "What do you expect in degenerate places like L.A. and Beverly Hills?" she asked.

An awkward moment passed. Alicia suppressed an urge to defend the places where she lived and worked, while dozens of other thoughts flitted through her overworked mind. She wondered if she would have been so amenable to helping cover Sternfeld's affair if it had been with a woman.

But then in the end, Alicia reminded herself that sexual affairs and the who's-servicing-whom of daily life were not what she was there for and were no one's damned business other than the frisky participants. Besides, to Alicia's increasingly jaded perspective, Sternfeld, standing there with a handsome wife and daughter, suddenly looked very connubial.

Lauren broke the silence by offering to make lunch for Alicia.

"Thanks, but I should be going," Alicia answered.

The interview was over and Alicia made her getaway as gracefully as possible under the circumstances.

C H A P T E R   1 5

Alicia spent the afternoon, or what remained of it after driving back to San Bernardino, prowling through California and out-of-state missing persons reports, still trying to peg a link between Joe Doe of the desert and the real world.

She made further inquiries by telephone with W.S., the lamentable White Snake of the San Bernardino ME's office, regarding her desert corpse. However, Dr. Sugarman, the pale serpent himself, had no new light to shed on the case. And not to put too fine a point on it, the doc seemed querulous and grudging with any support, spending more time whining about the blazing sunshine than offering up any proposed new paths of forensic discovery.

White Snake did announce that the cadaver was still in his overpopulated freezer, however, so he did leave the door—and for that matter, the mortuary drawer—open for further inquiries.

Then, to add to Alicia's vexation, at one point in the dying hours of the afternoon, Lieutenant Mott stopped by her office, which was an unusual and questionable occurrence.

Mott pushed the door halfway closed and grunted something about the overwhelming heat. He had rings of sweat at the armpits of his short-sleeved shirt to prove the point. It had turned into an ugly ninety-two-degree day in the Inland Empire, and the sidewalks outside were still sizzling at five-thirty P.M. But this was nothing new, as each of the last few days had hit the nineties in San Bernardino and had soared into the hundreds in the desert and up in Antelope Valley. But Alicia had the impression that Mott hadn't visited her to commiserate over an extended heat wave.

Mott nosed around with a couple of personal questions, to which Alicia chose not to respond. Her worst fears vis-à-vis Mott were confirmed. She arrived unhappily at the conclusion that Lieutenant Mott wanted to ask to see her socially, something that Alicia had already decided was not going to happen. She was already serving in a position beneath him in one way, and had zero desire to add a second, more intimate variation.

How to get past this without creating a professional problem was a further complication that she didn't need just now. It never ceased to amaze, even shock, her how many men—married and single, twenties through sixties—couldn't resist attempts to dip their pens in their professional inkwell. Was it, she wondered, that hard to bridle one's hormonal urges when working in close quarters with a female? Fortunately, when Alicia mentioned her ongoing fatigue and the huge amount of work she faced, Mott caught the message and steered the conversation in a different direction. At least for earth time present.

Mott had been separated from his wife for a long time, but had never divorced, something she might accept temporarily with the right man. No one arrived on a goddamn clamshell these days, anyway, not Aphrodite, not the man of her dreams, and not herself, either. But she surely wouldn't accept a haphazard legally married situation with the *wrong* man. And Mott was in the latter category. "Wrong man" should have been tattooed on his ass, one word on each cheek.

Then toward six-thirty, another man—this one less imposing—appeared quietly and stood in her doorway. Startled, Alicia looked up from her desk in haste, half expecting to see an unwelcome silvery vision from another world.

But this was someone new and different, even in a week when new and different had become the commonplace.

Before her stood a slight young man with mocha-hued skin. He was in full sartorial rebellion: red goggles, cut-off yellow jeans, Doc Martens in a paisley print, small gold hoops in each ear, a nose jewel, and an orange Dixie Chicks T-shirt. He had a pencil-thin Little Richard mustache circa 1956, spiked black hair, and looked to be about twenty years old.

The visitor held a motorcycle helmet in one hand, a package in the other. He stood there watching her, hesitating to knock.

"Yes?" she asked.

"Detective Alicia Aldrich?" he asked.

"Yes. That's me."

A beat, then, "My name is LeKeith," he said gently. "And this," he added, holding out the package and coming forward, "is for you."

Alicia blinked.

Warily, she signed a receipt and accepted the delivery. The man-boy's boots were big and tough enough to kick a hole in the side of a Humvee. And yet LeKeith moved delicately across the floor, hardly making a sound. Alicia watched him until he was gone. He seemed to be from another planet in the more figurative sense.

But *everyone* she encountered these days was at least a little strange, she concluded. She wondered if that included her, as well. But she turned her attention to what was before her, and at least initially the encounter had a happy conclusion.

The youth was a day courier from the airport and he had brought an unexpected treasure from Sacramento. It was a response to the request that she had almost forgotten she had placed into the CHPs system.

When she opened the parcel, she had what she needed to build her evening. It was a thick file on an at-large suspect believed to be in California, an escaped murderer named Amos Joy.

Mr. Joy was wanted in several states and was last seen fleeing a maximum-security state crackerbox for the criminally bonkers in Tempe, Arizona.

Alicia eagerly spread the material on her desk, set herself up with an obscenely large cup of coffee, and bent over the documents like a latter-day nun, pent up with her new catechisms for a solitary evening, and seeking enlightenment from on high.

Like a swimmer wading into unknown waters for the first time, Alicia began her journey into the history of Amos Joy. She had no idea where the currents would lead her.

Disorder reigned within the files. Someone had been there already, probably several someones. There were five envelopes of records, but two were empty.

Alicia looked to see if the missing material had been receipted. It hadn't. She wondered if someone was currently taking a hard look at Amos Joy elsewhere in the state. It would have been damned helpful to know. She wished the material at least had been placed on the police computers.

Where Amos had been for the first two decades of his life was a mystery. He had first locked horns with law enforcement in Arizona. Homicide. Amos, a university student at the time, had been picked up following the death of Dr. Richard Pareles, a professor of English. Pareles had been decapitated with an unidentifiable instrument.

Since it was known that Amos had threatened the professor, the police had interviewed him immediately. A three-hour-plus discussion proved elliptical, and Alicia read through the whole thing. Certain parts toward the end stood out. Police interviewer number one had been Officer Richard Hopkinson, PI, of the Tempe Arizona City Police. The second officer had been Officer Mary McLaren, PI2, of the same force.

Police Interviewer: Amos, did the professor make you mad?

Amos Joy: He made me sad. I only get glad and sad.

PI: Why 'sad'?

AJ: He was foolish.

PI: Why?

AJ: He wouldn't believe me when I presented the truth.

PI: What truth?

AJ: That I've come here from another world.

PI: Come on, Amos, let's cut that stuff.

AJ: You want to end up carved-apart dead, also?

PI: Don't threaten us, Amos.

AJ: Then don't deny the truth. Fa la la la la.

Second police interviewer (PI2): Why don't you treat us to the truth, Amos? Where do you come from? What's your real name?

AJ: You don't understand anything. When I sing to you, "Fa la la la la," that's a threat, too. But you don't see it, do you?

PI2: We're getting tired of this, Amos.

AJ: Can I leave?

PI: No.

AJ: You're wrong about that, too. I can leave any time I want.

PI2: We have as much time as you do, Amos.

AJ: You're wrong about everything.

PI: Tell us something that's true, Amos.

AJ: A massive invasion from space will take place in the Earth Year 2136. Nonmutant humans, the race indigenous to this wet blue rock, will provide a food source for the invaders—

PI: [unintelligible] . . . taking a [expletive deleted] break for five minutes. Mary, you can talk to this [expletive deleted] wacko alone if you want. Is he cuffed?

PI2: He's cuffed.

[Officer Hopkinson leaves.]

AJ: Now that he's gone, we can do sex if you like.

PI2: If you're trying to shock me, Amos, it won't work. I've seen things far more unusual than you.

AJ: No, you haven't.

PI2: Why are you so sure?

AJ: I keep telling you. I've tripped to this planet four times. This is the most recent.

PI2: You come from outer space, huh?

AJ: We all do. Is it pleasurable when a man puts part of himself inside you?

[Note: Following lewd gesture by subject, Officer McLaren secures subject with second set of handcuffs and leg shackles, leaves interview chamber. Lapse of two minutes. Returns.]

PI2: Amos, did you murder Dr. Pareles?

AJ: Yes, ma'am.

PI2: Why?

AJ: To look inside his neck. And to see how he would bleed if his head were separated.

PI2: So you're confessing?

AJ: Maybe.

PI2: Will you sign a statement?

AJ: Maybe.

PI2: What did you use to mutilate the body?

AJ: My hands.

PI2: Come on, Amos! To sever a head?

AJ: My space hands. Not my human hands. Want to see them? Want to feel them?

PI2: Amos, do you confess that you murdered the doctor?

AJ: Maybe.

PI2: Jesus Christ, Amos! You know we can pull down the shades and—

[Tape erased accidentally, first police interviewer returns at this point.]

AJ: I want to show both of you something.

PI: Just tell us why you did it.

AJ: No. I want to show you something.

PI2: We're not going to unlock you, Amos.

AJ: I want you to see how I look in my natural form. My silvery space form.

PI: Bullshit, Amos.

AJ: Watch me. Look at me.

PI: Amos, would you cut this—

PI2: Oh, my God!

[There are sounds of gasps and reaction from the interviewers. Interview was then terminated due to illness of both police interviewers.]

Officers Hopkinson and McLaren had curtailed their interview with startling abruptness, Alicia noted. Why? What had they seen? What had Amos showed them? What had he done?

She searched through the envelope containing the interview and found no further notation or explanation. Alicia made a written note. She would telephone both police officers. Surely they must have something further to say.

Oddly, only a supervisory notation was clipped on the

back of the envelope from a Captain Michael Ellsworth, Tempe Police.

It read, typewritten above the captain's initials:

> Background investigation of subject Amos Joy revealed that he had forged educational transcripts to attend Arizona State University. No actual high school attendance or record has been uncovered.
>
> Fingerprint identification provided no resolution to subject's actual ID. Assessment through FBI Bureau, Phoenix, of ridges and whorls from all ten fingers was attempted. FBI lab assessment of prints ranged from "computer-generated fakes" to "unreal" by officer in charge. Copies sent to Washington, D.C., for further analysis. Pending.

And it was pending to this date, Alicia noticed. The "second opinion" from Washington had never returned to Arizona. Or if it had, it had never arrived in this file.

She examined a second envelope.

Gore. Crime-scene photographs. Other victims attributed to Amos Joy: a female psychiatrist and her child.

The pathology fit the two murders assigned to Alicia, the one in the high desert, the one in Beverly Hills. She was grateful for that much. In a dark way, it was nice to have her suspicions confirmed.

She studied the picture of the psychiatrist's child who had been murdered. It wasn't just bloody it was . . . so . . .

Clinical! So perfect!

A small head crushed with such precision!

She put the photographs away. If Amos were responsible for the two deaths here in California, plus the English professor, plus the psychiatrist and her child, then

Amos was already past the number of four that would officially categorize him as a serial killer.

Thank God for that, too, she thought.

At least she might be able to get some help to bring him in. She cringed anew when she realized that she had come face-to-face with him. Then she felt something like electric shock go through her again.

Face-to-face. It'll happen again, Alicia.

Her head snapped up. She searched around, but couldn't find him. She wondered if he were there, anyway.

Invisible.

"When?" she asked. "When will we meet?"

She had an urge to shoot him on sight. After all, her sanity, she knew, was slipping away because of this case. Better to blow away the little devil and reclaim her mental health. The files she had been reading were a testament to the bad fortune of those who had hung around to do interviews with Amos.

"Did you murder all these people, Amos?"

All stories are true.

"So that means yes?"

Two-thirds of the wet blue rock are covered with water. The rest is considered suitable for craft landings from another planet.

"You're nothing more than a psycho," said Alicia. "Nothing more."

I'm a space critter.

"Go away."

Alicia waited for more. Nothing came. She felt buoyed a trifle by her verbal counterattack. She went to the final envelope.

It was a hodgepodge of doctors' opinions from the psychiatric hospital where Amos had been sent following his police interrogation. Included were lengthy interviews with the two psychiatrists who had eventually been slain. Their deaths matched that of the English professor. Yet Amos had both claimed credit and been incarcerated at the time of the second slayings.

I left and came back.

Alicia was again horrified and startled.

Someone had turned down the air-conditioning again and she was starting to sweat in her office. Or maybe the topic was making her sweat. Or the voice inside her head. She felt suddenly very hot. Almost crampy.

"How am I going to catch you and lock you up?" she asked aloud.

Fool! That's what I'm going to do with you!

She lost her temper. She stood suddenly and yelled.

"Get out of here, Amos!" Alicia screamed. "Out of my office! Out of my head! Now!" She picked up the materials she had been reading and was ready to hurl them. But she didn't.

Her voice echoed. The building fell silent around her. Not even the distant murmur of male voices could be heard. She settled back to her desk and sat down, her heart pounding, her face flushed.

Less than a minute later, a CHPs officer in uniform, a handsome blond man she had never seen before, arrived at her door. He was a strapping, hunky guy about five years younger than she. He looked in questioningly.

"I'm fine," she said.

He raised an eyebrow. "You don't sound fine."

"Thanks for your concern," she answered.

"I *am* concerned," he said.

"You've never seen me before in your life."

"Still doesn't mean I'm not concerned," he said.

She sighed.

His eyes searched the room, looking for unseen danger. He found none.

"Honestly. I'm okay," Alicia said, feeling calmer.

"Bad heat, huh?" he said.

"Yeah, murder," she said.

"Never seen such a strong sun," he said. "Bad day, too, maybe?" he asked.

"What's that mean?" she snapped.

He shrugged. "Don't mean nothing," he said.

"Make sure it doesn't."

He gave another little smile. "Well, nice to meet you," he said. Then he was on his way.

Alicia tried to calm herself for several minutes.

That damnable subliminal voice did not return. She finally had the emotional strength to study the last envelope, the one containing the psychiatric profiles. She spent an hour with them.

At this point Alicia's mood could best have been compared to that of a scientist who senses by instinct that she is on the brink of a discovery and is awaiting the logical connection. Later she would think of the situation as similar to shoving everything into a test tube to see if it exploded. In a way, she found the explosion in the final words she encountered in the file.

Strangely, the words went a long way toward bringing her back down to earth. They came from a summation written by a Dr. Richard Brillstein, chairman emeritus of the Arizona State University Department of Psychiatry. Dr. Brillstein tried to put Amos Joy in his rightful place, based on all known human knowledge.

. . . subject (Joy, Amos, Arizona. State Psychiatric Institute Case 00–J–385) is a unique case, but we must not lose sight of the obvious. Joy is a classic paranoid schizophrenic with delusional notions of being from "another planet." In clinically analyzed terms this is no different than if he were insisting he is Napoleon or Hitler. The dementia and delusion are the same no matter what "greater identity" has been chosen by the subject . . .

There is obviously sexual oppression lurking within the subject's psychosis, and my conjecture is that there is an extremely fragmented sense of identity, too. Taking into account that the subject has no traceable background, it is very possible that he himself does not know his true identity or provenance. A form of self-inflicted or self-sustained amnesia is not outside of the realm of possibility . . .

What makes this case more complicated is the subject's apparent success with both telekinesis and telepathy, that is, moving items through willpower as well as sending and receiving telepathic messages. It has long been held that free-floating electrical energy exists that we do not entirely understand but that can be released by the mind at times of extreme emotional turbulence. My analysis, based on forty years of psychiatric study, is that this element is at work in this particular case . . .

This in no way downplays Amos Joy's threat to both himself and to others. He should remain under maximum security and 24–7 supervision. He is a mortal man, deranged and dangerous. Institutions such as ours are in business to protect the public from such individuals.

It was signed by the doctor himself, two days before Amos Joy, the "mortal man, deranged and dangerous" apparently walked through the walls and exited the state nuthouse.

C H A P T E R 1 7

Alicia was deeply disturbed when she returned home to Venice that evening. She turned on her music system and played some jazz and blues. When that worsened her mood, she turned to loud stuff from the 1980s.

That didn't help, either.

She made herself a tuna sandwich, and opened a bottle of Carling Black Label. She knocked back that bottle and proceeded briskly to a second. The evening was as dark and sinister as this new presence in her life.

She broke out in a sweat when she thought of the little man she had encountered on Interstate 71. What was going on? Who the hell was he? On the kitchen counter, she picked up the receipt from the store. Nine dollars and seventy-five cents.

She stared at it for a moment. Nine seven five. That number kept coming up in her life. Same as the four eleven. Was she losing her sanity? Her shoulder throbbed again. She thought of taking a warm shower to try to alleviate the pain. Then she decided she would ice the shoulder instead.

Heat, cold.

Past, future.

Forward, back.

Four eleven. Nine seventy-five.

Her seemed to be heading in two directions at once.

A wave of loneliness surged through her and she wished that she had someone to come home to. It wasn't that she felt unsuccessful if she didn't have a spouse or a mate. It was just that she felt as if something big was missing.

There was noise outside her home. Outside and above. Some sort of strange airship. A small plane, perhaps. One of those sputtering homemade things: an engine that sounded midway between a lawn mower and a washing machine.

There was all sorts of strange stuff in the air off Venice. Los Angeles International Airport was just to the north. A US Air Force base was eighty miles to the south. And God knew what small strange private craft took off and landed from the countless small local airports that ringed metro L.A.

Then the aircraft was gone, reduced to a distant hum. Or was the distant hum something else in the air? She waited for that strange subliminal voice to answer her.

No answer.

"Well, then," she thought to herself as she finished the second beer of the evening. "No answer from my inner friend tonight. So maybe I'm finally alone."

She paused, still waiting.

She rallied around Dr. Brillstein's benediction: he was a mortal man. A complete Loony Tune, but mortal.

Still no answer.

"Well, at least I have *that* to be thankful for," she thought. "The voice is gone."

Funny thing was, she didn't feel so alone. And when she heard a creak from the next room, she placed her hand on her service pistol.

Just in case. If Amos was a mortal man and if he

turned up here tonight, well, by God, she'd blow the little fucker away, she decided. No California grand jury would hang a policewoman in her circumstances.

But she heard nothing more. And there was no one there. Or at least nothing visible.

What was that strange feeling that had inhabited her when she had been in the physical presence of that small man by the roadside? And why had his image flashed before her at her office?

Why, over the last few days, could she not shake the relentless memory of the time she had been shot and killed? What was that extra shiver of fear she was feeling these days?

She reached for a third bottle of beer.

She thought back to the afternoon when she had first been called to the John Doe in the Desert case.

She shuddered. There was something genuinely scary there. Something much worse than a murder-and-dump. Something that the first psychiatrists in Arizona had sensed but Dr. Brillstein had not.

What about Amos's strange fingerprints? Were they unearthly? Why were there no records of him that anyone could trace?

She lifted her damaged arm. The pins and needles flowed into her shoulder and down toward the elbow. She winced. Sometimes when she did this she couldn't even feel to grip.

Over the course of another quarter hour, she finished the third bottle of beer, wondering if she should chuck her police career.

It was one thing to endanger herself, another to potentially endanger the public or a partner. She went and found a fourth brew. It was nice and cold. She opened it and went to work on it.

Another aircraft passed above and—was it a coincidence?—there was another ground-level creak in her home, almost at the same time.

She kept her eyes open. She was getting a relaxing buzz from the beer.

She leaned back. She closed her eyes. The brightness started again, that yellowish white light that she had seen when she had been dying. Against her wishes, a small dark figure started to take form in the middle of the reddish hue, a figure that beckoned to her.

Had she been dead when she first saw this? Or alive? And which, she wondered, was she now?

She cried out. "No! No!"

Her words echoed in her empty home.

She opened her eyes, and looked around.

"Oh, God!" she said aloud.

She wondered where she had been. At least an hour must have passed because her CD had expired and the player had shut down.

Strange. She must have drifted off.

Her sandwich was finished.

Did she even remember having eaten it?

"Jesus," she muttered to herself.

She reached out for her beer. The bottle was warm. Where the hell had the time gone?

She then stood up and thought she understood. She was overtired and more drunk than she'd realized. She giggled, mildly amused.

She attempted to stand again. She failed.

Then, with the help of the armrest of her sofa, she got to her feet. She staggered upstairs.

She lurched into her bedroom and flopped onto her bed. She managed to pull off her weapon and lay it at her bedside. She pulled off the rest of her clothing. She stood, completely naked, and wandered into her bathroom. She turned on the shower full blast and stepped in.

She showered long and luxuriantly, washing her hair, scrubbing and massaging her skin. The aches and pains and some of the fatigue in her body started to dissipate.

She felt better. Vastly better, almost as if she had cleansed her soul and her spirit along with her body.

She stepped out of the shower. Stark naked, she toweled her hair. The booze she had consumed was still giving her a buzz, but now it was a comforting one, one that would ease her into a sound sleep.

She combed out her hair. She toweled her body, then walked back to her bed. She put her watch back on, out of habit. But otherwise, she would sleep naked tonight.

She liked the feeling of being all bare and clean. It made her feel both sexy and pure. She collapsed onto her sheets and relaxed. Her fumbling hand found the light switch and she put herself in darkness.

She lay there, listening to herself breathe. Her eyes flickered again. They found the luminous dial of her watch, inches away from her face, in the dark.

Ten-fifteen P.M. She closed her eyes again, a contented drunk at last.

A few minutes later, Alicia was aware that she was falling asleep. She managed to relax, to take herself out of the day's events. She could feel her mind, her body, and her thoughts drifting.

The feeling was a pleasant one.

A sense of contentment washed through her, a feeling of well-being. She pictured herself in a cabin in the mountains. She had just met a new man and he was gorgeous. In her fantasy, she didn't ask the man's name. She didn't want to know. Instead, she whispered to him one question.

"Will you make love to me really hard?"

"Yes, I will," he answered.

Her desire built.

"Will you do it to me all night?"

"Yes."

"If I beg you to stop, will you keep doing it to me?"

"Yes!"

She saw his face. It was the big blond trooper who had come to her office when she had yelled.

She giggled. Well, why not?

Ninety percent asleep, she allowed her right hand to drift across her lower abdomen until it stopped between her legs.

Her breathing deepened. Her fingers found the places that would give her satisfaction.

Alicia felt as if she had been drugged. She felt herself drifting again, as if she were visiting a part of her mind that she had never previously known to exist.

The picture in her mind became clearer and she saw herself sailing into space. The feeling was liberating, as if she had broken free of earlier ways of thinking.

She spoke aloud.

"Yeah," she said. "Chrolystron. Gonna get some in my own bloodstream, damn it."

I know how you think! What you repress the most, you want the most!

Hours passed, but it seemed like only a few heartbeats. Her sense of time seemed out of whack these days.

Her eyes flashed open. Her heart was beating loudly. She knew something had roused her, but she wasn't sure whether the noise had been in the dream or in her home. Alicia saw the dark bedroom around her. She looked around and found nothing amiss. She shut her eyes again quickly, seeking the pleasant feeling that she'd had in her dream state. She tried to recapture it.

There was a lightness around her, then a darkness. She again felt as if she were traveling somewhere.

She turned in her bed. Now she was being transported involuntarily. Wherever she was going, it was a place she didn't like. A place she feared. A place she did not wish to visit.

Her dead father was standing before her, pointing to the door of the decrepit bungalow belonging to Hernando Cordero, her would-be executioner.

In her dream, she walked down the same garbage-strewn hallway and got shot again and again and again. Maybe someday she would suffer a heart attack while asleep, she wondered from time to time, and Cordero would get her after all.

"Dad, I don't want to go up there," Alicia insisted in the dream.

"Oh, but you have to, my little angel. You're a policewoman. You have to be brave."

"I don't want to go."

Her father's expression turned grave. "Don't disgrace the family."

"But . . . ?"

"Go up there and get shot. That's your fate. To get shot."

"You've not forgiven me for becoming a cop?" she asked him.

"I never understood why you would do that," he answered. "Never understood."

"But Daddy . . . ?"

She was back in Irvine.

Her partner was firing bullets at Cordero. The latter was spinning and falling. Alicia was firing a final bullet, also. In the dream, Alicia screamed. She threw off her flak jacket, her bad arm failed her, and she was riveted in place while Cordero emptied an automatic pistol into her chest.

She spun in her bed.

She shuddered as if a cold current of air had come in to fill the room.

Then she opened her eyes a second time and was shocked.

She was still naked.

But now she was standing, as if roused while sleep-walking. The room was filled with an unusual light, one that created strange shadows across the room. She didn't know where the light was coming from, but she knew she wasn't imagining it.

A multitude of thoughts and sensations flew through her mind. She thought back on a picture she had seen in a *National Geographic* as a little girl. In it, a naked woman was on display at a slave auction. The woman was on display on a scaffold and several dozen men were bidding for her.

As a little girl she hadn't understood the sexuality of the painting but she had certainly understood its implications. She had felt so sorry for the woman in that picture because all of the men in the painting, all of those who were bidding for her, looked evil.

And now she felt like that woman, being assessed by some evil force. Then to her further horror, she thought she saw movement at the doorway to the hall.

A cold terror gripped her. She froze in her tracks. In the darkness, she saw the figure of a small man just beyond her doorway, partially concealed by the door. But his eyes were bold and bright, like a couple of little suns. He devoured her with his eyes.

"Oh, Jesus," she thought to herself. "Oh, holy Jesus!"

Alicia managed finally to uproot herself. She back-tracked slightly and reached for her service weapon, keeping her eyes focused on the form beyond the door.

Then a greater fear was upon her.

The body of the man behind the door took on a recognizable shape, the one she feared the most.

Five feet six. Thin and wiry. Large head.

Alicia's gaze rolled through the darkness. Her tingling right hand embraced the weapon. She looked back to find the intruder. But Amos, or the vision of him, had already withdrawn.

Alicia readied the weapon.

"Amos?" she said aloud. "Answer me or I'll shoot you."

No response.

"What are you doing?" Alicia asked. "Why are you here?"

In the dimness of the room, Alicia could no longer be sure if she saw the physical shape. But she heard a floorboard creak.

"Amos! Answer me!" Alicia demanded. She struggled with a robe and pulled it around her body, keeping the gun poised.

Then, finally clothed, Alicia reached, with her other hand, toward a light switch. A blinding overhead light flashed on.

There was nothing beyond the doorway. Alicia walked to the door and pulled it wide open. It banged as it struck the wall.

Alicia felt the wetness of her palms against the handle of her weapon. For several seconds, she waited, her heart thundering. Nothing happened. Then she walked slowly through the second floor of her house, waiting for something else to happen.

Nothing did.

Her shoulder throbbed. Her right palm now tingled with the acute pins-and-needles numbness that suggested a miniparalysis.

She went cautiously downstairs. She moved to her front door.

It was locked, just as she had left it. She turned and searched the first floor. She found no one.

She moved to her front window and peered out into the darkness. She saw nothing. She remained at the front window and switched on the large outdoor light. The light swept across her front lawn.

No Amos.

She checked her back door, too. And the door that led to the garage. All had been locked and bolted from within. No window had budged. No one could have humanly entered the house and departed.

The word repeated on her. Humanly . . .

Alicia stood very still by her front window.

She thought about her many recent dreams, and what she thought she had experienced. She tried for perspective and failed.

She felt the need for air. A lot of it. In fact, she reasoned, after an evening of boozing, the cool ocean air might do her good.

She pulled on an old coat as she unlocked her front door and stepped out into the night. It was crisp, with a breeze coming in off the Pacific. Fifty degrees maybe. She glanced at her watch. Four-eleven A.M. A completely inhuman hour to be awake, she figured. Then she recoiled from those numbers again.

Four-eleven. Why did those digits keep coming up?

Alicia settled onto the wooden front steps of her home. She sat perfectly still and listened to the night. She felt sober again and looked to the sky.

The night was bright. The stars were clear. The moon, reflecting the light of the sun, was at three quarters.

She heaved a sigh.

This night's episode, real as it may have seemed, must have been the product of a hyperactive imagination. There could not possibly have been an Amos in her house, she told herself. The door was *chained* from the inside. Amos, little weirdo that he was, simply could not have walked through a locked door.

Could he?

Alicia wondered why she had even asked herself such a question. Dr. Brillstein had him pegged. Bless Dr. Brillstein! To even entertain the notion of the extraterrestrial was ludicrous!

Wasn't it?

Then Alicia's eyes settled. She could barely see into the darkness beyond her lawn. But when her eyes did adjust, and when she could focus on a dark stand of eucalyptus and palm trees across the street, Alicia thought she saw movement.

She couldn't be sure. She kept her eyes trained on the place where she thought she had seen something. And then from somewhere—without any doubt—the figure of Amos Joy inevitably came into view.

Amos was standing across the street watching her.

"Amos?" Alicia asked softly. "Talk to me. What do you know? What are you leading me to?"

The vision was about fifty feet away. But Alicia was convinced that she saw Amos smile.

No spoken response followed.

"What do you want?" Alicia called out into the darkness.

Again, no verbal answer.

The minutes passed. Then a quarter hour. A bluish hue finally came up across the predawn horizon. The palm trees across the street formed an eerie backdrop to what she saw.

Alicia grew impatient. She drew her weapon and brandished it, flipping it from one hand to the other, pretending that she might suddenly go psycho and start firing. Amos was unmoved.

Distantly, Alicia thought she heard laughter. A mocking, haunting laughter. The thought came to her: Amos was glad.

As Alicia would recall it later, she had entered an almost hypnotic dreamlike state.

The quarter hours seemed to pass as single minutes. Alicia was next aware of the sky becoming much lighter. And yet with the advent of dawn, Amos was still there, not stationary but a solitary pacing figure on the opposite side of the road, one who seemed to be waiting for her, and yet oblivious of her at the same time.

Alicia reached to her wrist. She removed her watch and set it down on the porch next to her. Five-twenty A.M. She raised her eyes again to Amos. He smiled now. He raised a hand, beckoning her.

To her death? Or to some other state of awareness?

Alicia kept her eyes trained as the first fingers of morning embraced the sky and the earth.

"It's you, isn't it?" she asked him aloud, her voice barely more than a whisper. "It's you in my head."

Alicia settled into her spot, highly conscious of her nakedness beneath her robe. She leaned forward slightly and stared at the humanoid form, the vision, in front of her.

Amos started to move.

First he seemed to recede and diminish to her view. Then she realized that—at least to her perspective—the form had reconfigured itself. It was slowly moving but couldn't seem to decide upon its direction.

Then, with painful slowness and resolution, it approached her. And yet, despite the fact that Amos was in the form of a man, the being did not have the gait or cadence of something walking. It moved like a body on coasters, like something on wheels.

Or like something floating on air.

A new fear paralyzed her.

For a moment the vision was just on the other side of the street. Then it stopped. A strange light filled the road in front of it, which startled Alicia and frightened her even more. Then she was relieved, as she recognized the illumination as headlights from an approaching car.

She had the sense of being within one of those familiar nightmares where one is stuck on a railroad track, a train is approaching, and one can neither move nor cry out for help. She wanted to break free from this vision, but couldn't. Nor could she signal the car that came nearer and nearer. She was frozen in place, unable to move or speak.

The sound of the engine heightened. A Mustang passed, its ragtop down, its radio blaring.

The headlights dazzled her eyes. She tried to focus again, hoping that the vision was gone.

She gasped.

It wasn't gone at all. It was thirty feet closer. It seemed to have passed directly through the car and was now on Alicia's side of the road.

And it moved nearer. The same damnable gliding, sliding otherworldly forward movement.

She whispered aloud. "Please . . . please leave me alone . . . please leave me in peace . . ."

You'll be mine.

"Please don't touch me."

She hadn't been so scared since she realized that Hernando Cordero's bullets had struck her and she was losing blood and consciousness, wondering if she'd ever regain consciousness.

This won't hurt at all, Alicia. This won't hurt at all.

The vision before her was no longer that of a man.

Amos was gone and some other identity had emerged. It had human form but seemed more like a twenty-fifth-century evolution of a human being.

The head was disproportionately large for the body, and slightly triangular, as if the brain area were augmented beyond human proportions. The face was murky and unclear, though it did have two very large dark eyes. It was as if Amos had shed his disguise and emerged into his true form.

The vision was ten feet away from her. Then five. It was shimmering, changing colors, and even incorporating colors that she never knew existed, while effusing a rancid odor unlike anything she had ever experienced.

She wanted again to scream, but couldn't.

She wanted to turn her head, but couldn't.

She wanted to die rather than face this foul creature.

But couldn't. Or hadn't.

Look upon me.

She raised her eyes to where his face should have been. But there was no face. Just a surface.

Then two huge dark eyes emerged. Big and dark. No whites. Only massive bulging pupils. They blinked slowly, with see-through membranes.

That's good. Very good. Now come with me.

"This is not real! I'm dreaming! I'm dreaming!" she said aloud. She knew she was saying it aloud because she could hear her own voice.

No. Very real.

Something resembling an arm, or a tentacle, came from the humanoid's uneven torso. She was petrified. Then it touched her.

It was extremely cold.

And immediately upon contact, she experienced a bright flash that absorbed and contained her.

She closed her eyes.

There was a heavy burden upon her and she felt herself transported. Another sense of flight, as if the dream this same evening had been only a prelude.

This time the transporting had a ponderous rushing aspect to it, however. Somewhat akin to the feel of an airplane taking off very rapidly then making a very steep ascent into a turbulent sky.

She felt a sort of vertigo, as if she were rising, rising, rising, and had the impression that she was being catapulted or carried far from the surface of the earth.

C H A P T E R   1 8

The bright light still surrounded her as her trip began. She felt no pain other than mental anguish. But she felt herself rising relentlessly until—again, much like in an airplane—she had the sense of leveling off. The overall feeling was very serene, as if she had been tranquilized.

Sedated.

She had no idea where she was—or where her mind was—but it was her impression that she was far above the surface of the earth.

Yet she was not afraid. Fear seemed to have vanished and given way to tranquillity. Gradually the light began to clear and fade. She sensed movement around her. She became aware of a high-pitched whining just within her range of hearing.

There was for a moment no such thing as up or down. But then points of reference began to emerge and she was lying down on something that she would remember as being a very comfortable cot.

Silky to the touch of her bare skin.

Cool.

Refreshing.

Much like a waterbed.

She was aware of being naked, laid out like a corpse. And then she realized that she was being examined. The brightness cleared further and she realized that there were about a half-dozen of these beings surrounding her—shiny, shimmering grayish-green beings that resembled the one Amos had turned into—and they were examining her.

She was not held by any sort of physical restraints, but was unable to move. And these beings were examining her with their vision, both inside and out. Their large eyes were intently focused, flicking in one direction and then the next, and she could feel their individual gazes upon her bare flesh, like beams of warm light running up and down her.

The feeling upset her greatly, and then was strangely soothing. And while at first she wished to resist, that feeling too changed and she wanted to please them. She hoped they liked her body.

She also realized that they were communicating with each other, but didn't know how she knew that. She just did. She also knew that one of them was Amos. And she didn't know how she knew it, either, since they were all identical, but she did.

The next thing she knew, she had been turned over, and was lying facedown, her arms at her side. She started to feel fear, and then for some reason didn't feel that any more, either. It was as if each time she reached for a human emotion, they knew how to intercept it, quell it and change it.

Instead, in fact, a surge of contentment filled her, as if she had been given a strong warm narcotic. But it was physically satisfying, much like the feeling a woman has after having made love passionately and having enjoyed a series of strong orgasms.

Then she was on her back again. All of the beings were crowded around the lower portion of her naked body. They were examining her genitals. Again, there was no pain, no physical intrusion or trauma. Rather, a benign and thorough examination. Involuntarily, she spread her legs apart to aid their inspection.

One of the space beings turned toward her and she knew it was Amos. His eyes slowly blinked and were again covered with celery-colored membranes for a moment.

Yes, thank you, Alicia. Yes, thank you, you will be able to breed with me. Yes, you will be very perfect, thank you.

She tried to say again that she didn't want to breed with him. But as soon as the thought occurred, it was intercepted and she was forced to dismiss it.

Involuntarily, she found her mouth moving, words coming out. "Yes. I'd like that," she heard herself say.

The high-pitched whining, still just at the edge of her cosnsciousness, intensified. It became busier. She took it to be an expression of excitement. Amos was going to breed with her and all the others were pleased.

She wondered if it were going to happen right now.

Brightness followed again.

She found herself in another place.

She was on something that resembled a circular platform. The furnishings upon it were just like those on Earth. A bed. A table and a chair.

The brightness withdrew. She saw other platforms and each was inhabited by a woman, naked as she was. Each platform had a single woman on it, and the women all seemed sedated and listless, as if in captivity. And Alicia realized that she could not escape. The limits of how far she could go were the perimeters of her pedestal. She had the sense that there was an invisible barrier there, and she also had the sense that she was being held there for one captor in particular.

There must have been dozens of other women around her, but then—as far as her vision could travel—the dozens expanded to hundreds and the hundreds expanded to thousands, much like mirror images held up to mirror images. Too many to count. They were of all human colors—white, red, black, brown, and yellow—and most were young.

Breeding age. A space-station human slave auction!

Then this image faded also. Or at least her vision of it did. The strange light surrounded her again and she felt herself traveling once more. This time the journey was a reverse of the previous one.

She had the sense of drifting downward, tumbling, but in a carefree way, almost floating peacefully. The bright light seemed to escort her.

"What was this about?" she asked aloud. "What was this all about?"

I've shown you the future, Alicia. Your future. Like it?

"No!"

Shame on you. You'll learn to.

Then she felt something that might have been similar to an airplane coming in for a landing, though without bumps. It was a matter of speed decelerating, and light diminishing along with it.

She closed her eyes and as her hands and arms tried to cover herself, she realized that her body was now covered with cloth.

Her blue bathrobe was back in place.

Her eyes flashed open in surprise. She was back on the front step of her home.

She blinked.

She had the feeling of having emerged from a dream. But she wasn't so sure. It had been incredibly vivid. And she remembered every detail.

The morning was bright. She pulled the robe protectively to her body and tried to get her bearings. Across the street, Amos remained visible, back in human form. She was startled anew to see him.

Then, right before Alicia's eyes, the figure of Amos faded into nothingness.

He was gone.

She tried to convince herself that Amos had walked away, had disappeared among the trees while Alicia blinked. But she knew that wasn't the case.

She knew it in exactly the same way that she knew Amos had been within her home, and for that matter, she knew that it was he who had been somewhere else, too.

Alicia was left alone on her front step with disbelieving eyes, a trembling hand clutching a pistol, clothed only in a worn bathrobe, and her nerves rubbed raw. Everything she had ever believed in was complete chaos, every orthodoxy destroyed.

She looked down next to her and saw the face of her wristwatch. The timepiece was exactly where she had placed it. But the time was now seven twenty-six A.M. More than two hours had disappeared since she had last looked.

To where had it disappeared? she wondered. And for that matter, to what spacial or metaphysical location had *she* disappeared? Or at least where had her mind gone for those two hours?

Had she been asleep and entertained another dream? Or had she entered a trance state? If so, what had brought her out?

Then again, the larger question: Had Amos even been there at all? And had he guided her on some fantastic journey that had actually taken place?

The new day, as it happened, broke with an astonishing clarity. Alicia was left with a pair of final thoughts.

First, she would have to go visit her old friend and mentor, Ed Van Allen, with whom she had worked on a case in Los Angeles that had touched upon the supernatural. And second, perhaps it was a coincidence, but Amos had departed in the direction of the sun.

Alicia arranged to meet her one-time partner at their reg-
ular meeting place, on a bench in Santa Monica, down by
the beach. Their rendezvous was set for eight A.M. but she
was there early. She wore a light blue sweatsuit, with her
gun strapped to the leg on the right side. She wore a blue
Dodgers baseball cap to shade her eyes. It was her day off
from her four-mile workout but was not Ed's.

She and Ed Van Allen had known each other for six
years. He had hung the affectionate nickname Double-A
upon her, premised on her initials, and had taken her under his wing when she had gained her detective's shield
on the LAPD.

A mentor. A confidant. A friend.

He was a strong presence in her life and, twenty-two
years older than she, a source of wisdom and experience—even if it was tempered sometimes with a world-
weary cynicism.

She liked to think of herself as an independent
woman who made her own decisions, structured her
own life, and came to her own conclusions. Yet she was

aware that Ed Van Allen had affected her in more ways than she could readily count.

She had taken up running at his suggestion. She had taken up listening to jazz, Sinatra, and Pigpen-era Grateful Dead because of his enthusiasm for all three. And she had properly navigated the tricky waters of the LAPD's detective division through his guidance. Then, when the opening came in the California Highway Patrol, four months after she had received promotion to lieutenant first grade in L.A., she had run the possibility past Ed.

"You're only twenty-nine," he had advised. "There are damned few female detectives in the CHP. ahead of you. As a career track, it's a solid step. If that's what you want, go for it."

She applied.

Two weeks later, working with a different partner, she'd been shot, had died and returned. When she was wounded, Van Allen had been among the first to arrive at the hospital, was the first to give blood, and, according to her brothers, had maintained a vigil during all his off-duty time. He hadn't left until she was out of danger. Then he had visited every day.

It wasn't love between them, though there was some physical attraction. They had never dated or even flirted with the notion. The subject had never come up between them.

No, it wasn't love but it must have been something close, Alicia reasoned. A professional intimacy? A friendly sort of love?

By knowing Ed she had understood for the first time in her life why women get involved with older men. He had even sometimes made her wonder—divorced as he now was, with a daughter who was four years younger than she, and a son who was six years younger—what it would be like to be involved with a man that much older.

The familiar voice came softly from behind her.

"Hey," he said.

Startled slightly, she turned from where she sat on a bench. And there he was, walking toward her with a towel across his shoulders and a one-pint plastic bottle of Arrowhead water in his hand. He wore a gray sweatshirt soaked at the chest and the armpits, and a matching pair of gray Champion shorts.

She smiled broadly.

"Hey," she said in return. "Welcome."

"I'd make you as a cop any day," he said, kidding. "What are you doing? Working the parking lot?"

He slid onto the bench next to her. He placed a hand on hers and gave it a squeeze. She leaned to him, maybe a little too readily.

Graciously, he kissed her left cheek.

"I'm here to do cardiopulmonary resuscitation. In case some old geezer like you drops after his four-mile run."

He laughed.

"Hey. It's me who'll be doing the CPR on you, kiddo. I took off a few pounds of suet and I'm doing four miles under thirty-five minutes."

"Jesus. Don't kill yourself."

"I haven't yet," he said.

"So I see."

"How far 'under' thirty-five?"

He glanced at the stopwatch mode on his Timex. "Thirty-four fifty-nine point ninety-one," he said. "But it counts."

"It counts," she agreed.

She felt immeasurably better just seeing him.

His face was moist with sweat. He had more gray hair at the temples, but was still lean and strong. His arms looked chiseled and she had to admit that in addition to being a bit eccentric for a cop, for a Vietnam vet, he was a rock of his generation. They didn't make that many men like Ed Van Allen, and the world was poorer for it.

"So, Double-A?" he said after an appropriate pause and a bit of shop talk. "What brings you the whole two miles down here from the slums of Venice? Confess. What the hell are you working on?"

He opened the bottle of water and drew a long gulp.

"Double murder," she said. "One body dumped out in the high desert near Lancaster. Similar MO in Beverly Hills."

"High desert and Beverly Hills," he scoffed. "There's an unusual link."

"My thoughts also," she said.

"Been only one in the Hills recently that *I* know of. We talking about the one on Canon?"

"Yes," she said.

"He was a television exec, right?"

"That's the one," she said. "Not my precinct. Or yours."

"So what's it linked to?"

"A dump job in the high desert north of Lancaster. Obvious links. Might be serial. And I got a wacko suspect."

He shrugged. "These things happen on our fair planet," he said.

She recoiled. "Why did you say it that way?" she asked.

"How?"

" 'Our fair planet,' " Alicia said.

"I use that expression all the time. Figure of speech."

The sun brightened. Van Allen unfolded a pair of sunglasses and put them on. "You're jumpy this morning," he said. "What's going on?"

"Want to take a look at some stuff for me?" she asked.

"Sure. For you, anything."

She handed him an envelope. He opened it. Background on both murders, including photographs. He glanced through it while she ran through it verbally.

"What you have there, what's on paper, is all the basic stuff. But it's not what's troubling me," she said.

He continued to scan the material. "So talk to me," he said. "What is troubling you?" His eyes rose to meet hers.

She hesitated slightly. "Ed," she began, "I'm going to sound like a lunatic."

"From time to time we all do."

"Have you ever had a voice in your head?" she asked. "Something you couldn't get rid of? Aside from your own thoughts?"

Van Allen's brow furrowed. He nodded remotely.

"Like an unconscious voice telling you something?" he asked.

"Yes. Almost," she said. "Except the voice is more distinct."

He looked away for a moment, appearing as if he were studying the ocean. Then he looked back to her.

"It's the Cemetery of Angels case, isn't it?" he asked. "That's what you wanted to talk to me about?"

"Sort of. As a starting point," she answered. "But it reflects on my current case. Now answer my question, Ed."

"The voice, huh?"

She nodded.

"Yeah," he said. "In the Angels case, I heard a voice coming from somewhere. I don't know why it picked me. It scared the living hell out of me."

Alicia held a hand across the bill of her cap. The sun seemed intensely bright this morning.

"So then you wouldn't think I was crazy if I told you I was experiencing something similar now?" she asked.

"No. I wouldn't think you'd gone crackers," Van Allen said. "Although I know how much stress you've been under. Things like stress contribute, you know."

"I know," Alicia answered quietly.

A Pacific breeze caressed her hair as they sat in silence.

"So you're hearing something, right?" he asked.

She nodded.

"Where do you think it's coming from?" he asked.

She held a moment before she answered. "I think the source is a little man named Amos. My suspect in the case. I don't know."

"Have you interviewed this guy?"

"I met him once. He's creepy beyond belief."

"Want me to take a look at him with you sometime?"

"I wouldn't mind. If we can keep it unofficial."

"We can keep it any way you want," he said.

"Thanks."

"What else?" Ed Van Allen asked.

She shook her head defensively. "Nothing else. Why?"

He studied her. "You know something, Double-A? I know you pretty well."

"And?"

"You're holding something back on me," he said. "There's still a big something about this case that you're not telling me. Why?"

She let several seconds pass before she had the nerve to summon up the honest answer to his question.

"Why don't you let go with it, okay?" Ed asked gently.

"Because you're really going to think I'm a screwball," she said.

He held up his right hand, two fingers raised, two fingers folded down over the thumb.

"Scout's honor. I promise not to," he assured her.

For a moment her gaze buried itself into his. She knew that he had picked up on the terrible dread that was within her. She had to lay it bare.

"Come on, Alicia," he said. He placed an arm around

her. "Whatever it is, I won't think less of you. And you need to tell me."

"The man who owns this voice," she began. "He appears and disappears. I think he was even in my home. See, he was in one of my dreams. But then I pulled myself out of my sleep and my dream and opened my eyes and he was there."

Van Allen blinked. "He was *where?*"

"In my home. But when I went after him he disappeared into thin air. Only to reappear again. Ed, he's real but he's not human."

A beat, then, "So what do you think he is?"

A cloud rolled over the sun. A funny shadow crossed Alicia's face, one that made her look astonishingly old for several seconds.

"Judging by the visions I've had?"

"Judging by anything you think is significant."

She turned and looked him dead in the eye.

"He terrifies me. I think he's from another planet," she said. "I mean that literally. And I think he has plans to abduct me."

For several seconds, Van Allen made no answer at all.

"And I know how crazy that sounded," she concluded.

Van Allen looked out over the surface of the ocean. "Why would he want to abduct you, Alicia?" he asked.

Again, she had difficulty with the words.

"Go for it," he said softly. "Tell me what you're thinking."

"I think he wants to breed with me," she said.

He leaned back on the bench and sighed. He shook his head.

"Wow," he said. He fumbled slightly. "Alicia, you really know how to push the credibility envelope, don't you?" he asked gently.

"Ed, I'm here because I'm confused. I'm frightened. I'm barely able to cling to my rational mind. Do you understand that?"

"I do."

She paused again.

Her gaze went far away and then returned.

"On the night that he came into my home," she said, "I followed him outside. I watched his figure across the street. It was stalking me. Haunting me. Whatever you want to call it. But it was there. Then it did something very strange."

"What was that?"

"I saw it approach me. It approached me until I felt it was right in front of me, nearly making physical contact."

"Then?"

"Then there was something that I can't describe. Something almost electrical. A jolt. A shock. Then there was a flash."

"And?"

"I had this sensation of sailing," she said. "High up. Definitely a sensation of rising until we went through this screen of light or brightness or whatever. Then the next thing I knew, I felt I was . . . The only way I can describe it is that it was similar to the time that I nearly died. Similar but very, very different. I felt a weightlessness. And saw a light that was surreal."

"Then what?"

"I felt I was . . ." she sighed. "Oh, Ed . . . I can't believe that these words are even coming from me."

Van Allen was leaning forward slightly, a consoling look on his face. "Tell me, anyway," he said.

"I was being examined by these beings from another planet. I was naked and on an examination table. They were probing me with their eyes. Then I was in some sort of room that was like a cell on a platform. Except it had no walls. There were other women; they had abducted a whole bunch for breeding purposes. No one spoke. The other women were like zombies—neither living nor dead. But prisoners. The other women were of various ages and shape. But I felt as if I belonged to this one individual. He *owned* me. I was his. He wanted to breed with me."

"Did he?" Van Allen asked. "In your dream, I mean?"

"No," she said, shuddering. "That was something that I understood was in my future. As if he's saving it for a particular time. He had flashed me into the future. He wanted me to know what was going to happen because there's no way I can prevent it."

Van Allen looked away for a moment.

A pair of girls walked by and his eyes followed them absently, then turned back to Alicia.

"So it's sort of an outer-space abduction-rape fantasy. Right?"

"Is that what you think?" she asked.

"Maybe."

"Ed. This was more than a weird dream. I was sitting on the front porch of my home when he touched me. Two hours passed and I returned. I don't think I was sitting in that place on my porch for those two hours. I was taken somewhere else. At least mentally."

"May I play devil's advocate with you?" he asked.

"Of course."

"You're involved in a very strange case," he said. "And look at what you're telling me. Analyze it. The whole scenario is fraught with the possibility of self-hypnosis, of stress-related abuse fantasy. Alicia, there's not a single spaceship sighting in your story but there was enough in what you told me to keep a shrink busy for six months."

"So that's what you think?"

"That's my initial reaction," he answered carefully.

"You're forgetting how you and I have been trained: always look for the simplest, most logical explanation for anything. Start there. Then work your way to the spacey stuff."

She sighed.

"Why, for example, would this alien being have picked on you?" Van Allen asked.

"Because he's involved in the murder investigation that I'm working on," she said.

"Alicia?" he asked. "Don't get mad. But do I need to lean over and shake you? Do you know how wacko you're sounding?"

It was obvious that Van Allen agreed with Brillstein. Amos was mortal and dangerous but no more than that. The rest was stress fantasy. It all should have come together as good news for her. But somehow it didn't.

"Do you think there's a chance in a million that something really happened to me there on that porch?" she asked.

"Do I think that you were really transported somewhere?"

"Yes."

He opened his mouth to answer. She halted him.

"This is a philosophical question, Ed," she said. "Tell me whether you can categorically say that you disbelieve anything like that could possibly happen."

He thought for several seconds.

"Let's put it this way," he said in a gentle tone. "Your mind was transported somewhere. Exactly how and why is open to debate."

"What about my body?" she asked. "Could I really have been on this examination table?"

He shook his head. "Jesus! I'd like to give you a firm, no-bullshit 'no.' But I don't know," he said. "I used to be in denial about anything touching on this type of stuff:

the occult. The paranormal. The whole supernatural world. UFOs. Aliens. Then I had my own experiences. I saw a ghost myself. I *know* I did and when I tell most people they think I'm a fruit basket. So, no, I don't think you were, but I don't discount anything anymore, Alicia. I don't."

"Should I be scared?" Alicia asked.

"You should be careful," he answered. "Very careful. And any help you need from me will always be there for you."

"I want to at least know what the hell I'm dealing with."

"Of course," he said sympathetically. He gave her hand another squeeze.

"Have you ever heard of a chemical substance called chrolystron?" she asked.

He shook his head. "New one on me. Why?"

"It was found in the bloodstream of both my victims," she said. "It's a mystery chemical. No one knows where it comes from. But it turns up in the blood of astronauts. People who have flown in space."

"And your victims are not astronauts, I assume."

"You assume correctly."

He paused again.

"Well," he said quietly. "That throws an interesting light on things, doesn't it?"

"It does."

"And I also assume that neither victim could have picked up the chemical at some aerospace plant. Boeing, Lockheed, and McDonnell-Douglas are all in this area, plus some smaller subcontractors."

"First thing I thought of, too," she said. "The chemical doesn't work that way. You have to have been in space."

"Can't be injected?"

"Not from what I know."

Moodily, he assessed her situation. "The fact that 'experts' tell you something doesn't mean it's gospel, Alicia," he said. "What they're saying is they haven't figured how something could be possible yet. We always see stuff on the street that hasn't hit their labs yet."

"Good point," Alicia allowed.

But the moment disquieted him. Then, after several seconds more, "I'm wondering if you need to go see my friend Madame Olga. Madame Olga Karmalakova," he said.

"Who in hell is Madame Karmalakova?"

His mood lightened. "My 'cigare volante' lady. My favorite 'space cadet,'" he answered. "Arrived here from Russia or some damned place twenty years ago. An expert on all unidentified things that fly."

"Oh. A saucer nut, huh?"

"No," he said quietly. "Madame Karmalakova is an immensely bright woman. She's vastly knowledgeable about UFOs, ufology, space, heaven, and every damned thing in between."

"Uh-huh."

"She's also psychic. Helped the LAPD on a few cases, including some of mine, though damned if we'd admit that in court. Very New Age, or at least that's what people tell me she is. She's a piece of work. Calls me 'Van Halen,' by the way, not 'Van Allen.'"

"And she's local?"

"She lives up in the hills above Malibu. And she might be able to help you."

"How?"

"Insights. Background. Knowledge of similar occurrences." He shrugged. "That's my hunch," he said. "Based on what I know and what you've just told me."

He wiped a final few drops of sweat from his brow. "Talking to her might get you some perspective on your suspect. Might bring you down to Earth a little. Know what mean?"

"I don't want to make this any kookier than it already is, Ed."

"I know that. See, I had a so-called flying saucer case, too, one time. I went into it as skeptical as you are now."

"And what happened?"

"It turned out to be hoax. Some merry pranksters from the UCLA Law School had a superhigh-flying kite done up like a saucer. I did a little digging on this, and I advise you to do some, too. I discovered, for example, that the government keeps records on these things. About forty percent of UFO sightings each year tend to be misidentified aircraft or balloons. Another thirty-five percent are hoaxes, like the UCLA kite. Another fifteen percent are attributable, at least in theory, to something called 'the ionization phenomenon.' "

"What the heck is that?"

"Various forms of ionization around air molecules surrounding natural heat and light from the earth. Ball lightning is an example. More commonly in our neck of the woods, the heat that escapes the Earth after an earthquake is another example. The ionization phenomenon, if I'm remembering this properly, is what accounts for 'earth lights,' a luminance that sometimes appears brightly on the horizon and then dissipates and disappears. In other words, it looks like it hovers in place then zips away. See what I mean?"

She smiled. "You still have a percentage missing, don't you?"

"Yup," he said. "When you're finished with all the rational explanations, you're still left with five percent that are completely inexplicable. That's five percent out of ten thousand reported sightings. That reduces to five hundred unexplained incidents every year in the United

States alone. Let's say ninety-five percent of those should be in one of the previous categories. Swamp gas. Weather balloons. Airplanes. An early evening star. That still leaves you with a few dozen incidents that defy any kind of rational explanation."

He sipped his bottle of Arrowhead.

"See what I mean?" he asked.

"I see."

"Know what you should also do? There's a section of the L.A. Public Library dedicated to this type of stuff. I think it's called the LoBrutto Paranormal Research Collection. It's in the big building on Third Street. Been there a few times myself."

"Who was LoBrutto?" she asked.

"Some literary guy from New York who was fascinated with anything weird. He gave his collection of books and writings to the public library."

She nodded.

"Anyway, I've been to the collection a couple of times on a couple of cases. There's a woman named Mildred Canary who's the curator. You might spend a little time there, checking out your terrain. Look, even if you're dealing with some sicko flying-saucer nut, you'll get an insight into his warped psyche. You'll learn how he thinks and you'll sharpen your own thoughts."

"Very good advice," she said. "I'll try the Internet, too. There should be some insights there, as well."

He nodded. "May I be a philosopher for a moment?" he asked.

"Aren't you always?" she answered.

He smiled.

"Based on my fifty years on this planet, based on the Cemetery of Angels case, based on what I learned when I had my own saucer hoax: we live in a universe where nothing is inherently impossible. There's no law that says that everything we encounter in our lifetime must be explicable in human terms."

"Ed, you sound like you're doing a late-night FM station lead-in for 'Ripple' by the Grateful Dead."

He laughed. "Well, that Jerry Garcia knew a thing or two before he died of 'natural causes' while in drug detox."

Alicia laughed with him and then thought for a moment. "Okay. Where do I find Madame Karmalakova?"

"I'll make a phone call," he said, "I'll set up a meeting for tomorrow or the next day. How's that?"

"That would be good."

He smiled. "Keep in mind that she's a psychic, too," he said. "Don't dismiss that. She personally cracked a case for me once. That's how I know her."

"I'll behave."

He glanced at his watch. They both needed to get going. Van Allen stood. Alicia followed his lead.

"You might want to do two more things, too," he said.

"What's that?"

"By way of getting started with Madame Karmalakova," he advised, "ask her about the Ammon Society."

"Ammon?"

"Local cult. They claim there have been alien landings in this area for the past forty years. Decide for yourself how seriously you want to take them. At least it will get Madame Karmalakova talking."

She froze. She remembered the group Ted Sternfeld had mentioned. Amen. Almond. The little clique of "saucer nuts" that he'd said Bill Sands had hung out with.

"What did I say?" Van Allen asked.

"You're the second person to mention those people this week," she said.

He raised an eyebrow. "No such thing as coincidence, huh?"

She shook her head.

"They take their name from Ammon Ra. Ancient Egypt. God of the Sun." He laughed. "I busted one of them one time. About a year ago in Culver City. Whole damned carload of them weaving all over the place on 405 South."

"What planet were they coming back from?" she asked.

"Let's put it this way. They were sailing pretty high that night. But it had more do to with some stuff they had rolled into their cigarettes than to any trip in a rocket ship."

She laughed, relieved.

"Okay," she said. "What else?"

"Are you still going to the department psychologist? Posttrauma stress counseling?"

"Oh hell, Ed—"

"Answer me."

"I go when I have time," she said.

"Promise me you'll make time," he said. "No matter what you're dealing with, you want to go into it as balanced as possible. There's so much weird stuff out there. I don't want you to lose it completely."

"Lose it, huh?"

"Yes. Complete crack-up. I'm concerned."

"Ed . . . ?"

"Promise me," he insisted.

After a long sigh, "I promise."

He embraced her, long and firmly.

She didn't want it to end. But after several seconds, it did.

They walked to their respective cars and went to work.

CHAPTER 20

Later that same day, in the early evening, Alicia sat down at a table in the research annex of the Los Angeles Public Library on Third Street. It was the first time that she had ever filed call slips at the LoBrutto Paranormal Research Collection. She was embarrassed to even be there.

Several minutes after she sat down, a short, slight woman with tightly bunned gray hair approached her. Mildred Canary, assistant reference librarian, cradled an assortment of books in her thin arms.

"Here we are, my dear," Mildred chirped breathlessly as she arrived. She set five books upon the table. Two of the volumes seemed very old. Only one had a jacket, one was very slim, and all were worn.

The librarian, clad in a pale yellow dress, arranged the books in front of her so that Alicia could see the titles on their spines. "Detective Alicia. File request number 163. Correct?" she asked.

"Yes. Thank you," Alicia answered.

"The sixth book you requested is not on the shelves. Subject matter was UFOs and alien abduction? Was that it?"

At the words "UFOs and alien abduction" Alicia noticed several heads jerk up around the room. She could feel them looking at her. She could see it.

"Yes. That was it. Thank you," Detective Alicia said to Curator Canary.

"Flying saucers. Mmm, yes," the librarian said. "We see them all the time, don't we?" She arched an eyebrow like an old-fashioned schoolmarm.

Then Mildred Canary abandoned Alicia to her research. The detective drew a breath and scanned the room as she prepared to examine her books. Arbitrarily, she took up the thin book first—it was on top and was the closest.

Alicia scanned through it. There were several sections on the Egyptians. The Pyramids along the Nile. The curses of the Pharaohs. Alicia flipped through several chapters which discussed hieroglyphics that addressed incidents involving "visitors from the sky."

Ancient religion, she wondered, or an actual account of an inexplicable occurrence? She tried to keep her mind open to anything, as Ed had advised.

From a document written during the fifteenth century B.C., during the reign of Pharaoh Thutmose III, she found an intriguing incident:

> A circle of fire, coming from the sky, several rods long, circular. After some days there are legions of these, inhabited by small creatures, nearly human in form, gray, green, shining with the intensity of Ra, the Most Holy and Revered God of the Sun.

She continued to read. She switched to a second book on the ancients.

Alexander the Great—ruler, wise man, historian—apparently had had several experiences with UFOs. For example, while he and his forces were in the process of crossing the river Jaxartes into India in 329 B.C., he saw:

> . . . several round silver shields, diving repeatedly upon my army, gleaming, orbicular as the full moon, and causing horses, elephants, and my shamans and soldiers to panic. The round shields retreated at a high altitude into the sky, then vanished . . .

Alicia continued.

Alexander's close encounters did not end there. Seven years later, in 322 B.C. during Alexander's siege of Tyre, he wrote that

> . . . a large flying shield or disc led a formation of six smaller flying shields above Tyre, circling. While my encamped army watched in incredulity, the large disc shone a beam of light upon the walls of mighty Tyre, causing them ruin. More beams were fired from the four diminutive airships, causing the rest of the walls to crumble. My attackers, not ones to ignore a gift from the sky, poured into the city. [See also: Mogul Art; British Museum, p. 445]

Alicia followed the cross-reference.

It led her to a famous painting of Alexander: Alexander's "flights to the heavens on the back of an eagle." The "eagle" carried the Macedonian leader so far aloft that he was able to study and re-create the topography of the Earth well enough to plan his world conquest. The accuracy of Alexander's maps were something no modern historian has ever been able to explain.

Alicia closed the book.

"No one rides an eagle," she said to herself.

A thought came to her.

Americans did. To the moon.

"What?" she asked herself. "Americans did what to the moon?"

The eagle has landed.

She tried to ignore the voice. She wasn't sure if it was Amos again or her own subconscious.

Disturbed, she moved on to *The Anglo-Saxon Chronicle,* a collection of documents written independently in various English monasteries between A.D. 450 and 1150. The priests who wrote the chronicles made several references to astronomical phenomena that were correctly identified: eclipses, comets, meteors, parhelia. Then there was the following entry:

> *On the eve of Cena Domini, the Thursday before Easter, two moons were seen in the sky before daybreak above Sussex. One to the east, one to the west. They moved in tandem to the Plains of Salisbury where they set down two miles from the megaliths. They glowed yellow and passengers perhaps from God's heaven were seen to escape. They stood on the plains until dawn when their moon-craft took upon itself the red-gold color of dawn. Their passengers boarded, the craft lifted and hovered and departed toward the west country more rapidly than anything any mortal man has ever seen in the sky . . . God save us all, Judgment Day is nigh . . .*

What had the priests observed? Alicia wondered.

Whatever it had been, chroniclers in Wales made similar observations on the following date and others in the north of England and Scotland observed similar phenomena all within the same week, strongly suggesting a succession of celestial visits witnessed by countless observers. Particularly noteworthy was the fact that the priests, the learned men of the day, had recorded the sighting.

King Henry I, the last of the Norman kings, even dispatched knights into his realm to search for the creatures that had come from the sky. If any were found, no record of the capture was kept.

"It might be duly noted," the journal continued,

> . . . that the appearance of visitors from the sky had a devastating effect upon Britons of the day; it is no coincidence that the bishopric was moved from Old Sarum to Salisbury during the ensuing years, and the great Cathedral at Salisbury, which to this day in the twentieth century has the highest spire (404 feet/123 meters) in England, was constructed in the decades (1220–1260) that followed, no doubt beseeching the heavens to send their otherworldly visitors again.

Bemused and intrigued, Alicia went on to the next volume.

This one was much more modern and suggested current-day relevance. Alicia found an account of an expedition to the Tibet-China border during the years 1928–1930, headed by the German scientist, explorer, and adventurer Heinrich Henigman, a one-time Nobel prize winner in physics.

The area, in the midst of the Himalayas, with the highest peaks on the planet, had always been a hotbed of anomalous sightings: demons, nonhuman creatures, and strange lights in the sky.

Henigman unearthed a set of 112 stone discs. The discs resembled then-modern phonograph discs; a hole in their center formed a double groove that spiraled out to the edge. The groove was a form of writing that would take archeologists another dozen years to decipher. Even then, in 1942, the translation was so startling that the Peking Academy prevented its publication until 1948. In the final days of the Chiang Kai-shek regime, the document was published under the unwieldy title *The Grooved Script Regarding the Spaceships Which Landed on Planet Earth 10,000 Years Ago*.

In part, the text of the script said:

> *There was a devastating explosion of unknown origin. The earth quaked and shuddered and there were fires. Then human-shaped Beings descended from the clouds in their craft while the native Ham people [Ed. note: Tibetan tribe] hid in their caves. However, the Beings knew the language of the Hams and communicated telepathically with them, assuring them that they meant no harm. They wished to retrieve the pieces and beings in one of their airships [Ed. note: Chinese characters meaning "grand elliptical stones that ride upon the sky" were used] that had crashed. It could be observed that even one hundred centuries ago, before the dawn of modern history, the concept of "crash retrieval" was known upon the earth. [See also Alwin, Baher: The Night the Sky Caught Fire, WH Allen, London, 1983; and Corrigan, Patrick: Mysteries of Tibet, Doubleday, New York, 1978]*

Alicia read with accelerating fascination.

From ancient times on, for those with an open mind, the universe had been a place where nothing was impossible. Since the dawn of history, it seemed, there had been accounts of airships around the earth created from nonhuman intelligence and technology. Sure, some of the accounts came from myth, folk belief, or various religions. But how could one explain away the accounts of Alexander the Great or the German scientist Henigman? What were the limits, Alicia wondered, of what one could see if one kept one's eyes on the heavens and one's mind wide open?

Henigman's expedition was comprised of ten European adventurers, plus a dozen native guides and bearers. They were obviously a group that kept both minds and eyes open, particularly in that high Himalayan region so noted for the inexplicable.

Not long before the journey's end, Henigman wrote:

While we were returning to civilization by crossing a remote stretch of western China, we pitched our camp sixteen kilometers south of Ulan-Devan. Shortly after dawn, on the morning of 7 June, in the Year of Our Lord 1929, Dr. Philbus noticed the presence of what appeared to be a large black vulture circling in the sky about a hundred meters to the west of our camp. The presence of the large predator threw our bearers into a frenzy of near panic. We needed to calm them before we could put our field glasses upon the bird. More than one party of explorers has been abandoned in the mountain wilderness by a jittery crew and we had no desire to join the list of those unfortunate souls who have perished through the cowardice and lack of discipline of our heathen servants . . .

However, when calm was restored and the scientists of our party had trained their oculars on the great and unusual bird, one, Dr. Bauer-Koizim, I believe, noticed something very high in the sky beyond the vulture . . .

It was not visible to the naked eye. Only the most powerful of our field glasses were initially able to track it. But we passed the glasses among us and all witnessed it: a massive, and I would say beautiful, spheroid body, shining in the morning sun . . .

Dr. Philbus, as has been previously stated in this journal, is an expert aviator, and a major in the Luftwaffe. His credentials—which include the Distinguished Flying Cross during service in France—are well known to the German National Aeronautical Academy in Berlin. The good doctor states categorically that the craft was moving faster than any known winged aircraft of this day. Nor was it similar to any flying craft of his experience.

It also ascended, descended, and veered in patterns that none of us had ever before witnessed. Most bizarre, it disappeared by approaching us at an astonishing speed, growing larger, just close enough so that we could make out a design pattern resembling windows, then ascending in two seconds' time into the blue firmament above us. If a man of average size held a golf ball in his hand, and extended his hand as far as he could reach, the ball would be as large as this spaceship was to us in the instant before it vanished . . .

The entire incident, from discovery to abrupt disappearance, lasted aproximately eighty-five seconds. Photography proved futile, as we were not quick enough with our equipment . . .

Dr. Philbus suggested that the craft's maximum air speed might have been as swift as fifteen hundred kilometers per hour . . .

Some members of our party also recalled hearing a distant high-pitched humming while viewing the craft. Sadly, I recall no such stimuli myself, though my own hearing was grievously impaired while serving as a major in the artillery on the Russian front during the Great War. It might also be noted that all of our bearers and guides seemed to treat the appearance of the aircraft with a certain routine insouciance; the black vulture caused them greater unease

Nothing that happened farther along on our journey served to demystify this incident. We broke camp the next day after attempting once more to locate the unidentified flying object, and descended the Halti-Piri glacier to the southeast.

Alicia sighed.

The Henigman discoveries conformed to the most stringent requirements of accuracy: in a written account multiple witnesses of good character and high-powered binoculars to aid the participants. The books before Alicia were stuffed with such reports, ancient and modern.

Not that it wasn't memorable stuff.

In another book, *UFOs in the Bible*, for example, half crackpot, half brilliant:

> Many episodes in both the Old and New Testaments lend themselves to ufological interpretation, the most significant being the "star" that announced the birth of Jesus ... Christian theology points out that the word "magi" is a name for astrologers and magicians ... The Bible narrative also indicates that the "star" moved, not as the other heavenly bodies did, but under its own steam, and "came to rest" above the birthplace of Jesus ... A fifteenth-century Russian translation of an even more ancient document states that the "star" was watched by many astronomers in the eastern countries and that one particular night it lit up the sky as if it were the sun. The document continues to state that this star then hung over Mount Vans for a complete day, after which it landed on the mountain "like an eagle." This text then refers to others that allege that the Savior "came down from" the star. This would seem quite probable if we are to believe the New Testament when it says that Christ ascended to Heaven "in a cloud" ...

Alicia wanted to stop reading but could not pull herself away. The literature of ufology seemed endless, relentlessly interfacing with religion, art, and literature.

The beat went on. Another intriguing section in the same book:

Unquestionably, also, images of flying saucers appear in much of the art of the Renaissance. Of the most particular interest is the world-famous fresco in the Dechany Monastery in the former Yugoslavia, which apparently depicts angels, but without wings and looking as though they are pilots of a spacecraft. The monastery was built in the fourteenth century, but not until the advent of sputnik and the first artificial earth satellites of the twentieth century did the visions of these paintings make sense to the "modern" eye. It is extraordinary that our world had to wait for the advent of modern space technology, and the concomitant expansion of contemporary ideas, before images of our "prescientific" ancestors could be given a less than supernatural interpretation.

Alicia pursed her lips. She found an article published by an English literary critic named Nigel Richardson, a don at Oxford, who had written in the early nineteen eighties. The article focused on the fiction of Jonathan Swift and in particular one of Gulliver's travels.

While most readers will be familiar with Gulliver's adventures in Lilliput and Brobdinag, they are probably unaware of a third place called Laputa. The story there opens with Gulliver sighting "a flying circular island" driven by a magnetic motor. This strange island lands and Gulliver is "abducted." The vehicle is named Laputa. One is left to wonder where Swift got his inspiration, as there were no circular islands known to the English of Swift's time. Similarly, where did Swift get the information that he imparts to the inhabitants of this island on the subject of Mars?

We all know now that Mars has two moons, but these were not "discovered" by Asaph Hall until 1877, as there were no telescopes powerful enough until then. Yet Swift

*wrote in 1726. Further, the Laputans told Gulliver that
the moons orbited Mars at three and five diameters re-
spectively. Swift calculated the orbits of these moons and
arrived at figures which were not "known to modern science" until the twentieth century . . .*

*Was Gulliver's Travels actually "faction," and was
Swift the beneficiary of knowledge gleaned from an alien
encounter in the 1720s? Such speculation is unacceptable
to the modern scientific mentality; yet the strange syn-
chronicity remains, and permeates all of Swift's later writings.*

Alicia flipped forward and she spotted a section that
someone had highlighted. Nearby, the librarians were
readying to close the annex. She hurried to read the ruminations of some writer—probably now long dead, Alicia reasoned—from several decades earlier:

*Any genuine skeptic should be able to argue from
the data as convincingly for the existence of UFOs and
alien life-form on earth as for their nonexistence, because all skepticism should really be about the nonaccep-
tance of unproved absolutes, and not disproving ideas and
possibilities that do not conform to the accepted cosmo-
logical wisdom of the day. So let us have no more skepticism, particularly in regard to UFOs and aliens, which
is based mostly on social and intellectual prejudice,
and which is little more than an arcane belief system itself.*

Alicia closed the book and spent several moments in
deep thought. Mildred Canary trundled past Alicia's
table. "Five minutes, ma'am," she said. "We're about to
close."

Alicia nodded, thanked her, and slid all five books back to her. But she remained sitting for a moment, lost in thought. So where did all this leave her and her investigation?

Ufology had been there all along, throughout human history, for anyone ready to believe. Fanciful as some of the accounts she had read might be, they seemed less fanciful to her today than they might have a month earlier.

She rose from the table and left the library. In the sunlight outside, an alien idea skittered through her head.

Someday the people of the future might look back in astonishment at our prescientific superstitions that there were no such things as flying saucers!

She blew out a breath. She couldn't even tell where that idea had come from. Had it been Amos? Her own subconsciousness? Or a an unavoidable intellectual conclusion from all that she had read?

"Belief?" she now asked herself. "Is that all it takes? The ability to see what is so obvious?"

An answer arrived like words whispered on starlight . . .

Yes . . .

A deep shudder gripped her. That alien voice? Those bizarre iconoclastic thoughts? She couldn't tell if they were hers or someone else's now. She began to ask herself questions to which the answers bordered on the unthinkable.

Point: There had been hundreds of thousands of UFO sightings and alleged alien encounters over the course of centuries. But weren't these centuries just seconds in the lifetime of the universe?

Point: In all cultures, ufology existed. And yet conventional beliefs, be it organized religion or state socialism, had always sought to suppress it or discredit it. Why?

Where was the danger? What was the social heresy? All over the world, would the existing system of social values crumble with the discovery of an ufological holy grail?

Point: Was Alexander the Great an alien?

Further point: Had Jesus been one?

She smiled, knowing how these thoughts, even as facetious conjectures, would have offended so many. But interpret either man in that vein, and their powers, their sway over people, became much more comprehensible.

From somewhere in her youth an idle thought flashed. Her father had known a man who had served in the United States Air Force at Los Alamos, New Mexico. She thought she recalled his name: Major John Devereux.

The major had been a pleasantly profane, prematurely aged man who eventually smoked and drank himself to death at age fifty-five after a career in the military. He had also been a neighbor of the Aldrich family when Alicia had been growing up. He had had nothing but time on his hands in his final years, and used to wander over to the Aldrich house on summer evenings to sip beer and watch the Dodgers on TV with Alicia's dad.

One night, Alicia had overheard the major talking to her father over some Pabst Blue Ribbon. Alicia had been a teenager at the time. The words had always stayed with her.

"You know, Peter," the major had confessed, "there's this storage area they have there in New Mexico. CIA runs it. Or air force intelligence. Or someone. It's underground, about a full half mile square. I got in there once. You wouldn't believe your goddamned eyes. They got every strange space item they've ever found, stashed there in that hanger and classified top secret."

The major hadn't even been speaking of the celebrated Roswell incident of 1947, the weather balloon with test crash dummies that the flying saucer kooks had pointed to for years as "proof" of an alien invasion just after mankind had entered the atomic age. The major had dismissed the Roswell incident thoroughly, calling it a U.S. Army experiment that had been "thoroughly fucked up with usual army precision."

Rather, he had been talking about "the real stuff" that was in that top-secret storage area. Real stuff. Strange stuff.

"Scary stuff," Devereux had said softly. "Stuff I can barely believe myself. Be funny if that Commie Orson Welles turned out to be some sort of prophet. You know what I mean? War of the frigging Worlds, and all that?"

Two nights later, standing outside, Alicia had asked her father what Major Devereux had meant. Her father had motioned his head to indicate the full, clear, and beautiful starry sky above their heads.

"Take a look up there," Ken Aldrich, vice-president of the First National Bank of Pasadena and backyard astronomer, had said. "What do you see?"

"The sky," she had answered.

"What's in it?"

"Stars. Millions of them. So?"

"Wouldn't it be the height of presumption to think that we are alone?" he had said.

"That's scary," she said, trembling.

He placed a strong arm around her shoulders.

"No," her father had said. "It's cozy. Comforting. You just have to think of it in the right way."

She wondered. The way she was thinking now?

She started her car.

She drove, her mind a controlled clutter of theories, suspicions, nuances, certainties, and heresies. Yet in her fatigue, she knew that intellectually she was ready to open her mind and move forward.

After having read the material in the library, she had the sense of having sailed forward and back through a clear open sky. Soon, if she were very lucky, she would start assembling little pieces of the puzzle and start forming a picture, or at least a mosaic. She was looking—intellectually speaking again—for a place to land, a peaceful little cloud that would offer her, if not enlightenment, then at least tranquillity.

At least now, in other words, she was ready to go see Madame Karmalakova, Ed Van Allen's mysterious expert on all inexplicable things that flew through the air.

CHAPTER 21

Mid-afternoon the following day, Alicia drove northward along the Pacific Coast Highway from Venice. For some reason, images from her adolescence flashed before her as if they were suddenly emerging out of the clouds of her memory into an eerie sunlight.

She could remember the evenings spent during summer vacation from high school, hanging out at the In-N-Out Burgers in Ventura and Thousand Oaks. She recalled a time with her first serious boyfriend when she was seventeen years old. His name had been Kevin, and he took her swimming and surfing one day at the McGrath State Beach. The surf had been heavy. Her bathing suit had not been up to the challenge of heavy surf and, much to Kevin's delight, the top had been lost in the water, and she had refused to come out of the water until he found her a T-shirt. Later in the summer they had had sex.

It was only the second time in her life and Kevin had plied her with booze and, in retrospect, it had been midway between a clumsy seduction and outright date rape.

Afterward, Kevin had shown no interest in her and moved on to another girl.

After high school, Kevin had gone to work and Alicia had gone to college to obtain her degree in criminology, eventually garnering the appointment to the police department at Long Beach. Life came full circle a year later. Alicia had been on duty with a partner named Bill Flynn when they were called to recover some surfboards stolen from a shop in Redondo. She and her partner had nailed the three perps with sixteen short boards. One of the suspects was Kevin.

"Can't you cut me a break, Ally?" he'd asked.

"I don't remember you ever cutting me one."

"Oh, come on, Ally."

"It's Officer Aldrich now, anyway," she had answered as her partner had cuffed him. "Do you want to hear your Miranda from me or Officer Flynn?"

"Neither, fuck it."

" 'Neither' is not one of your choices."

Flynn did the Miranda and Kevin did ten months on probation. It was a strange memory, a strange experience, busting a former lover. It had taught her, however, that life would be a succession of such strange experiences.

Alicia's car left the highway at Malibu. She pulled to the side of the road to consult a map. The address she had for Olga Karmalakova was on Mountainview Road, up in the hills past Pepperdine University. Judging by the map, she was within two miles of her destination.

Another five minutes of driving time took her up a hilly winding road that led toward the Santa Monica Mountains. Her route brought her through a winding stretch of low pine trees, then past a mobile home settlement. Several families had laundry out to dry, and one had a rusting old refrigerator out, too, also presumably to dry. Two trailers had massive new satellite dishes, aimed at the southwestern horizon.

This was not the beachfront Malibu of celebrities or multimillion-dollar homes. No Madonna, no Streisand, no Jay Leno in these parts. Rather, this was gritty hillside Malibu, an area sometimes singed by the fires, pock-marked by small settlements of squatters like these, little poor-white enclaves that had been here for decades.

Mountainview Road was more a rural lane than a street. The address she had for Madame Karmalakova was Number 12, but when Alicia arrived at the large 12 that marked the address, she had not yet seen numbers one through eleven.

Instead, she abruptly stopped her Jeep before an un-even lot that had been cleared and carved out of earth and stone at the summit of a sloping hillside, complete with boulders and fallen trees. There in the midst of the rubble was a structure unlike any that Alicia had ever seen.

It took Alicia several seconds to decide that this was a dwelling. The building had been forged together from various low-maintenance materials. Scrap aluminum sheets had been used for walls and roofing. Large sections of plate glass formed sturdy windows and two slid-ing panels of the same formed what Alicia suspected was the front door.

Alicia stepped out of her car. Wedged unapologeti-cally against the curb, presumably the property of the oc-cupant at Number 12, were a pair of motor vehicles. One was a rusty green Mercury van, easily two decades old, maybe three, that looked like it never moved, at least not under its own power. The license plate itself was of a vanishing breed, the old black California plate with the bold golden letters, a plate treasured by longtime natives, but not issued since 1975.

Alicia looked at the van carefully and saw that some-one had applied the decal JESUS: THE MESSIAH HAS ARRIVED! to the left side of the rear window. More recently, someone had tried to scratch out the JESUS, but vestiges of it were still visible. The MESSIAH boldly remained, its message loud and clear, on the far right of the same window.

The other vehicle, much newer, was a bright red Saturn with a moon roof. It appeared to be properly registered and seemed more likely to be in full working order.

Alicia's attention returned to more immediate matters.

She looked back to Number 12 and did have to marvel at the rudimentary simplicity and functionality of the place, not to mention its scrappy California-hilltop flair. The building blended in perfectly with its surroundings and expanded into the landscape. Alicia surmised from the design that its occupant was probably a bright eccentric. She cautioned herself that the prisons and mental hospitals of America were also full of bright eccentrics.

For a moment, she saw herself as a younger woman, knocking on strange doors in Long Beach, responding to calls ranging from homicides to shopliftings to lost dogs, her right palm sweating as it perched apprehensively on the handle of her sidearm, never knowing exactly what lurked beyond the next door.

She shivered.

As she took her first step toward the building, a cloud slid across the sun. Alicia was still in daylight, but not sunshine.

As she walked, there was an unsettling crinkling sound underfoot. She looked down.

Beneath her feet, a whimsical walkway made from flattened beer cans led to the front door. Alicia followed it. Budweiser Boulevard. Stroh's Street. Lager Lane. Rue Rheingold. At the front door, she knocked once. When there was no answer, she knocked again. Her knuckles hit the plate-glass door harder the second time.

Alicia could see directly into the house. There was one large room and in the middle of it something big, hulking, and colorful roused itself from a chair and started to move.

A massive mother bear of a woman in a tie-dyed caftan removed a pair of headphones from her ears. She looked like a lady grizzly rising from hibernation. Summoned by her visitor, she flowed across the room like a wave. The woman had a wide, round moonish face and closely cropped blond hair with pale green highlights.

Idly, Alicia wondered how Lieutenant Mott would react if she fixed up her own hair with verdant nuances. Maybe, she wondered further, it would be enough to disengage Mott's raging midlife hormones. Then again, such a touch might cause his juices to pump all the more arduously.

Alicia tried to put herself back in the present time and place. Damn. She was having trouble concentrating these days. Not a good sign.

The big lady came to the door. She stood about five ten in her bare feet and must have weighed three hundred pounds. But she looked even bigger.

The door opened partly, held by a chain bolt, not that she needed it. The woman smiled tentatively. "Yes?" she asked.

Her voice was basso-melodic, sweet and deep, a Muscovite Mama Cass, but with a tad of perestroika. Her eyes were curious and round as coins.

Alicia had her shield ready and showed it.

"Detective Alicia Aldrich. California Highway Patrol. I'm looking for Madame Olga Karmalakova."

The woman, unlike many visited by state police detectives, smiled broadly. Her large brown eyes flicked over her visitor's shoulder for a second, then settled softly back into Alicia's gaze.

"Oh, yes," the woman said. "Oh, of course, yes, yes. Eddie Van Halen," she said, teasingly referring to their mutual friend, Ed Van Allen. "I knew to be expecting you, friend of Ed. I'm delighted. Delighted. Mmm."

"You're Madame Karmalakova."

"Yes."

The door closed again for a moment as the woman fussed with the bolt contraption on the door and disarmed it. Then the door opened wide.

"Come in, darling."

She held out a fleshy pair of arms that somehow emerged bare from under the caftan. They looked like giant loaves of French bread. There was a red and blue mark on the woman's left forearm, but Alicia couldn't see it well enough to identify it.

Madame Karmalakova embraced a slightly unwilling Alicia, who kept an elbow firmly upon her service weapon.

"I'm Olga Karmalakova. I've been expecting you. Come, come. Sit down. Be comfortable. I will educate you and change your life. Come in, yes?"

Alicia entered the structure, a cathedral in aluminum, a best-case scenario of personal recycling. As the door closed behind her, Alicia wasn't all so sure that she wanted her life changed. She was seeking enlightenment, however, and the resolution to a pair of homicides.

And she had the distinct notion that in meeting this woman, she had come one step closer to an understanding of what was going on around her.

"You are so welcome here," Alicia's hostess said, drawing her visitor into her home. "Sit down."

"Thank you."

Madame Karmalakova wore one massive gold hoop earing in her right lobe and appeared to be in her forties, though it was tough to tell. The caftan looked all the more Technicolor up close and, for that matter, widescreen, too.

"You're here to talk to me about ufology? Well, won't I be damned! That's wonderful. Wonderful, yes?"

"I'm glad you have the time," Alicia said.

"Time?" the woman retorted. "Time! Time for me is nothing. No one visits me out here. I make my own time, mmm. Tea?"

"What?"

"I'll brew us some tea, mmm? How would you like that?"

Madame Karmalakova nearly overflowed her caftan, but overflowed with hospitality, too.

"Tea would be wonderful," Alicia replied.

Like its exterior, the interior of Madame Karmalakova's home was a medley of functional items. She obviously had a lifelong love affair with aluminum, because all the furniture seemed to be forged from that material, one way or another. A steel framework held a trio of large red pillows that formed a sofa, and a coffee table had been fashioned out of three trash cans and a flat pane of glass. A large-screen TV was in one corner, sitting on a steel trolley that looked as if it had once been hospital equipment or a drink trolley on an airplane.

Alicia sat down in a rocker that was an exception to the room's own rules. It was made of wicker. Alicia guessed it was something that Madame Olga must have picked up from a garage sale, as it seemed out of place.

While her hostess went to her kitchen to brew tea, however, Alicia had a minute to assess the rest of the interior. The one-story home had been fashioned at the very top of the hill. The back of the house afforded a magnificent view of a wooded valley that led to the mountains, as well as the sky. And speaking of which, in the center of the living room ceiling was a vast skylight, a triplet of huge glass panes fitted to the aluminum roof. The center panel had a mechanical latch to it and Alicia guessed that it could slide open.

Madame Karmalakova returned with the tea, a small steel pot and two ceramic mugs on a round red steel Coca-Cola tray. The Russian lady caught Alicia gazing through the skylight.

"Oh, darling, it's *spectacular* at night," she said softly. "I sit here inside and watch the heavens till I fall asleep. In this room, the planets come and go. Like Michelangelo, yes, you know, in the poetry of T. S. Eliot, or the women who talk of Michelangelo? I sleep here sometimes if I do not sleep on my porch. No bugs. A little warmer. Sugar? Milk? Lemon?"

"What?"

"For your tea, darling. Sugar? Milk? Citron?"

"Just a bit of milk," said Alicia, returning to earth.

Madame Karmalakova poured. Alicia could see past a room divider that led to the kitchen. Plates and cooking utensils rose high in the sink. She drew the impression that Olga Karmalakova used everything until it ran out, then hosed it down all at once.

Maybe.

Beyond that, out past the kitchen door, Madame apparently kept a large round tank of water. It looked like a huge aquarium, rather global in shape. As Alicia looked more carefully at it, she saw that it *was* a fishery of some sort, holding maybe a dozen finny creatures swimming casually, pleasantly, going nowhere in circles.

"This is quite something, I tell you that," Olga Karmalakova said. "It's been a long time since 'Van Halen' had anything to do with me. Mmm. I can hardly imagine this, yes."

Alicia accepted a mug of tea. It was jasmine with a gorgeous bouquet. Suddenly she was starting to like her Russian lady.

"I was hoping you'd bring Van Halen with you," her hostess said. "Surprise Olga. You know?"

"Ed's pretty busy. Working some tough cases in L.A."

"Yes, I know, for sure, for sure," Olga said. She seated herself on the center red cushion of the sofa. The steel supports heaved a dismal sigh as she sat.

"You tell him I said hello. I need to talk to him about ufology, too. He's a doubting Thomas. Or a doubting Edmund. Whichever. He needs to believe, too." She smiled.

There was even something weird about Olga's smile. Maybe it was just too fleshy. Or spacey. Or perhaps it was just the context.

Simultaneously, in the back of her mind, Alicia recalled a case from when she had worked up north. It hadn't been Alicia's case but she had heard all about it from her peers.

A Sausalito lady had welcomed two Oakland policemen into her home with hash brownies and tea laced with LSD when they had responded to a complaint. Then she had popped John Coltrane's *Blue Train* onto the repeat function of her CD player and sat there and tripped with the cops for twelve hours before they informed her why they were there to start with: her thirty-two unneutered pussy cats were creating a neighborhood nuisance.

"Why do you call Ed 'Van Halen'?" Alicia asked, backtracking.

"Because that's what I think of when I conjure up him," she said. "Van Allen. Van Halen. Eddie Van Allen, Eddie Van Halen. Allen Van Eddie, Halen van Eddie Allen. And finally Van Allen Belt, mmm?"

She laughed indulgently. "Eddie is my rock-and-roll policeman, darling. That's what I call him, yes?"

"I see."

"And he calls me his 'space cadet,' " she continued. "His 'psychic mama.' I take that as a great compliment."

Alicia smiled.

"What does he tell you about me?" Madame Karmalakova asked.

"Exactly what you just said. You're his space cadet and his psychic lady."

"I'm flattered greatly." Her expression changed slightly. "What else does he say? Does he say I'm strange?"

"Madame Karmalakova, Ed and I are police officers in southern California. Some days *everyone* we meet is a little strange."

"Yes, yes, please. Anything else he says?"

"He also says you can tell me about the possibility of

extraterrestrial life on earth," Alicia answered with some hesitation.

The notion hung in the air uneasily. But she forged ahead. "He said you'd have some things you could share."

Madame Karmalakova drank her entire mug of tea in one long slow thoughtful draw. She uttered a slight laugh.

"I can tell you everything you need to know," she said. "All things, plus things you *do not* need to know. Madame Karmalakova is *the* earthbound expert, yes?"

"That's what Ed said."

"Mmm. Ed does not lie, young lady," Madame Karmalakova replied acidly.

"Then where shall we start?" Alicia asked, picking up the conversation without missing a beat.

"What specifically did you want to know?"

"Maybe you could tell me a little about the Ammon Society," Alicia suggested.

"Suppose I do not," Olga Karmalakova answered immediately.

It was as if she were on the edge of a threshold but would not step past it. Somewhere, it seemed, there was a line drawn.

"I do not know if it's a good idea to discuss the Ammon Society with a skeptic," Madame Karmalakova continued.

"How do you know I'm a skeptic?"

"I'm a psychic, too, remember? I know exactly what you think."

"What am I thinking now?" Alicia asked, wondering just how crazy or how authoritative the woman was.

"You're wondering just how crazy or authoritative I am," Madame Karmalakova said. "Am I correct?"

Alicia was startled. She felt a pang of warning. "You're correct."

"I know I'm correct," she snorted. "I did not even have to ask. Psychic, mmm?"

One side of Alicia's mind told her that she did not believe in psychic stuff. The other side was in open revolt against such reasoning, and she even recalled that Ed had once successfully used this woman. She wondered if—all things considered, psychic stuff, ufological stuff, southern California kooky stuff—Madame Karmalakova might have greater insight into Alicia's two open homicides than Alicia had dared to hope. But Alicia filed away the thought.

Madame Karmalakova leaned back and shook her head. Her large arms folded behind her skull, cradling it.

"Psychic, mmm. You'd like to believe but do not know if you can, yes?"

"Correct."

"Americans!" Madame Karmalakova said. "Strange breed of people, you are. The shelves of your supermarkets and electronic stores are filled with goods to buy. In Russia, where I live before America, the same shelves are empty. But your American spiritual and psychic shelves are empty and in Russia they are full. Explain *that*. You are the detective, so you should have answers."

"I'm not sure where you're going with this," Alicia said, "or what it has to do with why I'm here."

"In America, unless an idea can be marketed in book or magazine, it does not reach the individual. In Russia, this is not the case. Due to tradition. Soviet history."

Madame Karmalakova rambled into a mini-lesson on Russian history. Alicia sat patiently and helped herself to more tea.

Meanwhile, Madame Karmalakova talked first about the great atomic explosion—fifteen hundred times the force of the Hiroshima bomb of 1945—in Tunguska, Siberia, on June 30, 1908, a blast that turned the skies fiery then black for a week, left a crater four miles wide, and remained officially unexplained to this day.

"Not difficult to understand," Madame Olga said.

"Visiting spacecraft explode by accident three miles above surface of earth."

She cited this nonchalantly, as if talking about a day of scattered January showers across the Los Angeles River basin.

"Explosion in Tunguska?" she said. "Covered up by Soviet regime. Gave rise to all my knowledge about this planet and others."

"Uh-huh," Alicia said.

Then, abruptly, Karmalakova threw her whole train of conversation in reverse. She talked about witchcraft in Russia and how through the centuries accused Russian witches were burned at the stake, courtesy of the Christian church, same as they were in western Europe.

"Perhaps three million women were incinerated by organized religion when the church was at the height of its power, yes?" Madame Karmalakova said. "Most were burned. But in rural provinces, witches were buried alive up to their breasts and left to die. Horrendous unforgivable genocide! Mostly young women who had not borne children yet. And many probably had psychic powers."

Those mental and intellectual powers, she said, were then driven out of mainstream society at the behest of churches, which wanted no part of any such competition for the serious job of salvation.

In the West, Madame Karmalakova said, those with psychic powers were largely eradicated, suppressed, and replaced by organized religion. But in Russia, the seers were driven underground. Psychic and paranormal research, including ufology, thus never aspired to circulate in the mainstream Russian media. In the days of the Soviet empire, such ideas were heretical to the political order as well as the underground religious order. But, unlike anywhere else in the world, she asserted, they already had a vast tradition of genuine antiestablishment intellectual movements that would consider all new ideas. Students, scholars, and private groups would form secret cults around new beliefs. It had worked this way from the time of Catherine the Great to the present.

"The ground has always been fertile in the Russian psyche," Madame Karmalakova said, "to develop 'the paranormal,' which is actually only the act of taking one's brain to a higher power."

Madame Karmalakova paused.

"And similar, the intellectuals in Russian society were free to consider alternative interpretations of the universe," she continued, "including the possibility of extraterrestrial visits. See? This particularly became clear in this century, ironically under Stalin. Americans were in public enjoying *their* century while Russians in private looked to the future with a naïve passion."

Alicia's attention faltered. Her gaze drifted over Madame Karmalakova's shoulder. There were a pair of oil paintings of her on the wall. In one she was smiling; in the other she was frowning. Under the former, there was a handwritten sign saying, GOOD KARMA. The other said BAD KARMA.

Alicia's gaze completed the round trip and found Madame Karmalakova looking directly into her eyes.

"They're self-portraits," Madame Karmalakova said softly.

"You paint?"

"I have many talents. Far more than you imagine. And I express myself in many ways."

"I can see that."

"And I'll start by expressing a warning," she said. "This is our departure point. You might lead a much happier life if you do not go any farther with this."

"Why?"

"It's just a warning."

"Madame Karmalakova. I'm an adult. I'm a police officer. I want to hear what you have to say."

"Of course. But that does not mean you'll be better off for it." She was speaking very quietly now. "To me it's perfectly natural to have a foot in two worlds. For others, it can be very dangerous."

"Please?" Alicia asked.

Madame Olga thought for a moment, then shook her head again. "No," she finally said. "Not at all a good idea for you. Sorry."

"What you mean, Madame Karmalakova," Alicia continued patiently, "is that you won't tell me. Are you protecting someone?"

"Yes. You, dear."

Alicia stiffened.

"I do not wish to be protected, Madame Karmalakova," Alicia insisted. "I came here to learn and I'm still waiting."

Exasperation overtook the hostess. "Call it as you will," Madame Karmalakova said. "You died and came back. So you've already experienced two worlds. So maybe you be okay with this."

"I only remember the one world. This one. I don't remember anything other than light in the other."

"You were not there long enough. You returned in minutes."

Alicia felt a surge of anxiety. "And how did you know about that?" she asked.

Her hostess smiled. "I can tell by looking at you. You been places and back." She grinned. "More tea, maybe? It's jasmine. Out of this world, do not you think?"

"Please don't toy with me."

"I would not dream of it, Alicia. You're Ed's friend. I'm trying to be hospitable."

"Then try being cooperative, too. I have two murders to investigate and I need your help. I might not be a believer the way you are, but I have an open mind. I want to hear what you have to say."

The Russian woman said softly, "A voice you hear in your head. Is that it?"

Alicia felt a slight chill. "Yes," she said.

Expecting more anger or evasion, Alicia was surprised when Olga Karmalakova seemed to be thinking, very deeply.

Then, abruptly, as if reaching some distant psychological threshold herself—and passing it, making a decision as she passed—she folded her hands before her. She was settling herself, preparing herself for what she had to say next.

"I think, in this instance, dabbling in the extraterrestrial can be dangerous," she said. "But you insist, so we will do it." She pondered another elliptical point. "Were you raised as a Christian?"

"Yes," Alicia said. "A Catholic."

"Ah! Do you still practice?"

"I've lapsed," Alicia said.

"Good for you. You have to acknowledge that mainstream religions have failed in order to consider an alternative."

"Yeah. So?"

"Are you willing to throw wide open your mind this evening?" Olga asked. "Are you really ready to drop any preconceived notion of God and the universe?"

"Yes, I am."

Madame Karmalakova laughed again.

"Let me tell you something, Alicia. Take this promise and remember it. By the time your current investigation is over, you'll no longer be a skeptic. You'll see the window into the other world and you will believe in it. And then you'll be in the unenviable position of being the believer among the doubters. It will be your task to do missionary work for the future, while others insist you are, how do you say, 'a nut case.' "

"I'll remember that," Alicia said quietly.

Madame Karmalakova seemed pleased.

She leaned back in her chair and her eyes drifted through the skylight again. By now it was early evening. Daylight was gone. The nearest stars were visible.

She sighed. "I love to track the planets, do not you?" Madame Karmalakova asked.

"Track them?"

"Follow their flow and flight across the night sky, yes?" she said. "Look, there's my friend Mars, the tiny red one with the pinkish glow. And oh, Venus . . . Venus is not visible now, but I know where she is. Much more visible before dawn. *Der Morgenstern,* yes?" she laughed. "Sometimes I love to wake up just before dawn and look for Venus in the morning sky, my dreams still fresh in my head."

Several seconds passed. There was a twitter from some birds outside, then it quickly stopped.

"Look closely, though," Madame Karmalakova said, raising a hand and pointing. "That little dot right there? See it? That's Jupiter. You can see it with the naked eye."

She smiled. Madame Karmalakova's gaze returned from the heavens. She reached across the table and placed a hand on Alicia's hand. "Stay for dinner, would you?" she said. "I'll feed you well. Culinarily and intellectually. I have so much to tell you that you'll be bursting when you leave."

"Couldn't we just continue our conversation right now?" Alicia asked.

Madame Karmalakova's face reddened instantly with anger. "No!" she snapped, furious. "A thousand times, no!" Her words were loud, echoing off the glass and metal walls. She was silent for a moment as Alicia, greatly startled, felt herself recoil slightly.

"Everyone thinks I'm a nutty fat old lady! Just talk to me, take my knowledge, then get out of here fast! Well, I resent it! This is important; if you want to know and hear you have to stay!"

She was leaning forward on the cushions now, her eyes wide. Alicia had rarely seen anything quite like this, and didn't know if Madame Karmalakova was going to rage further or collapse into a pathetic show of tears.

"I merely didn't wish to put you to any trouble," Alicia lied. "I'd love to stay for dinner, if it's not inconvenient."

"First I fix dinner," said Madame Karmalakova said softly. "Do you have dietary restrictions? Fish? Pig?"

"No restrictions," said Alicia.

"Then we will talk more about Tunguska, 1908, in Siberia, and the first journey of extraterrestrials in this century. And we will discuss the Ammon Society, in our current year, as you wish."

Alicia suppressed a sigh. "That would be wonderful," she said. "Maybe I could use the washroom while you're cooking."

"Naturally, dear," Madame Karmalakova said. She directed Alicia to the wash facilities, which were a separate cubicle at the corner of the house.

The bathroom, which had a steel toilet bowl, much like on an aircraft, was decorated in a Hollywood movie motif. Three large posters, all with the same subtopic. *Star Trek, the Movie. Close Encounters of the Third Kind.* Then an oldie. Vintage Hollywood. *The War of the Worlds.*

Above the towel rack was a framed letter from the head of the Department of Astrophysics at Cal Tech, thanking Madame Karmalakova for a series of lectures she had delivered. Alicia read it as she dried her hands. It appeared to be genuine.

Then, in an area of bookshelves off from the sitting area, Alicia was not surprised to find hundreds of texts on psychology, parapsychology, witchcraft, and various other forms of the extraterrestrial and the so-called para-normal. Eclectic stuff. From *Dune* and *Fahrenheit 451* to *The Vampire LeStat* and *The Exorcist*. In addition, a huge collection of the Russian poets, in Russian and English. Curiously, the books were pristine; they appeared untouched by human hands.

"You're wondering if I've read them, are not you?" came the voice from the kitchen, startling Alicia.

"Yes, actually. That's exactly what I was thinking."

Madame Karmalakova laughed. "Do not be embarrassed. People notice that all the books are in such very good condition. Do not have to be a mind reader to know what people are thinking then."

It all figured. Alicia's hand rose and she withdrew a book from the shelf and glanced at it. *Stranger in a Strange Land.* Robert Heinlein.

Alicia opened it and discovered it was signed. She closed it and put it back. Then she was fingering an early edition of Gene Roddenberry when she heard her hostess's foot step heavily upon the floorboards of the living area.

Alicia returned to the living area and stood by the floor-to-ceiling window that overlooked the front of the property. She pulled her cell phone from her purse and phoned Ed Van Allen, to tell him that she was at Madame Karmalakova's and would be staying for dinner. She did this overtly so that Madame Karmalakova, whom she guessed was eavesdropping, would know she had called.

The ploy worked.

"Say hello to Van Halen for me, too," Madame Karmalakova shouted from her cooking station.

Alicia extended the good wishes and hung up the phone.

Van Allen had been surprised that Alicia was visiting there already and also seemed slightly concerned that

Alicia might be getting in so deep with Madame Karmalakova. He said he'd call back on some pretext in two hours, to make sure things were still fine.

Alicia liked the idea and left that plan in service.

She returned to the sitting area of the living room and found a comfortable spot on the sofa. She sat down and attempted to relax.

"So what's your feeling?" Alicia finally asked. "Are visitors from other planets here on Earth?"

Madame Karmalakova laughed.

"Oh, darling," she said. "You start with the easiest, most simplistic questions first. Well, dear, I'll give you the most straightforward answer. Of course they are! And is not it wonderful?"

There was a time when Alicia would have found Madame Karmalakova's assertion laughable. Today, it made her queasy.

"How about some proof?" Alicia asked.

"Ah! You're one of those!" she said.

"That's how I'm trained as a policewoman," Alicia said.

"Oh, yes, yes. Let me show you something," Madame Olga said.

The heavy woman took Alicia to a stockroom crammed with fifteen file cabinets.

"I did all this by hand. I do not completely trust computers," she said. "Worldwide, more than nine hundred thousand UFO sightings, all these in the last ten years. I pulled these off the Internet. These things happen every *day* and every night, darling. Hundreds each day. The sightings are all over the planet but no one wants to give them any significance."

Alicia tried a file drawer and rambled through the various files. A clipping about a strange set of lights in the sky in Montana. Something over Sicily. Something else in South America. A round greenish craft in the sky that hovered and silently tracked a cruise ship at sea eight miles south of Bermuda—the craft was seen by six hundred passengers— then flew off into the night at astonishing speeds. Madame Karmalakova let Alicia browse through the files for several minutes, until the detective looked back up.

"Interested in humanoid sightings?" Madame Karmalakova asked next.

"I probably would be if I knew exactly what a humanoid was."

Madame Karmalakova laughed. "You already do. A humanoid looks like a human, but then again does not," Madame Olga said. "A head. Two eyes. Two arms. Two legs. A torso."

"So a chimpanzee is a humanoid?" Alicia asked.

"Sure. So is fucking Bigfoot and so is the goddamn Yeti up in Nepal," she said with an edge. "And so are the robots from those awful sci-fi films in the 1950s, mmm?" She winked. "Then again," she added more ominously, "so are the creatures that have come to this planet from other places."

"Uh-huh," Alicia answered.

A flash of the silvery beings who had abducted her, or at least possessed her subconscious, then jolted Alicia. For a second she was stunned. Madame Olga watched, as if she knew something was happening. Then all was normal again, except something silvery caught her eye right then in Earth time present, too: the flap of a fishtail in the tank of water out beyond the kitchen.

"Three thousand humanoid sightings since 1988 alone," Madame Karmalakova said, forging ahead. "Many near Kilimanjaro in Africa. *Thousands* in the United States and western Europe. And this despite the "laugh factor," as Madame Karmalakova called it: the fact that people would laugh at anyone who tried seriously to say he or she had seen a spaceship or encountered a humanoid.

"Three thousand sightings. That's many. Very many, very many, very many. Oh! I have a stellar idea. Do you like trout?" Madame Karmalakova asked.

"What?"

"For dinner? Trout. Very fresh, fresh, fresh."

"Sure." As soon as the word was out of her mouth, Alicia had a hunch she would be sorry.

Madame Karmalakova smiled. She turned and lurched to her kitchen. Then she stepped out her kitchen door.

Alicia watched with astonishment as Olga picked up a fisherman's hand net and splashed it into her backyard fish tank. The net swished rapidly through the water. The woman's reactions were much faster than Alicia expected. The net came up within a few heartbeats with a live quarry.

Four flapping struggling fish.

"Sturdy little buggers," Madame Karmalakova said. "There are two in particular I want."

She reached with a massive hand into the net, where there were four backyard rainbow trout. Madame Karmalakova grabbed one by its tail, held it up for inspection and dropped it back in the tank. She threw back another in the same way. Then she emptied the net and dropped the other two—the two in particular she wanted—onto the ground.

The two grounded fish flapped in terror and wriggled across some flagstones. Madame Karmalakova picked up a long knife. She stepped on the body of one fish to hold it in place, then sliced its head off with one deft stroke.

She nudged it aside with her foot and found the other fish, which had worked its way under a backyard gas grill. Alicia's hostess decapitated the second smaller fish just as swiftly.

Then she removed the tails with two more swipes of the blade, and brought the remains indoors. As Alicia continued to watch in a mild state of horror, Madame Karmalakova went to the sink and, under a stream of cold running water, methodically cleaned and filleted the rest of the bloodied trout. Then she assembled her pots and pans and cooking ingredients.

"You'll know the little finny ones are fresh, will not you, darling?" Madame Karmalakova asked.

"I sure will," said Alicia, lacking in enthusiasm.

"No frozen crap here, mmm?" She wiped her hands on her sunburst caftan, leaving scarlet stains.

"Obviously not."

Madame Karmalakova set about her work in the kitchen, seemingly pleased to be cooking. And the vision of her busy in a domestic task eventually seemed settling to Alicia.

Okay, Alicia concluded. The woman seemed a little spacey, a trifle nutty, and thoroughly eccentric. But probably harmless. Alicia would just keep her eyes on her while she was cooking.

"You do not have to watch me so intently, darling," Madame Karmalakova said a few minutes later. "I'm not going to poison you."

Alicia sighed again. There was no way to keep one's thoughts to oneself around a psychic.

Olga went back to work. Dinner began to take shape in the kitchen. Fillet of trout, rice, a green pepper, some peas and carrots from her garden, and a bottle of California Chardonnay. It actually seemed normal. More normal than anything else around. The fillets sizzled in olive oil and the unorthodox home was filled with the fragrant smells of *haute cuisine*.

Alicia volunteered to set the table.

The table was steel and glass. The forks and knives were stainless steel with lime-green handles. And all the time she was working, Madame Karmalakova kept humming a Beatles tune.

Alicia couldn't place the melody at first. But just before the meal was served, she had it. "All Across the Universe."

Of course, Alicia concluded. What else could it have been?

Then, as she added the final touches to the meal, Madame Karmalakova engaged Alicia in a freewheeling round of chitchat, mostly a monologue. She spoke again of Tunguska in 1908 as the seminal event in this century, the clear indication that humans were not alone in the universe. And she talked further about some of the intellectual motivation behind the Soviet space program: the quest to discover life in deep space.

She emerged from the kitchen long enough to call Alicia's attention to an oversized framed photograph on the wall near one of her sitting areas.

The photograph, in color, showed a large thick clump of empty trees with their tops sheared off, under a vacant sky. Across the bottom of the picture was an inscription in Russian, an array of bold Cyrillic letters that made no sense to Alicia.

"I once visited the 'City of the Stars,'" Madame Karmalakova said. "The Soviet training facility for cosmonauts. The office of Yuri Gagarin, the first human in space, has been preserved from the time of his death in 1968. He crashed his MiG on a training flight."

Olga indicated the details of the picture as she explained. "These trees? These were the trees his MiG hit as it crashed to earth."

Alicia looked at the photo a second time. It now had added poignancy.

"What does the inscription say?" Alicia asked.

"It says, 'The path to the cosmos is never easy.'"

Alicia smiled thinly and felt apprehensive. She sensed that Madame Olga had something further to say. She sensed correctly.

"Gagarin was made a hero of the Soviet Union by Khrushchev after his ride on *Vostok 1* in 1961. You remember? He rode into the cosmos. Then later, Gagarin proudly said, 'I looked everywhere and did not see God.' Mmm? What Soviet authorities never revealed was what he *did* see. When he came back to earth, he became alcoholic and depressive. He saw much in space that the Communists would not let him discuss. He drank heavily, divorced, and was flying drunk when he crashed his MiG."

"Sad," Alicia said.

"Predictable." The Russian woman shrugged.

From there she rambled, firing a shotgun assault of space tidbits and theories, stepping in and out of the kitchen to elaborate on her points. "Cosmonaut Nicholas Protkin saw his *Soyuz T* craft ringed by seven brightly lit airships for three orbits of the earth in 1981. The craft were bright and glowing and had winglike appendages . . .

"U.S. astronaut Gordon Cooper saw several airships that he could not identify during his trip to the moon and return . . .

"Alien interest in the earth increased dramatically after 1945, the time when humankind entered the atomic age . . .

"In the future, the cities of the earth will be lit at night by giant sky mirrors in orbit around the world, mirrors that will reflect the light of the sun the same way the moon does.

"In the constellation Pegasus, a planet exists named Bellerophon upon which life exists with astonishing similarity to that on earth . . .

"An unidentified round object flew over the main television transmission tower in Moscow in August of 1988, knocking out all television transmission for two hours . . .

"Lieutenant Colonel Andrei Semenchenko, a hero of the Soviet Air Force, fired on two bright lights that flew near his aircraft over Murmansk in 1994. Semenchenko and his jet were never seen again, and never found, though he was flying southward across the interior of Russia . . ."

And finally, to Alicia's temporary relief, "I'm almost finished in this kitchen. It is almost time to eat, yes?"

CHAPTER 23

"So! Angels or flying saucers?" Madame Karmalakova asked as they sat down to dinner some ten minutes later.

"What?" Alicia answered.

"This is a hypothetical," Madame Karmalakova said. "If you look in the sky at night, and see a yellow light peacefully, poetically, gliding across the horizon, no sound, which would you wish it to be: an angel or a spaceship? Mmm?"

"Why couldn't it be an airplane? Or a helicopter?" Alicia asked.

The heavy woman pursed her lips.

"I suppose it could be," she allowed. "But of course, there's always the chance that it's not, yes? So if it were one or the other, angel or alien spacecraft, which would you prefer?"

Madame Karmalakova asked the question with a wink. She rose from her seat for a moment and went to a music system. She inserted a CD and stood back for a moment as she let it play. Now Alicia knew that the woman was playing subtle mind games. The music was Dvorak's *The Planets*.

"I'd prefer it to be an angel," Alicia said.

"*Really?* And why is that, darling?"

Alicia shrugged. "More reassuring, maybe. The presence of an angel suggests heavenly guidance. An afterlife. Spiritual redemption."

"Mmm," Madame Karmalakova parried. "But perhaps there is no afterlife. Then the angels would be useless."

Catholic school kicked in. "But if they *were* angels," Alicia countered, "that would presume that a spiritual afterlife *did* exist. Thus I would be legitimate in my hope that they *were* angels."

"Mmm. Clever, are you not?"

"Sometimes."

"Is that what you believe? An afterlife. Christian values? All that?"

"Yes," said Alicia.

"Mmm," the other woman said again.

There was a medley of vegetables on Alicia's plate, freshly picked from Madame Karmalakova's garden. They, like the fish, were prepared perfectly. Olga apparently liked to eat well. She obviously liked to philosophize, too.

"And so what would be so terribly wrong with a visit from another planet?" Alicia's hostess tried next.

"Maybe nothing. Maybe a lot."

"The visitors from another planet could bring knowledge that could aid humanity. Why would not they be welcome?"

"It depends on what price one has to pay for their knowledge," Alicia parried. Quietly, in the back of her mind, she realized how far she had traveled from a murder investigation.

"What do you mean by that?" Madame Karmalakova asked, her mouth full.

"It would depend on whether the visitors were peaceful. Whether they brought germs or disease with them. Their intentions."

"Suppose they wanted to use the Earth for a few Earth centuries as a stopping place on a journey through the stars. Maybe it would bring some much-needed order to the planet."

"It would also be frightening," Alicia continued.

"Why?"

Alicia sipped some wine and replied. "Fear of the unknown. Fear that human survival is going to be imperiled."

"Humans die in a short time, anyway. Why fear the inevitable?"

"Most people want to live as long as possible," Alicia argued.

"Most fish do, too," the Russian lady answered. "And yet no one misses a few when they disappear."

With a plump thumb and forefinger, Madame K picked up an entire half-fillet of trout, cocked her head back, and fed herself the entire piece of fish. She barely chewed. It was gone.

"Tasty, are not they?" she asked. "This was a pair of females. A full-grown one and a smaller adolescent."

"How do you know they were females?" Alicia asked.

"You can't tell? By looking at them."

"No." It wasn't exactly the discussion Alicia might have hoped for while she was still eating.

Madame Karmalakova shook her massive head. "Well, I can tell. And I wonder why humans wish to live as long as they do, by the way. The quality of most human life is so low."

Alicia let the remark pass. Why was it, she wondered, that a high intellect sometimes accompanied a low sense of morality?

"Mmm," Madame Karmalakova said again, scrutinizing her guest carefully. "So you are a very thoughtful lady, are not you?"

"I like to think I am."

"University educated, I assume."

"How did you know?"

Her round eyes narrowed. "I guessed."

"I went to the University of California for six years at night," Alicia said.

"Berkeley?"

"Los Angeles. I earned my bachelor's degree."

"Your field of study?"

"Criminology."

"Ah! Suppose there were no more crimes. Would you be out of business?"

"I don't think that would happen," Alicia said with a rueful smile. "The human condition being what it is."

She finished her first glass of wine. Madame Karmalakova poured her a second.

"You've only been here an hour," she said. "Already you're sounding like me with my pithy dismissal of humankind. Hmm. I do make myself unpopular."

"Unpopular opinions can do that."

Alicia finished one side of the trout. It was excellent. The meal was a tough break for the trout, abducted from the placid sphere as they had been, but the meal was thoroughly delicious.

"So, in light of the things you've told me, I can't help but ask about you," Alicia said.

"What about me, how?" She raised an eyebrow.

"Tell me where you came from."

"Which planet?" she asked, making a joke of it.

"We could start there."

Madame K laughed. "Here you see me. Solid Russian girl. Ufologist and expert."

"So you're not going to tell me you've come here via a spaceship, are you?"

She shook her head and laughed. "Why would I tell you that?"

"Don't know."

"I do not tell you anything at all like that," Madame Olga said. "I just teach you. Teach you to think straight. To consider—"

"The extraterrestrial?"

"Yes. Consider the extraterrestrial in your investigation. Police need more like you. Consider the extraterrestrial and you will resolve your questions."

"Uh-huh."

"You take offense?" The big woman's plate was clean.

"I don't take offense," Alicia said. "But I came here for answers and explanations."

"So then, Detective," Madame Karmalakova said after a pause and a sip of wine. "You're here to talk with intelligence about Earth invasion by creepy beings from other times, planets, dimensions, universes, are you? Is that it?"

"I'm investigating two murders," Alicia said. "The background is pulling me in a peculiar direction. I want some insights."

"Ever done much reading on the subject? Research?"

"A bit. Just recently," Alicia said.

"What about a book titled *Slaughterhouse Five*? Ever read that?"

"I think I saw the movie," she said.

"Figures," she said. "Donald Sutherland and Valerie Perrine dancing around nude."

"It's amazing how right that bizarre Vonnegut fellow got it. You know. Billy Pilgrim . . . living from time to time to time. That's what it's like at the higher levels, mmm?"

"Do tell."

Madame Karmalakova shook her head. "You come here and eat my food but you won't believe. Shameful."

Madame Karmalakova rose and cleared the plates. She reemerged from the kitchen with two smaller dessert plates, plus a basket of fruit and a plate of cheese.

"I'm going to tell you something, Alicia," Madame Karmalakova said conspiratorially. "Higher beings know how to conceal themselves in Earth camouflage."

"They conceal themselves in a human form?" asked Alicia.

"Usually. Occasionally animal form. Many of these higher beings are among us."

Alicia selected a pear and a small piece of Monterey Jack. Madame Karmalakova took a large wedge of Edam and two pears.

"It still goes against everything I've ever thought," Alicia said.

Madame Olga's eyes narrowed strangely, with only the whites remaining apparent, then opened again like moons emerging from an eclipse. Her face creased with a wide smile. "May I put a hypothesis to you?" she asked.

"Of course."

"Have you ever considered that when people describe seeing a strange light in the sky, what they are actually seeing are moving windows, moving electromagnetic portals between universes?"

Alicia blew out a long breath.

"What are you talking about? 'Electro' what?"

"You're educated," Madame Karmalakova said. "This part should not be difficult. If you go to a giant hologram and stick your hand in, it looks like your hand has been severed. Instead, your hand has intruded on another place. You cannot see your hand and you can't see the other place. But both exist and when you withdraw your hand it comes back into this time and space."

"I follow. So?" Alicia said.

"Consider that the lights in the sky might be electro-magnetic openings between time and space here and time and space somewhere else. Every once in a while, however, something pokes through from the other side.

Some advanced presence ventures into this realm from the other. Then someone from this side gets conveyed into the other time and space. People on Earth think this impossible because there is a complexity to this phenomenon that defies human understanding. But it would explain where these thousands of people who have reported being abducted have gone. And it would equally account for the disparity between Earth time and 'lost time.'"

Madame Karmalakova wiped her moist lips and finished her wine. Alicia was left pondering the hypothesis.

"Have you ever read anything by this man named Arthur C. Clarke?" Madame Karmalakova asked. "I read writers from around the world who speculate on space and space travel."

"I saw the movie 2001. That was his, wasn't it?"

Madame Karmalakova smiled indulgently and forged ahead.

"Clarke once wrote, 'Advanced technology is by definition magic,'" she said. "If you showed your great-grandfather a television set, a pocket calculator, or a fax machine, he would have thought it was magic. Or diabolical. Or miraculous. But all it would have been was the technology of the future breaking through to the past."

"So?" Alicia asked.

In whatever language, Madame K had obviously spent much time absorbing the hundreds of books in her collection, regardless of what their condition implied.

"Let me make further points," Madame Olga said. "In the 1700s, the most learned physicists in Europe categorically denied the existence of meteorites. 1903, Simon Newcomb, a great American astronomer, published a long treatise concluding that the only way man would ever fly was in a ship that was lighter than air. The Wright brothers 'flew' less than three months later. In the 1920s a respected English astronomer named Justin Krieger-McGhie 'proved' that it would be impossible to give anything enough energy to orbit the earth. And in the 1940s, the physicist Norman Hayden proved that the initial launch weight of a chemically powered rocket to reach the moon would have to be a million million tons. The trip was achieved less than thirty years later with a weight of three thousand tons. Hayden had been off by a factor of three hundred million. Why? Because he made all the wrong assumptions about technology that he did not understand."

"Okay. So?" Alicia asked again.

"Modern physics is fossilized," Madame Karmalakova insisted, her jowls shaking slightly, her face passionate. "The premises of the earth sciences are ancient. The scientists insist that if they cannot explain something, it cannot exist. That's where they are today with extraterrestrials," she said. "They don't know, they don't understand, so they don't believe."

"But if—"

"Quiet!" she snapped. "Look! You may not know how to float someone through a wall, or leave a psychic imprint on a place, or dip in and out of a time warp, but that does not mean it cannot happen. In Homer's Greece, the masses were pantheistic in their conventional accepted beliefs. Zeus. His kids, Apollo and Artemis. Helios, the sun god. But the educated men of the time knew these gods did not exist and surmised that there must be a higher order in the universe. Today, a similar situation. Wise men know that conventional religion and physics fail to explain the complexities of the universe. They too know that a higher order must exist."

Alicia understood Madame Olga's point. She finished her fruit. "So how does that circle back to the Ammon Society?" Alicia asked.

"Very easily. The members of the Ammon Society believe that extraterrestrials landed in the San Gabriel Mountains in 1975. One of many landings."

"Uh-huh," Alicia said.

"Aliens landed on the summit of Mount Baldy," Madame Karmalakova continued, "and left at least one being to live on the planet Earth for an indefinite period. The extraterrestrials also charged Mount Baldy with cosmic energy. It is a holy place, Alicia. A spiritual battery. Now, the Ammonites feel, it is the burden of humanity to channel the cosmic force and do good around the world."

"How many of these Ammon believers are there?"

"Maybe a few score here in California. A few hundred around the country. A thousand in the world."

"Are you one of them?"

She laughed dismissively. "No, darling, I'm not."

"Do they have a leader, the Ammonites?"

"Does not every movement have a leader?" Madame Karmalakova asked in response. "Human nature, I suppose."

"I was hoping you could be more specific," Alicia answered.

"I'll try to be. Ammonites believe all power and life comes from the sun. And they further believe that human life is merely an early step on the path of godly and universal evolution. A person can speed the progress by helping the environment. And mankind."

Alicia leaned back and listened.

"Many other planets, including three in our solar system, are populated by higher beings, some of whom have some human genes."

"What other kind of genes are there?"

"You are asking the wrong question. The question should be, 'At what point in evolution, and how, did they mutate?' This is the dialectic I engage my students in at university when I teach. Humans have common ancestors with the great apes of today. But the entire universe continually explodes and evolves. Suppose humans had common ancestors with human-type beings who were transported to another galaxy or into a warp in time billions of years ago, there to evolve in different ways, with different stimuli and at a different velocity. They might now have a higher intelligence, still be humanoid in appearance, and be capable of traveling back to this planet to temporarily rendezvous with their common ancestors."

Sometimes Madame Karmalakova sounded like a genius. Sometimes she sounded like a lunatic. Often, the distinction was vague.

She continued. "The most exalted of the higher beings—I'll use the yoga word *prana,* meaning life force—try to direct wisdom to mortal humans so that they can progress."

"Uh-huh," Alicia said. "Sort of a Heaven's Gate situation? Thirty-nine true believers commit suicide so they can enter a spaceship. Are we heading for something like that?"

Madame Karmalakova showed a flash of fury.

"Absolutely and positively not!" she raged. "Those individuals were misguided! It is a basic tenet of Ammonism that you will never meet or possess advanced intelligence by committing suicide. In fact, it is certain you will not."

Madame K sighed. Her eyes drifted up to her skylight, then returned. "Humph. Idiocy. Might as well start talking about Jonestown and vats of cyanide-laced Kool-Aid."

"Do you know of someone named Amos Joy?" Alicia asked.

The psychic's demeanor turned darker.

"Yes," she said. "Of course I know him."

"How do you know him?"

"I have lectured widely on the subject of ufology, as you know. An individual like Amos Joy would naturally come to my attention."

"He's a strange little man, isn't he?" Alicia asked.

Madame Karmalakova was silent.

"Would you call him an alien?" Alicia asked.

Madame Karmalakova laughed. "Lord, Lord," she answered. "I'd call him a former inmate of a psychiatric institution."

"I think he's dangerous," said Alicia.

"Very likely," Madame Olga said.

"He's getting into my head," Alicia said. "He seems to have some sort of . . . I don't know, telepathic powers."

"So I've heard."

"I saw him a few days ago," Alicia said.

Madame Karmalakova stopped short.

"You did, did you!"

"That surprises you?"

"Yes." She paused. "And what sort of messages do you feel that he's sending you?"

"Aggressive and threatening remarks, mixed with 'ufological' overtones. And I believe he's a suspect in several murder cases."

"More murders," Madame Karmalakova said, shaking her thick head. "The last thing this world needs, is it not?"

"It's certainly one of the last."

On a wall behind Madame Karmalakova, there was a clock. Steel rimmed, naturally. The clock showed that it was almost eleven P.M. Alicia was amazed at how time had flown by. Alicia excused herself for a moment and phoned Ed Van Allen, just to check in with him, let him know things were going well and relieve him of calling her.

Then Alicia turned her attention back to her hostess.

"Tell me," the Russian woman said next, moving toward a conclusion. "Do you really think that you, personally, are up to this?"

"Up to what?"

"Meeting a being from another planet."

"Is that what you're finally telling me that Amos is?"

Madame Karmalakova hesitated. Then, with great gravity, answered. "Yes," she said. "That is what he is."

Alicia felt deeply unsettled by her answer, but she recovered quickly.

"No matter what you think," she said, "it's still my job to locate Amos Joy, question him, and, if necessary, arrest him."

Olga snorted. "Of course it is," she said. "And twice before he walked away from such situations, leaving deceased persons behind. Dead, dead, dead. Is that what you want for yourself?"

"Of course not."

"Then why do you persist?"

"My job is my job," she said doggedly.

Madame Karmalakova sighed. "A collision course between two worlds," she said. "That's what I'm talking about."

"What?" Alicia asked.

"That's what you're embarked on, Alicia," she said. "Let Amos Joy run his course on this planet. Walk away from this right now."

"That's not my job, to walk away. This is a homicide investigation. Can you tell me how to locate Amos?"

"He'll find *you*. Same as he has in the past."

"Can you explain better than that?"

"No. And, darling, I've now warned you twice."

"Thank you," Alicia said, her irritation growing. "Yes. Twice. I appreciate your concern, Madame Karmalakova. Honestly, I do. But I can take care of myself."

"Can you?" Madame Olga challenged.

Then she told a final story.

"When I was lecturing up at Stanford two years ago," she said, "there was an interesting patient who was being interviewed by the psychology department. A former pilot for Eastern Airlines, he'd flown in Vietnam before he flew commercially. Air force officer, also. Retired man when he was a patient at Stanford. About fifty-five years old, serious and sober. Name was Captain James McTavish."

McTavish had remained an avid pilot even after leaving the defunct airline, Madame Karmalakova related. He had been flying along the coast south of Big Sur in his own Piper Cherokee, however, when he realized that there was a large craft above him that wasn't showing on his own radar but had been picked up by air traffic south of San Francisco.

From combat, Captain McTavish knew how to maneuver an aircraft to evade a threat. So he turned his own craft in a way that allowed him to see what was above him, expecting a 757 or 767, and wanting to get quickly out of the larger aircraft's slipstream.

What McTavish saw, according to the transmissions he made to the air traffic controllers in San Francisco, was a huge round craft, ringed with lights and windows. It must have been seventy meters in diameter. It was elliptical, disc shaped, he said, and was tracking him.

The aircraft dogged James McTavish, who requested permission to land immediately. There were several sightings of the craft from the ground. But then McTavish claimed he had undergone a change of heart. A different feeling came over him, he radioed, and he felt he needed to rendezvous with the larger ship, or at least to get a better look at it.

So McTavish put his Cherokee into an abrupt ascent pattern and rose in the sky. The disc kept its distance, then held its own position—hovering noiselessly—as McTavish turned toward it.

"As God is my witness, I've never seen anything like this. It's saucer shaped and I can see it moving. I'm going to attempt a flyby."

"Cherokee-7, we can't find the object on radar anymore. You sure you know what you're looking at?"

"I know I'm looking at something. I've just never seen anything like it," McTavish radioed back. He was guessing it was some giant balloon, but he also added that it seemed to be revolving. "I'm going to pass within twenty meters of the front of it if I can."

"Cherokee-7, we're still not seeing anything," San Francisco radioed back.

"Well, I do," McTavish answered.

The next transmissions were intermittent and laden with static, but it appeared that McTavish thought he was approaching the unidentified craft and was trying to look inside it.

Then McTavish came back on, screaming.

"I see him! I see him! I see a whole bunch of them!" McTavish yelled. "Oh, my God! Oh, my God!"

Eleven seconds later, McTavish's radio went dead. He disappeared from the radar screen.

A search followed. Nothing was ever seen again of McTavish's aircraft. The pilot, however, was found one week later, disoriented and walking in a remote section of the John Muir State Forest. Police who brought him to a hospital were initially unable to identify him and McTavish did not even know who he was.

He was treated for shock and hypothermia. Eventually, and only for a short time, he partially regained the ability to speak. That was when he was taken to Stanford University Hospital and interviewed. Captain McTavish told a tale of his aircraft being sucked into a flying saucer and how he was removed from it by aliens.

He said he was not in any physical pain. He said examinations were done on him, time stopped, and then he felt very sleepy. He passed out. Then, next thing he knew, he was in a remote section of forest. It was morning and he began to walk, hoping to be found by police but unable to articulate exactly what had happened.

Then, after a day of interviews at Stanford, after the above details were related, McTavish again slipped into a standing coma, even though his body showed no sign of trauma. All he could repeat were two thoughts, over and over.

"Silvery creatures in a reddish light . . . I saw them . . . I saw them . . . I saw them . . ."

For another week this was the only sentence McTavish would utter. Then, on the eighth day, he strung some bed sheets together in his hospital room, walked into the shower and hanged himself.

Madame Karmalakova let the end of the story sit in the air for several seconds. Alicia tried to sort it out, plus its implications.

"So what's your point?" Alicia asked Madame Karmalakova.

"Just this. When universes collide, there is usually some damage. If you do not want to be part of the damage, if you do not think you can look directly upon the face of a visitor from another dimension, then you must not consider it. And right now, that is the direction in which you are heading. Do I make my point?"

Madame Karmalakova let her words settle. And even Alicia, a rational woman by nature, felt her flesh crawl.

"That's all the knowledge I have to impart to you," Madame Karmalakova concluded. "If you're as intelligent as I think you are, you'll heed my warning. If not . . ."

She spread her wide arms and looked overhead.

Alicia followed the woman's eyes. They went to the skylight and beyond, into the stars.

CHAPTER 24

Recalling her evening as she drove back to Venice, Alicia had the sensation of having seen Madame Olga through the wrong end of a telescope. The closer she had come to her over the course of the day, with her hoop earring, platinum hair, and lofty celestial pronouncements, the more the woman had receded . . . sort of like the smile of the Cheshire Cat, which also withdrew as one approached it.

Driving home, Alicia again vacillated between whether the woman was inspired or wacko, or a bit of both. Near midnight, driving south through a crumbling stretch of the Pacific Coast Highway south of Malibu, Alicia experienced an even more heightened sense of paranoia about her hostess and decided that she would run her name through the FBI computers as well as the Immigration and Naturalization Service database. Above and beyond what she had served for dinner, there was something fishy about Madame K. And mentally, Alicia was kicking herself. The madame had kept Alicia so distracted, that Alicia hadn't even broached her two cases.

What Alicia *did* know was that Madame Karmalakova

had profoundly disturbed her. Somehow she had legitimized this whole extraterrestrial theme in Alicia's mind, and Alicia was profoundly uncomfortable with it. What exactly had caused that feeling?

Had it been the disquieting tale she had told at the end of their time together? Had it been the dead seriousness with which she had spoken of an extraterrestrial presence on the Earth? Was it the overall nuttiness quotient and *unusualness* of the woman? The seemingly routine decapitation of two trout?

Or had it been something more? Something Alicia had sensed?

For all of Alicia's adult life she had told herself to trust her instincts. Her instincts were telling her something here, and yet she was trying to *dismiss* what they were saying to her.

"And why am I doing that?" she demanded of herself, whispering aloud in the dark car as she drove through the California night. On the car radio she blasted Star 97. Shawn Mullins was singing the familiar ballad about a girl in a bar on Fairfax and the difficulty of playing a gig in this town and keeping a straight face. Well, Shawn, Alicia answered rhetorically, sometimes it was hard to be a cop in this town and keep a straight face, too.

Her cell phone rang. It was Ed Van Allen. "Should I compare notes with you on Madame Olga?" he asked.

"I'd compare notes if I knew where to start," Alicia answered. "Your saucer lady is one hell of a piece of work."

"Did she clarify anything?" Van Allen asked.

Alicia thought about it. "I'm not going to know till morning," she said. "After I think everything over."

"Call me if you need to," Van Allen offered, and signed off.

Alicia drove past the new Getty Museum, gleaming, wealthy, and floodlit high up on the cliffs to her left above the PCH. To her right, the Pacific Ocean glimmered in the moonlight.

"So!" she said to herself. "Am I afraid to accept what Madame Karmalakova believes? Am I afraid to alter the basic beliefs I've always held about the physics of this planet? Will I make a leap and follow this outer-space nonsense or will I—

You are afraid, Alicia!

"Go away!" she answered.

You know with whom you're communicating, don't you?

She paused. She hesitated.

"Yes, I know," she said.

What is my name?

"Your name is Amos," she said to the empty car.

Alanis Morisette followed Shawn Mullins. She had read recently that Alanis liked *Three's Company*. She had always suspected that Alanis was reachable. Now she knew.

The inner voice continued, clear as a church bell.

Then if you believe in me, why are you afraid to take the next step? Why can't you approach and pass through one of those windows that Madame Karmalakova described?

She thought back to that afternoon, trying to make sense out of what Madame Karmalakova had said during the chitchat segment.

Of Amos Joy: "I know there is blood on his hands. And yet no earthly prison will ever hold him."

Of Alicia, her visitor: "I sense a lot of loneliness. A lot of indecision. A sense that your youth is passing and you haven't done anything important in your life yet."

Of life and spirituality in general: "You are like most native-born Americans. You have no sense of the spiritual or the larger universe that surrounds you."

But what had Madame Karmalakova been saying?

Tunguska.

Sky mirrors.

Earth landings by quasi-aliens on Mount Baldy.

Human-mutant beings on earth.

A gaggle of information about UFO records in the former Soviet Union?

What in hell was this all about?

How in hell did it make any sense?

Was the Russian woman leaving Alicia no space to believe in *any* interpretation of recent events other than the extraterrestrial?

Suddenly Alicia felt a rush of anger sweep through her.

Who the hell was Madame Karmalakova kidding?

What did she *really* know? Where did the bullshit start? Where did it end?

Alicia tried to keep it in perspective.

There used to be an old saying about southern California, that one day earlier in this century someone tilted the United States and everything loose rolled to the southwestern corner. People like Madame Karmalakova were often held as proof of that theory.

Alicia was downright angry with herself. She had gotten swept away with so much strange loopy, kooky stuff in the last week that she could barely summon up any common sense.

"Want me to believe in a goddamn space alien?" she asked herself aloud in the car. "Then show me one!"

Olga Karmalakova was just another southern California fruitcake, she decided next. Highly educated, articulate in several languages perhaps, as eccentric as a four-dollar bill and maybe just as queer, also. But that was it. The fact that she was colorful and convincing didn't make her correct or believable per se.

And as for Amos?

For the lamentable Mr. Joy, it was time to see this whole

unseemly affair in the proper light and bring it down to earth. Amos Joy was a clever homicidal maniac. Nothing more. Nothing less. A Ted Bundy. A John Wayne Gacy.

The visions and nightmares that Joy had hurled in Alicia's direction?

Time to see them in the proper light, too, she decided boldly. Her dear friend Ed Van Allen had possibly come close to the truth, even though Alicia had not wanted to hear it at the time. Alicia's recent physical injuries had caused a neurosis, a quiet, deeply rooted hysteria that had manifested itself in wild fantasies and visions.

She thought back to the Psych 303 course she had taken at university and the courses in stress management at the police academy, and she managed to define and compartmentalize these visions, too.

God, she thought to herself. Here she was practically turning into something as nutty as one of those filbert orchards she used to see up north.

Well, she concluded south of the intersection where Pico hit Ocean Avenue in Santa Monica, at least she finally had her head straightened out.

Now she could proceed rationally. Finally!

Alicia finally neared Venice.

She left the Pacific Coast Highway and followed Venice Boulevard. Then her thoughts spiraled again, back to the religion she had grown up with and how she had lost it.

She thought of the nuns who had taught her in school as a girl. They had a special bell they used to ring and all the girls were supposed to drop to their knees at the sound of the bell. If the hem of a girl's skirt didn't touch the floor it was officially too short. Most girls solved that hemline conundrum by wearing a skirt of the proper length, then rolling it up at the waist after school. She smiled a second time at the memory.

She thought of the refracted light through stained glass, the devout old people clutching their beads, the incense in the churches, the torturous angels, the grueling confessions when she always knew which priest she was talking to, the way she had moved her hand the wrong way the first time she ever crossed herself, the incomprehensible masses, the cheerful baptisms, the interminable wakes, the painfully overwrought funerals, and the overall bitterly sorrowful sweetness of the whole Roman Catholic ordeal.

And from there she connected with how, when she passed her sixteenth birthday, much to her mother's horror and her father's knowing indulgent silence, she had rejected the whole damned Catholic boatload of it as so much latter-day superstition and hocus-pocus.

No more confession.

No more "Our Father."

No more having to fold her hands in a certain way if the "amen" to a prayer was to succeed. And no more having to negotiate for heavenly joys by bartering away earthly delights.

She had stopped going to church on Sundays, then she had stopped going on Easter, and it was only the social occasion of the midnight mass before Christmas—surely not the service itself—that now drew her in once a year.

Well, what was that if not a void?

She had been dead, after all, and she hadn't seen God or one damned chirping angel.

Same as Yuri Gagarin.

An odd thought struck her.

Had she seen an angel?

Amos?

Where *did* he fit into her universe now?

Then again, if she no longer believed in a creator—

"in the beginning God created Heaven and Earth"—then what did she believe in?

What *about* all that space out there in the sky above?

What *about* these electromagnetic windows into other dimensions?

Well, something to think about, anyway. But at least now she was thinking rationally.

At half past midnight, she was back in her home, when an unsettling conclusion coalesced in her head and found words.

Faith is something I do not understand, predicated as it is upon superstition rather than knowledge.

She turned the thought over in her mind.

And then she realized that she hadn't thought that at all. It had been another one of those flashes from Amos. She had to admit: the little bastard did have strong brain waves. Well, she had some positions of strength, too, and the little maniac hadn't yet faced some of hers.

Buoyed, she undressed, and stood nude before a full-length mirror in her bedroom for a moment. She was pleased with what she saw. The notion of seducing her old friend Ed crossed her mind—not for the first time—now that he was single and available, and the thought made her laugh.

She dressed for another night alone in bed. A baggy extra-large blue cotton L.A. Dodgers T-shirt and a pair of men's boxer shorts. A girl had a right to be comfy. It had been, after all, a memorable day.

She slept with the light on and with her service weapon by her bed. Not because she feared any extraterrestrial. But rather, she now felt she had a pretty good mark on Amos Joy and didn't discount the notion that he might find her again before she found him. And she wanted to be ready.

The funny thing was, the more she protested all of the

ufology that Madame K had thrown at her, the more Amos seemed small, mean, and earthbound. So Alicia would pursue him accordingly.

She settled in to sleep. Dispelled from her mind, Amos vanished. The night—cool and beautiful outside with a magnificent panoply of stars—was uneventful.

Alicia managed to sleep soundly, as if an angel were singing her a lullaby and drawing her onward into a peaceful slumber.

CHAPTER 25

One week after the burial of Bill Sands, while driving home across Lincoln Boulevard in Venice, Alicia spotted Amos Joy outside a bar called Conchita's.

The warm afternoon had almost expired completely. It was half past six in the evening. Amos was standing in the parking lot, staring at the road. He was waiting for something—Alicia, maybe—to catch his attention.

Conchita's was a ramshackle russet-roofed roadhouse by the highway. Above the entrance, atop the roof, there was a sign that was at odds with proper grammar and punctuation but nonetheless proclaimed:

Conchita's Bar
MexiCali Restaurante

The establishment had a primary reputation as a cheap place for the local office workers to get drunk after work, and it did a secondary business as a pickup joint. Its tertiary reason for existing was the burrito or taco dinner that sold for $5.95.

Alicia pulled her car into the parking lot. Amos gave her a look, turned and walked inside. There were five vehicles in the parking lot and she tried to guess which one was Amos's.

She failed.

Upon exiting her Jeep, her hand lingered on the police radio. Backup. She would definitely need backup.

Then her hand strayed from the radio. She pictured Amos guiding her hand away from it. Instead, she followed the little man into Conchita's.

She felt as if he had beckoned. She also felt as if he had a way of jamming her thoughts, almost like jamming radar. She thought back to the day when she had attended Janet's birthday party and had seen that flash in the sky, and how she had felt something boring into her brain on the eventual ride out into the desert.

Today, she was pretty sure what had bored into her brain that day.

Me.

"Yes. Goddamn it. You!" she said aloud.

Back to the present, or what passed for it: Conchita's.

Alicia looked around when she came inside. She took in the place. The interior never changed.

There was a long mirror behind a worn bar. Plenty of cheap whiskey and the predictable national name-brand beers on tap. Mexicali memorabilia all over.

A huge portrait of Pancho Villa.

Plenty of Cinco de Mayo stuff.

A basketball picture. College hoops, from the Wooden-UCLA sixties when UCLA stood for UCal with Lew Alcindor.

A couple of piñatas along the ceiling, waiting to be busted open, not far from an explosion of NFL stuff—including L.A. Raiders leftovers—and some Latin American soccer banners. The place was run by its bullish namesake, whom Alicia knew and who often took too keen an interest in Alicia.

Conchita's also had a noisy jukebox that usually blared godawful eighties-style Big Hair stadium rock, plus salsa. Today's selection, as Alicia arrived, was something by Freddy Fender, currently forgotten in most other sections of the country.

Also on the premises was an irritating little man named Manny Biancanegra, who tended bar. Biancanegra was a short stocky man with a bent nose and a personality to match.

Manny had locked horns with Alicia a few times before. Biancanegra liked to get ugly drunk with his customers and then go driving fast through Venice, Marina Del Rey, and Santa Monica. He kept a jacked-up 1977 Plymouth Duster and liked to give the car a workout. Three times Alicia had arrested him, once on a DWI, once with a suspended registration, and once for doing seventy miles per hour through a school zone. The Happy Motoring Trifecta.

There were only a handful of tables busy when Alicia walked in, populated mostly by men but with a few women sprinkled about. Amos was sitting alone at the north end of the bar. His narrow frame and the clear high forehead were not hard to find.

Amos's eyes slid in Alicia's direction as she entered the room. She wondered whether Amos had seen her through the window.

Eye contact immediately, back and forth, Alicia to Amos and slam-bang back again. An obvious connection. Again, Alicia felt something visceral, like an electric shock.

Alicia walked slowly to Amos's end of the bar and sat down next to him. Manny, the bartender, ignored her, which was fine, since Alicia didn't feel like drinking.

"Hello, Amos," Alicia said.

The little man did not answer. Conveniently, the juke-box came to a temporary rest. No more Freddy Fender.

Amos Joy's eyes sailed away from Alicia.

"Amos, I'm here to talk to you," Alicia said.

Time slowed.

Amos remained quiet. Alicia struggled against a sickening feeling.

"So talk," the little man finally purred.

"I want to know about the Ammon Society," Alicia said.

"Pioneers. Truth on Earth," Amos answered.

"Be more specific."

"What could be more specific than that?" Amos asked. "Visitors from another galaxy landed on Mount Baldy forty-one Eoots ago."

"Forty-one what?"

"Eoots. Earth orbits of the sun. Thought you'd know the concept."

"Forty-one years."

"Eoots."

"Why did they stop?"

"Left a messenger here."

"I suppose that's you," Alicia said.

"You suppose correctly."

"And why a messenger?"

"Intergalactic colonization. There are a lot of us here, passing as humans. You'll start to notice. You'll start to see who's who." He paused. "We're soon to start breeding with local females."

"You're a little maniac," she said. "Nothing more, nothing less."

She considered slapping handcuffs on him right then. She decided she would. She reached for the wrist bracelets and something akin to a minicoma came over her.

Her reactions slowed. Unbelievably enough, she felt Amos had jammed her thought processes.

She blinked and felt herself entering some strange spatial field. Her eyes drifted lower, then rose again.

Across from her, Amos seemed to be in an extraterrestrial form, silvery slim and shimmering. Then suddenly, the freeze-frame quality of time ceased and the vision was gone.

"Jesus," she said softly.

Something resembling a laugh came from Amos.

"And suppose I think you're a common criminal," she said, struggling, breathing shallowly. "Suppose I think you're a nut case with some sort of exceptional mental abilities. Suppose I told you that."

He laughed. "You wouldn't be much different from those psychiatrists," he said.

"The ones you murdered," Alicia said.

"The ones I butchered," Amos Joy offered amiably.

He paused, then continued.

"When I leave this planet shortly I'm taking two human females with me," he said. "You'll be one."

She drew a breath.

Manny passed by her on the other side of the bar. He gave her a withering look and tried to look down her blouse at the same time.

Alicia blanched slightly and exhaled slowly. The pain in her shoulder was as loud as a choir of demons.

"Let's just talk, all right?" Alicia asked.

"Want me to show you stuff?"

"What sort of stuff?"

"Stuff I can do and humans can't," he said.

A small smile slipped fleetingly across his face.

Manny Biancanegra had placed his cigarette in an ashtray within Amos's reach. Alicia watched in disbelief as Amos took the cigarette between his thumb and forefinger. He snuffed the burning end between his wet lips.

He set the butt back in the tray and looked toward Manny Biancanegra. As Biancanegra watched impotently, the ashtray flew over the back edge of the bar, crashing noisily to the floor. Biancanegra turned away. He had seen, but he hadn't believed.

Amos looked back to Alicia. He frowned ominously. His eyes glistened. They took on the shape of big black almonds, then became human again.

"Want to see another bar trick?" Amos Joy asked.

"Sure."

"Watch closely."

Amos turned and looked across the room. Alicia followed Amos's gaze, but failed to detect anything significant. The jukebox across the room suddenly went dark and silent. Several drinkers looked to see what had happened.

Amos turned back to Alicia.

"What say?" the little guy asked. "I did that."

"You did what?"

"Killed the music."

Alicia eased slightly and leaned back. "Come on, Amos. That's bull."

"Tell me when you want it back on," Amos said.

Alicia waited several seconds. "Now," she said.

Amos's eyes never left her.

Music filled the room again.

"Eight Miles High." "Mr. Spaceman." Amos smiled slightly as if he were playing games. He held Alicia virtually in a trance as the music played, one song after another. "Here Comes the Sun."

Then finally Amos rose without speaking further. He walked to the door. His gait was unusual, more gliding than strolling. Alicia's gut told her to get up, storm after him, or maybe even shoot him to stop him, but she felt frozen in place. She couldn't act in his presence. No wonder he could kill so easily. No wonder no prison could hold him.

Conchita appeared beside Alicia.

"That little twerp comes in here three or four times a week, Alicia," Conchita said.

Conchita's breath was like kerosene, her makeup like house paint. She draped an arm across Alicia's shoulders. "He drives a lot of the good customers out," Conchita bitched.

"What do you know about him?" Alicia asked.

"Everyone's scared of him. He gives everyone the creeps."

"Everyone including me," Alicia answered.

"Why don't you shoot him someday?" Conchita said.

It was more than an idle suggestion. It was well known in the neighborhood that Conchita kept a sawed-off shotgun in her office behind the dining room.

"I'm scared shitless of him," Alicia heard herself saying.

Alicia's gaze remained on the door until she was certain that Amos wasn't on his way back in for an encore.

Then finally she followed. But when she stood outside in the parking lot, there was no sign of Amos Joy. Nor were any of the five vehicles missing.

Alicia realized she was standing exactly where she had stood when she had decided to follow Amos into the bar. She wished she had noted the time. She had such a loose grip on her sanity right now that she wondered if she had imagined the entire incident.

It was only when she returned to her Jeep and flipped on the police radio that she heard of a report of a child missing. Then she learned the address.

C H A P T E R 2 6

At her desk early the next morning, Alicia opened the file on Amos Joy and reread every detail.

She moved eventually to the psychological conclusions of Dr. Brillstein, who had pronounced Amos Joy dangerous and deranged but mortal, and somehow possessed of telepathic skills. The point had an eerie resonance now, as Madame Karmalakova, in addition to so many other topics that she had touched upon, had spoken for a few moments about the parapsychological aspects of cosmonaut training. The Russians had been deeply into the meditative aspects of ufology, the concept of psychiatric bilocation and extrasensory awareness. All this while their empire staggered into financial ruin.

How all this tied in with Amos Joy, however, remained an open question. There were strings meandering in every direction and Alicia was still unable to tie any of them together.

Even the analysis of Amos Joy as a mortal human being left questions dangling.

Why had his fingerprints been abnormal?

How had he made his escape from the psychiatric institution in Arizona?

Why did he have no legitimate high school transcript and no background beyond his ill-fated appearance at a university?

How had such a small man overpowered his victims? Though Alicia—with a shiver—did recall the man's exceptional strength.

And what about Joy's supposed telepathic skills? Could she have an answer for that, please? Last night, driving home from Madame Karmalakova's tinfoil cathedral, she thought she had everything figured out. Now, in the light of day, things were murkier.

When it came down to it, all she had was theory. And instinct. She couldn't process the information before her. She didn't know what in hell she was looking at.

She picked up her telephone. Time to get some help. Time to make some calls.

The first was to Dr. Sugarman in San Bernardino. Still no ID on John Doe of the Desert, White Snake explained. The body still didn't match any local missing persons report and didn't fit into anything that Alicia could pull off the national listings, either. White Snake's office was getting irritated with her calls.

She hung up and pondered the victim's identity. He had been a well-dressed man. White middle class. And he'd been dropped off in the middle of the desert. No footprints. No tire tracks, though the wind could have removed any traces of either. She felt herself fighting the question she was asking herself. Had he been dropped off from the air?

She sighed.

That at least would explain the chrolystron!

She rubbed her eyes. Words came back from the previous evening, an early exchange with Madame Olga:

"Are you willing to throw wide open your mind this evening?" Olga had asked. "Are you really ready to drop any preconceived notion of God and the universe for at least a few hours, so that we can talk these things through on an intellectual level?"

"Yes, I am," Alicia had answered.

Madame Karmalakova had laughed again.

"Let me tell you something, Alicia. Take this promise and remember it. It's the most important thing you will hear from me today."

"What's that?"

"By the time your current investigation is over, by the time you've visited me for the last time, you'll no longer be a skeptic. You'll see the window into the other world and you will believe in it. And then you'll be in the unenviable position of being the believer among the doubters."

Sitting at her desk this morning, Alicia felt as if a set of little internal screws were being tightened. In her shoulder. In her head.

With growing irritation, she glanced back through one of Amos Joy's law-enforcement evaluations from Arizona. She read the section where the two police interviewers had curtailed their examination after having "seen" something that Joy had showed them.

What had it been? Was it akin to what Alicia had seen in her dreams? She noted the names. One had been Officer Richard Hopkinson of the Tempe, Arizona, Police Department. The second officer had been Officer Mary McLaren of the same force.

Alicia picked up the phone and dialed the police department in Tempe. This was a call, she told herself, that she should have made earlier. She was unable to get through to either individual, however, and left a voicemail message with a Captain William Gracie, the commander of both officers.

Then she rose from her desk and went to a CHP computer terminal. She accessed records from the Immigration and Naturalization Service and ran Olga Karmalakova's name and address.

She half expected the inquiry to pose more questions than it answered. Madame Olga's provenance would likely be as hazy as Amos Joy's; there would be no record of the woman entering the country legally; there would be something "wrong" or "off," even if Alicia couldn't quite tell what it was.

Then the screen filled and, once again, Alicia's suspicions were unwarranted. Madame Karmalakova's entry papers had been in order and she was the legitimate holder of a green card. She had emigrated from the Ukraine in 1988 and had, according to the INS records, a university degree from Kiev in engineering, with a minor degree in astrophysics.

There was even a picture of the ponderous woman, who hadn't aged much at all. Alicia stared at the screen for several seconds and the screen stared back. She downloaded a copy of the picture and printed it out. Then she rose and went back to her office.

In the afternoon she phoned her contact at the Beverly Hills Police Department to see if they could provide anything further on the demise of Bill Sands. Aside from a few details about his funeral, which had taken place the previous day, they had nothing.

Then, late in the day, Alicia drove out to Santa Barbara again to pay a call on Ted Sternfeld, Sands's former lover. Alicia arrived in the early evening. Sternfeld was home, his wife and daughter were not.

It was the perfect time for a frank talk, and Alicia had lucked into it, carrying a few documents with her in a neat folio that she kept tucked under the arm that didn't ache.

Sternfeld had been at his piano when Alicia arrived, tinkering with the Broadway scores he loved, and he showed her some music that he was composing. He was a free sprit locked into his insurance career, he mused to Alicia with unusual candor, and would love to have chucked it all to have lived in West Hollywood or in Greenwich Village back in New York where he was from, just to write for the theater. That had always been his first love, his passion, and in a way it had been a connection between him and Sands.

"Who knows?" Sternfeld said. "Maybe I could have been a star. Maybe not. Maybe there's still time, maybe there isn't. Sad about the life we want to lead but sometimes don't, isn't it?"

"Real sad," Alicia agreed, while Sternfeld, his fingers tinkling the keyboard with surprising skill, re-created the theme from *Cabaret*.

Alicia guessed that Ted Sternfeld had had a drink before she arrived.

Maybe two or three.

But she listened indulgently to the words and the music—which didn't match each other—for as long as it took to determine that the conversation was going nowhere. Not even a little alcohol-induced slip that might have opened the floodgates for her. Nothing. She was about to steer the conversation back to homicide when Sternfeld did the deed for her.

"Sorry," he said. "I've been in a very down mood since Billy was murdered. I know you didn't come out here to listen to my ruminations. What may I help you with today?"

Alicia produced a photograph of Amos Joy from the file on the demented little creature. She handed it to Ted Sternfeld.

His right hand carried the treble clef while his left accepted the photograph. Alicia watched his expression.

"Who's this?" he asked.

"Never seen him before?"

"No."

She gave him another couple of seconds. "You're sure?" she asked.

"I'd know. I have a good memory for names and faces."

She took the photo back. Instinct told her that Sternfeld was telling the truth.

"A potential suspect. That's all," she said.

"In Billy's death?"

"Maybe."

"Bastard," Sternfeld muttered angrily. "Hope you catch him, convict him, and shove him into the gas chamber. Is that how it's still done in this state? The gas chamber?"

"California and North Carolina," Alicia answered. "We're the last to still use lethal gas."

Sternfeld was still trying to make some sense out of that when Alicia asked her follow-up question.

"You mentioned an 'Amen' Society, or an 'Almond' Society, as you called it, last time we spoke."

"Yes, I did."

"Could it have been the Ammon Society?" she asked, accenting the second syllable. Then she spelled it. "A-M-M-O-N?"

"Probably," he said after a moment of thought. "Yes. That sounds right. That was probably it."

"And Mr. Sands was a member?"

"From what I could see, 'membership' was pretty informal. Not like they carried cards or paid dues or anything. They would just meet. People's homes. Bars. Then they'd go out to some mountain north of L.A. once a month, parade around like a tribe of latter-day Druids to pick up the vibes."

He held Alicia's gaze for an extra second. "First time I heard of it, I thought it was just some sex thing. You know, some California mountaintop orgy."

"Was it?"

"Apparently not, from what I was told. If it had been a sex thing that would have made it more comprehensible. But going out there just to commune with the supposed biological aura spewed off by some spacecraft that no one actually ever saw? Well . . ."

He shook his head hopelessly.

"Do you remember the name of the mountain?" Alicia asked.

"I'd know it if I heard it."

"Mount Baldy?"

"Yeah, that's it," he said immediately.

He stopped playing music.

"The whole nutty crew of them had this thing about that mountain. Something about a spaceship landing there. That make any sense to you? It's as nutty as peanut brittle to me."

"It corroborates what I've been told elsewhere."

"That's good."

"Ever go to any of the Ammon meetings?"

"No."

"Ever meet any Ammon members?"

"You asked me that last time."

"I'm asking again."

He shrugged. "One or two," he said. "But look. I don't remember names, honestly I don't. And I met them at some bars in West L.A., so I can't even steer you to anyone's home."

"Did they have meetings there? In those bars?"

"They met there. There was no such thing as a formal meeting, other than their crazy field trips to Mount Baldy to soak up the so-called electrobiological force or whatever. That's what I understood."

Sternfeld paused, as if considering whether to add something. Alicia seized the moment.

"Something else?" she asked.

"Well, I had *arguments* with Billy about this crap. I'm not ashamed to tell you, I majored in physics at Princeton University. I know a thing or two about energy, forces, and so on. Billy claimed the energy out on Mount Baldy carried information on the fate of this planet in the future. I tried to argue rationally, based on physics, based on rational knowledge. I told him, look, anyone who knows diddly-squat about the study of matter and energy and the relationship between them knows that in order for energy to be equated with information, it has to have a carrier. A vector. And some dumb-ass field on a mountaintop is not a vector."

"What did he say to that?" Alicia asked, curious.

"He said that Ammonites knew more than the uninformed, the uninitiated," Sternfeld said with a short smile. "That they had higher knowledge because they had been in touch with extraterrestrials. He said there were maybe seven, eight or nine, levels of carriers. Kinetic motion is level one, which he was right about. Identified in the eighteenth century. Level two would be an electromagnetic field, which became known in this century. But then he started talking nonsense about biological fields and higher levels of energy and being able to float people through walls and stepping into other dimensions to stop time. Sonoluminescence."

Sternfeld shook his head sadly.

"A lot of horse shit, as far as I'm concerned," he concluded.

"Based on what we know now," Alicia heard herself saying.

Sternfeld looked up, catching her square in the eye. "What?" he asked.

"If you had described a fax machine or a color television to your great-grandfather, he would have said it was magic," she said. "Advanced technology is the 'impossible' or the 'magic' of previous generations."

Sternfeld looked stricken. "Good Christ! Are you a real cop or are you one of them?" he snapped.

"I'm playing devil's advocate with you," Alicia said politely. "We don't know about a mountaintop till we've been there and understood it."

Sternfeld had traveled a great distance since the Tigertown physics labs near Nassau Hall. He looked at Alicia as if she had lost her mind.

"Do you remember which bars?" she asked smoothly.

"What?"

"Which bars might the group have met at?" Alicia asked, backtracking. "In West L.A., as you were saying."

"Oh. Quentin's was one. That's at Santa Monica Boulevard and Crescent Heights," he said. "And Hawkeye's up on Sunset. It's near the House of Blues."

"I know the area."

Alicia reached again into her folio case. She withdrew a copy of the picture of Olga Karmalakova that she had pulled off the INS files. She handed it to Ted Sternfeld.

"Recognize this woman?"

Sternfeld curled a lip.

"Oh, Lord. What a porker. She's a queer-looking old bag, too, isn't she?"

"Recognize her?"

"Wow. Look at that double chin."

"Do you recognize her?" Alicia insisted.

"Never seen her before. Should I have?" He handed back the photograph.

Again, instinct told Alicia that Sternfeld wasn't lying, though she couldn't be sure.

"You're probably lucky you haven't," Alicia said. And with that benediction, her visit concluded.

C H A P T E R 2 7

Alicia drove directly back to Los Angeles, intent on hitting the bars that Sternfeld had mentioned.

Hawkeye's didn't exist anymore. It had been closed and turned into a pricey clothing boutique for women. There, a tall ginger-haired girl named Monika greeted Alicia with a Scandinavian accent. Today, Monika was done up in purple-frosted lipstick, knee-high red leather boots, and very obviously no undergarments of any kind under a microshort black dress.

Monika told Alicia that the Hawkeye's had been gone for more than a year. Some scandal about four years' worth of back taxes due to the City of West Hollywood. The Nest had been a popular place with great music and twenty-something crowds that overflowed onto Sunset every weekend. Then one deplorable day, the joint had been boarded up by some iron-fisted city marshals, never to reopen. The owners quickly vacationed to Brazil. End of Monika's information. There was no biological aura around Monika, other than the obvious one, but there was the scent of Juicy Fruit gum.

At Quentin's on Santa Monica Boulevard, Alicia didn't do much better.

There was a short, unshaven stumpy bartender on duty who said his name was Widgy. His hair had been cropped severely—much like the trees in the photograph of Yuri Gagarin's final flight—and also freshly gelled. Widgy had on an open Hawaiian shirt that featured jubilant naked people, male and female, dancing, riding surfboards, and, if Alicia was seeing things properly, copulating in groups.

Widgy also wore a thin gold chain around his torso. When he leaned forward, Alicia caught a glimpse of a left-side nipple ring and the pinkish nipple that it adorned. Behind the bar was an old presidential campaign poster for Ronald Reagan. Someone—maybe even Widgy—had put lipstick on the Great Communicator and a pink bra across his chest. Above it was an unrelated sign:

SOAKING WET SHORTS CONTEST
EVERY THURSDAY 9 P.M.

Alicia was going to miss out; today was a Tuesday.

Widgy answered questions politely but cautiously. He knew a cop when he saw one, female or male, but he said he knew nothing about the Ammon Society, Ammonites, Mennonites, meteorites, stalagmites or stalactites, or any informal group that gathered there.

"Ever had any groups that focused on flying saucers? UFOs? *Star Trek* type stuff?"

Widgy shook his head again. "Some of the people who come in are strange," the barman said. "But not *that* strange."

"It's not as nutty as it sounds," Alicia heard herself saying.

Widgy wasn't buying it.

"Our customers are local West Hollywood people. They like to be left alone and meet their friends," Widgy explained. "You know, it's not like we get the Kiwanians in here or nothing."

Standing there neatly dressed in a blue blazer, blue blouse, and khaki pants, Alicia was starting to feel out of place. She moved to the show-and-tell part of her inquiry.

That flopped, too.

Widgy didn't recognize either picture that Alicia had to offer, but mentioned helpfully there were other bartenders who worked other nights. Maybe they could tell her something and maybe they couldn't.

Alicia said she would be back.

She phoned into CHP headquarters from her car and spoke briefly with Lieutenant Mott. She didn't tell him exactly the directions in which the case was leading but she did say she was running down a few things.

Then, before going home to Venice, she switched into her voice mail and listened to a call back from Captain William Gracie of the Tempe Arizona Police Department.

Neither officers Hopkinson nor McLaren would be available in the foreseeable future. Mary McLaren was on psychiatric sick leave, the captain explained. And Richard Hopkinson had, after eight and a half years of exemplary service as a police officer, not shown up at work a month earlier. He had been missing since. An investigation was ongoing, but Captain Gracie declined to give any details.

Alicia felt her heart flutter.

She listened to the message twice, kept it in her in box in case she wished to hear it again, then set down the phone.

Once again she was certain: there was no such thing as a coincidence. She would sleep with the light on again this evening, she decided, and would have her weapon at bedside, too.

She began to wonder if she should get a dog. A big, tough, jittery territorial beast that would sleep with one eye open, so that Alicia could sleep with both eyes shut.

CHAPTER 28

Janet lay in her bedroom and listened to the quiet of the house around her. She heard nothing stirring, no sound but her own breathing. The neighborhood beyond her walls was equally quiet.

So what had roused her from sleep? She was normally a solid sleeper. What was different about tonight? Why did she have a sense of something unsettled around her?

She looked at the clock near her bed. It was 4:39 A.M. according to the digital readout on her clock radio.

Outside her home, the night was bright, chilly, and quiet. A light rain had fallen earlier, unusual in southern California at this time of year. Janet rose from where she lay in the bed and went to a window. She pushed aside the curtain and glanced out.

The sky! Oh, how the sky glowed so invitingly tonight!

She had rarely seen it so alluring. The stars were scintillating in their sparkle, and the space between them was dark and deep. Janet, half asleep, fantasized about rocket ships that would voyage from one star to another. Someday, she thought to herself, she would like to ride through the stars with a man who was her husband.

Janet pulled her hand away from the window. The curtain silently glided back into place. She turned and stood.

She felt funny.

She knew something was wrong. It was as if something alien were present nearby. Something bad.

She wanted to go into her parents' bedroom and lie down with them. Something was beckoning her. Did she have a ghost visiting her tonight? She believed in God and Jesus because her parents had taught her to. She wondered whether God and Jesus were able to protect girls from ghosts and the other scary things that fly through the night.

Ghosts.

She shivered. She was scared.

But she had a feeling that this wasn't ghosts tonight.

This was something else.

It was almost as if, she realized, someone had planted a notion in her head and it was trying to take form. She didn't know where it was coming from. She only knew that it was there.

She looked out the window again, feeling compelled to look up at the sky. She practically felt as if she were being drawn up into it.

Wow! This was some strange feeling!

Tomorrow, she would call her friends Patricia and Tanya, and tell them about this. She would also tell her aunt Alicia, who was on the California Highway Patrol. Aunt Alicia knew about all sorts of strange things because she was a policewoman.

Janet walked to her bedroom door. She stood in the doorway for several seconds. Then she raised her eyes and stepped into the hallway.

She had been standing there for several minutes when she realized that her eyes hadn't moved. They were set upon the half-open door to that led to the guest room on the second floor.

Janet became aware of movement. She smiled and grew fearful at the same time. She wondered if it was "Eloise."

Eloise didn't really exist, of course. Eloise was her imaginary girlfriend, the two of them against the world.

There was a flickering change in the lighting. A shadow crossing the floor. She couldn't see into the room because the door was blocking her vision. But she knew something had moved.

Janet whispered. "Eloise . . . ?"

Something surged inside her. She walked quietly across the hallway to the room. She arrived at the door and listened.

What had she heard? A high-pitching whining, like some piece of electronic machinery functioning somewhere in the distance?

No. Not exactly.

A voice? A heartbeat?

No. Neither of those, either.

In fact, nothing. Dire silence. How, then, did she know that something was there?

She pushed the door open. The hinges uttered a little tortured wail, but the door gave way easily.

Janet braced herself, expecting to see a human figure standing before her. But there was none. And now she realized what had been affecting the light in the room. It was a reflection of the moonlight through the branches of a large tree outside. The light from the moon filtered through the wavering branches and then through the window. A cloud may have passed over the moon to affect the brightness.

Or so it appeared. Janet stepped into the room. She still had the sense of something. "Anyone here?" she asked softly.

A visitor.

"From where?"

From the sky.

"From where in the sky?"

A beat, then, *From the star Sirius in the constellation Canis Major.*

Janet began to giggle nervously. What funny thoughts were playing and unraveling within her head! She had neither heard of such a star or such a constellation. Nor had it ever occurred to her that someday she would receive voyagers from space.

Nor did the reality of it even occur to her now. Things like that, she reasoned, didn't really happen.

All stories are true.

Janet walked to the center of the room, then turned in every direction. She tried to lure the voice into communicating. In her sleepy state, she wondered if Eloise were a little more real in this dream. Maybe it was Eloise who was saying such unusual things.

"Come on," she said aloud, her words echoing in the quiet house. "Talk to me. Let's be friends."

Silence answered, a painful silence because now silence was exactly what Janet did not want. Then, beyond the perimeters of her consciousness, as she tried very hard, she *thought* she heard something more. Then:

Fa la la la la.

And then an inquiry floated to her invisibly through the night.

Why have you laughed?

"Because your thoughts are funny," Janet whispered.

No they're not!

"Stop hiding! I want to see you," Janet insisted.

A creak responded on the wooden floor before Janet. A creak that made her heart soar but that led nowhere.

She looked all around, toward the ceiling, across the walls of the room. "Eloise?" she implored. "Come on. Please come out. If it's you and you're real, please show yourself."

I'm not Eloise.

"Then show yourself no matter who you are."

She cocked her head, listening more intently than ever. Then from somewhere another thought came to her.

Are you sure you are ready? Not everyone can accept a visitor from another galaxy.

"From another *what?*" she asked softly. "Did you just ask me that question? Did you send me that thought?"

There was another creak, this time over her head.

A response? Or just a tick in the old ceiling boards.

Yes. I sent you that thought. Come to me.

Janet felt a shiver.

Then quickly another image was upon her, a vision of mind-numbing intensity. It came across her so strongly that all she could see for a few moments was what was in her mind's eye. It controlled her while it lasted, blinding her to her physical surroundings.

In the vision, Janet saw herself seventy years into the future as an old woman, wandering from room to room in some sort of gray prison. There were other women, young and old, but they shuffled around like zombies, dressed in tattered garments. All personality and humanity had been extirpated from their bodies.

They wore tattered coats, some of them, their buttons were crooked, their hair unkempt. They talked to friends unseen. Some of the younger ones wandered about half-naked, as if still traumatized by some momentous incomprehensible event. Some very young girls walked about completely naked, frightened and crying, but still manifesting some small bit of humanity. On their otherwise flawless young bodies were scars and bruises, as if they had been subjected to some sort of rough experimentation. The vision repelled her. She felt very sad for the lonely, isolated women in this strange gray tomb. In the background behind the cells was a panoply of stars.

What was this all about? Janet wondered. Was this how craziness started?

No. Places like this exist in other dimensions, upon other stars. With Earth women captured for breeding and mutation stock.

"What?" Janet whispered. Someone had answered again! "Talk to me!" she demanded, her voice louder. "Where are you? Say something again!"

You will be fine.

"*Who* are you? *Where* are you?" Janet asked.

Come back into your room.

"Why?"

I await you.

"But who *are* you?

Don't ask. Just come to me. Fa la la la la.

Janet felt a scream rise in her throat. She caught it and stopped it. Or maybe something within her caught the scream and stopped it, like one of those nightmares where one wants badly to scream, but can't.

She walked back toward her bedroom. She had the sense of gliding. The air around her had a different feel. She couldn't place exactly what it was, but it was like when a storm is approaching and the barometric pressure drops.

She returned to her room. The room was empty. Her sheets and blankets were where she had left them. On the wall was a poster from her favorite television show.

Keri Russell. "Felicity."

Nothing seemed strange. Yet.

Keep walking. You'll see me soon.

"But . . . ?"

Keep walking. You'll see me soon.

She went to the window. She gazed at the night. Then, as she raised her eyes again to the heavens, her jaw fell wide open. There was something shimmering in the sky. It didn't look solid. Just a light of some sort, like the round part of a beam.

It moved slightly, much like a spotlight sweeps a night sky. But it was much larger. It looked like the beacon of a huge flashlight, maybe a hundred feet up.

It came closer. It first looked round. Then it was elliptical. It scared Janet, particularly when it came to rest above her home.

Now she knew she was not dreaming and wanted to call out. But she was no longer able to form words. She was transfixed.

The diameter of the light grew above her home. It now looked like a giant soccer ball, all yellow, bright like a flame.

She watched it like a terrier tracking a bird.

Then in the snap of a second it was gone.

Completely gone from the sky.

"What the . . . ?" she asked herself. It was as if the luminous circle had ducked behind something, or tumbled into a hole in space.

Gone!

She started to wonder where a light could go.

But then she had an idea where it had gone, even though the thought was preposterous.

Whatever the light was, it had dipped down to earth and had entered her house. It was in her room, right behind her. She knew because her room was brighter suddenly, glowing unnaturally.

She wanted to turn, but was afraid to.

She wanted to scream, but was still incapacitated.

Then she realized that a little bit of physical control had come back to her. So she started to turn to face the interior of her room and the strange source of light.

Now you will see me. Now you will come with me.

Janet turned fully. A vision from another world was before her, a humanoid form, greenish-silver it seemed to her, glowing dully but with enough reddish-hued light to illuminate her room.

The creature was about her height, standing less than two feet away. It had a head with dark almond-shaped eyes. She stared into the unyielding dark crescent eyes. The eyes seemed to be slowly blinking, membranes descending and ascending at even intervals. There were two small holes where a nose might be. A slit for a mouth. There was a torso and arms and legs.

In Janet's soul, in her gut, in her heart, was the most wrenching scream of terror that a nine-year-old girl could possibly muster. But it was nowhere in her lungs or in her throat.

The creature raised its right arm.

Janet felt something very cold and very strong touch her wrist. In a moment that had no measurement in real time, she felt her consciousness start to drift, and she felt herself being transported up, up, up from the room until the room was no longer there at all and she knew that she wasn't there, either.

There are no relationships between earthbound human beings more complicated than those between mothers and daughters. Mothers, for example, have instincts that defy comprehension by any known science. Mothers can sense when their children are in peril.

Moments after the humanoid hand touched Janet's wrist, her mother, Alicia's sister, bolted upright from a nightmare.

The details of the nightmare slipped immediately away from her. But the terror was still in her throat.

For a moment, she couldn't move forward or back, forward into the present—her home, the bed she shared with her husband—or back—into the creepy details of the nightmare.

She only knew that the nightmare had been bad, one that touched upon something otherworldly. That, and the fact that she thought she might have heard some sort of strange thump.

Her husband was snoring placidly beside her.

No point in sending him to investigate. He wouldn't see anything even if he were staring right at it.

So she rose from bed herself, and walked to her daughter's room.

The first thing that struck her was the deserted bed.

The second thing was the wide-open window.

The third was that Janet was gone.

The irony was that during the precise moments of the abduction, Alicia had taken the occasion to work at her home computer.

She had bared her own soul and heart in writing an updated report on the case before her, the case she now referred to as the King of the Sun case.

She had put in writing the ideas that were in her head. Twilight dreams of silvery humanoids. Thought transference. Tunguska. The Ammon Society.

Aliens landing on Mount Baldy.

Extraterrestrial forces.

She poured into the computer every thought and notion she had about the case. Then she saved the file and marked it for the attention of Lieutenant Mott, closed it, and signed off.

CHAPTER 29

Alicia parked behind the LAPD car that was already at the curb before her sister Linda's home. She stepped out of her Jeep and drew a shaky breath.

This neighborhood was not the type of place where she was summoned for anything violent. Housebreakings weren't uncommon, nor was the occasional auto theft. But those weren't usually the cases that Alicia drew.

She walked to the front door.

Her shoulder was troubling her again. The pain made her feel old and battered. Not as fast, not as flexible, not quite as complete as she used to be.

Aging, she concluded, was a pain.

But she steered her thoughts in another direction. Her niece was missing, just as Amos Joy had promised. How in hell was Alicia going to tie this into everything that she knew and felt about Amos Joy and his extraterrestrial links?

How, and still sound rational?

She knocked on the door and waited.

Maybe Janet had turned up alive and giggling in the

time it had taken Alicia to drive over. But somehow she knew it wasn't going to be that simple.

James, her sister's husband, loomed into view, looking haggard. He'd aged from thirty-six to sixty since she last saw him.

"Yes?" he asked.

"Hey, Jim," Alicia said.

"Oh. You," James said. "Glad you came."

"Where's Linda?" Alicia asked.

"Inside," he answered. "And there are already some other cops here," James said. "In uniform."

"That's standard," Alicia began. "They took the 911 call. The follow-up on the case is done through the detective bureau. Are there other detectives here yet?"

"No." James led her into the house.

"There will be soon," she said.

A silvery voice fluttered into her subconscious. *Not that it will do any good.*

"Get out of my head," Alicia grumbled.

James turned. "Say something?" he asked.

Alicia shook her head.

James looked and walked forward again. A grandfather clock she had never noticed before stood in the corner of the room. Sun and moon logo for day and night. The sun looked menacing. The moon looked resolutely evil. Humanized faces on planets. Whose idea had that been so very long ago?

She cringed at the thought that little inanimate objects—if they *were* inanimate—were mocking her.

James exhaled hard. "I'll go get Linda," he said.

James disappeared into another downstairs room.

Alicia stood alone in the living room, waiting.

One of the uniformed men came into view, gave her a nod and went out to work the radio in the car.

A few moments later, Linda came into the living room with her husband. Her eyes were red, wet and moist, but she was composed.

Alicia pulled her into an embrace and then stepped back, automatically reaching for the stock lines of reassurance that she always used in cases of disappearance. As she spoke, her hands went into the familiar motions of their own accord. She retrieved her fountain pen and a small notebook from her inside pocket.

The first pages of the notebook were covered with her jottings from the visit to Madame Olga Karmalakova. Other pages were dedicated to the tattooed corpses, one from the high desert and the other from BevHilz.

Alicia did a double take.

She—or someone—had drawn a little sketch of the sun on one of the pages, high on the page as if in the sky. On the bottom of the page, below her notes, were stick figures of two bodies.

Stick figures with detail. They were female bodies.

She felt a rush.

Time seemed to hold still around her. An eerie, heavy silence. Alicia flipped the pages to try to escape that section of the notebook.

But she couldn't.

Her fingers only found pages that continued the previous notes. And now, with a deeper, more terrifying rush, she saw a similar sketch on the next page.

Same sun.

This time, *four* bodies at the lower section of the page, each lying in deathly repose. Two males. Two females. One of the females was smaller than the other.

Then Alicia realized that the doodlings were not hers. The hand had come from somewhere else.

My hand.

Time remained still in the room. Her sister and brother-in-law were not moving. Alicia glanced at her watch. No movement from the second hand.

"Jesus. Time frozen! Why?"

Why not?

"How! How can you make time stand still!"

Dearest lady, it happens all the time.

"I'm hypnotized! Is that it? Is that how you control my mind?"

Don't be absurd.

She turned and saw Amos.

"Why were you in my notebook?"

To show you the future.

"I don't wish to see it!"

Come to Mount Baldy and you will live it.

"Go away!"

Alicia shook herself, trying to break the spell. Linda and James and everything else in current reality remained motionless. Like cigar-store Indians.

She looked down and the second hand on her watch strutted one notch forward, then another.

It stopped again.

Want to see another trick?

"No."

You will anyway.

"Please don't . . ."

Laughter. Then, involuntarily, Alicia lowered her head, as if a pair of hands were upon her, moving her, making her look downward.

The watch face again.

"Oh, Holy Jesus!" Alicia said.

The second hand strutted again. *This time backward.* Time in reverse. The universe going backward.

"Not possible."

It certainly is. Happens all the time.

More laughter.

She felt herself frozen for God knew how long. Time shut down completely. Amos, silvery and lithe, moved around the room. He showed her Janet, a scream of horror set on the girl's face, then he took the girl away again.

Then he vanished, and Alicia was jolted back to what she hoped was reality.

And time was moving again, manifested by the watch hand and by James and Linda.

Like solid ice turned to water in a heartbeat.

An image was in Alicia's mind: fish.

Two trout stuck in ice, then bursting to freedom as the ice was gone. A silvery rainbow, a flapping of fins.

"Alicia?" Linda asked. "Alicia!"

Jolted finally, Alicia replied.

"I think we need to have a discussion," Alicia said to her sister and brother-in-law. "Is there a good place to talk?"

"Right here's fine," James said. He motioned toward a new sofa.

Husband and wife sat down.

Alicia pulled forward a chair.

She kept her injured right shoulder upright. It was starting to pain her particularly right how.

She grimaced. She had a pounding headache now, too. A silver hammer, rap, rap, rapping in her head.

She envisioned the little spaceman ever smaller, tucked inside her head, pounding a hammer to an anvil ever since that day when she'd seen the flash in the sky.

Her mind hopped. Flipped and flew.

No holding back her normal rational senses now.

The hammer in her head: *Lucifer's hammer! Glad you're thinking spatially.*

Alicia whispered aloud. "Please, Hammer. Don't hurt 'em."

"What?" James asked.

" 'Maxwell's Silver Hammer,' " Alicia said next.

"Alicia! Are you okay?" her sister asked.

"Fuck it. I'm fine," she answered.

Linda and James were staring at her.

"Alicia, what do you think has gone on here?" Linda asked.

All she was capable of these days: a stock answer. Police department bullshit. "I have no way of knowing," Alicia said, "until you've told me as much as you know. Then we'll do everything we can. That much I can promise you."

Linda sighed, trying to stifle the terror, in addition to the unbearable sense of violation. Who could have been in her home? Who could have taken her child?

During the first minutes of the meeting, Alicia sought to maintain a grip on sanity and cover the earthly details.

She wrote a description of her niece and immediately put it out on the police radio. Linda also provided a recent photograph. Two additional uniformed men arrived a few minutes later.

Alicia sent one of the men to police headquarters immediately so that a copy of the picture could be transmitted to all counties in southern California, and posted on the Internet.

"What are our chances?" Linda asked, her voice starting to falter. "To find Janet alive?"

Amos again, in Alicia's head: *None, you cow.*

"The sooner you give us everything we need to work with," Alicia said again, "the better the chances."

Liar! You know the truth!

"You make it sound so routine," Linda said. "And my daughter is missing."

James gave her hand a squeeze.

More CHP horse manure: "The disappearance of a child gets the department's highest priority. We also call in the FBI. They have magnificent computers. Nationwide networks of information. Informants. Thousands of very dedicated people. We want as many available people and resources as possible on your side."

Distant laughter.

"Of course," James said. "But Janet could be right in the neighborhood somewhere. She could have just wandered off."

Or she might be out of this world, already.

"Any particular reason you suggest that?" Alicia asked.

"No," James admitted after a slight pause.

Alicia eyed her sister and brother-in-law. "Now I need to ask you some questions," she said, almost apologetically. "May I?"

James nodded, but his approval was grudging and impatient.

"Please go ahead," Linda said. She tightly clasped her husband's hand.

"What time did you see Janet last?" Alicia asked.

"She went to bed at eight o'clock," Linda said. "Sometimes she stays awake a little. You know how kids are."

Alicia nodded. She knew. "Did you go upstairs with her?" she asked.

Linda looked at her husband and let him answer.

"We both did," James said. "I put Janet in bed myself. That would have been about quarter past eight."

Alicia pressed onward. "Anything unusual happen last night?" she asked softly.

"No," Linda said. She paused. "The only thing that's been at all unusual recently is—"

"Let's not get into this," James said softly.

"I need to know everything," Alicia said.

Linda sighed.

"Janet's had this fixation recently. A series of bad dreams."

"About what?" Alicia asked.

You'll like this, Amos said from somewhere.

"Spacemen," James interjected angrily. "Been watching more of that damned science fiction stuff on TV. Or hearing stories at school."

"Spacemen?"

Linda exhaled long and hard. "She's had this recurring dream. Or nightmare."

"We should never have given her that fucking telescope," James said bitterly. "It only made everything worse."

"Tell me about the dream," Alicia asked.

Linda paused.

"This spaceman comes and carries her away," she said. "She told us about trips to other planets."

"I see," Alicia said softly. Yes, she saw, all right.

"He even has a name," Linda acknowledged.

"Janet said he had a name?" Alicia asked. "This . . . this character in a dream?"

"Yeah. Her space buddy has a name. Janet said he claims he's the 'king of the sun,'" James said, his irritation turned to anger now. "The king of the fucking sun, all right? Goddamn fucking sci-fi fantasy, okay? Now! Can we discuss where my daughter is and how we might be able to get her back from the pervert who stole her?"

Linda shuddered. She placed her hand on her husband's.

The couple was so preoccupied with the rush of their own fear and apprehension that they missed the abject expression of horror on Alicia's face.

King of the Sun, King of the Sun.

Fortunately, the detectives who would be officially

handling the case, an LAPD man and woman from the kidnapping/abduction unit, arrived at the door moments later. Alicia turned the questioning over to them.

As the assigned detectives took over the questioning, Alicia prowled the house. She thought back to the last time she had been there, the day of Janet's birthday party.

Was it coincidence, or was there something to that, too?

That was the same day that the mutilated John Doe had been discovered in the desert, her first step into the "King of the Sun" case, her first step toward contact with Amos Joy.

Contact.

Not to mention the flash in the sky that she had seen through Janet's telescope.

Eventually, Alicia found herself in her niece's bedroom, standing at the window, looking upward.

Alicia gazed toward the sky. Lost in thought, her mind drifted toward an image of a plateau on a mountain. A place she had never been before but seemed to be seeing very clearly for the first time.

Then the voice came to her again, by way of explanation.

Yes. Baldy. Mount Baldy.

"All right," she said softly. "All right, Amos. I'm ready for you."

You're certain?

"Yes."

Then say it loud for all the world to hear. And I will have your resolution ready for you.

"I'm ready," Alicia said boldly. "I'm ready for any planet you want to take me to. You hear that? I'm damned good and ready."

No answer from Amos. Instead, a response from this world.

Sister Linda, standing behind her at the door to Janet's room.

"Ali?" Linda asked, her brow furrowed in a frown. "What is it with you these days? What in hell has gotten into your head?"

"Why?"

"You're not the same."

"Sorry," Alicia said, her cheeks flushing. "Just thinking aloud."

"Sure." A pause. Still staring. Not convinced at all. "The other detectives want to see you."

"Of course."

Linda wore an expression that suggested that yet one more worry was now added to her burden. And as for Alicia, her expression was one of humiliation. That, and pain, since her shoulder was throbbing as if clutched by an invisible hand.

The silver hammer in her brain pounded on and on and on without remorse.

CHAPTER 30

The next morning, with Janet still missing, Alicia ran a computerized historical check of various missing children throughout California. She sought in particular anything that could draw a parallel to her niece's disappearance. Any suggestion of a psychopath like Amos Joy. The factor of the missing child having dreams of space travel.

Anything.

A fellow CHP officer came by and asked Alicia what angle she was working. She lied. She couldn't admit that over the last weeks, she had turned into a latter-day spaceman hunter, a devout believer in the otherworldly.

She spent an hour on the research and came up empty. The computer told her that nothing of this sort had ever happened elsewhere in the United States.

She leaned back in her chair and was staring off into a different world, trying to sort things out, when the phone rang on her desk.

Her commander, Lieutenant Albert Mott, wanted to see her as soon as possible. And the lieutenant didn't sound amused.

Alicia's shoulder throbbed as she got to her feet.

Moments later, Alicia arrived in the commander's office. Lieutenant Mott was leaning back at his desk. His jacket hung on the back of his chair. He was in white shirtsleeves and a dark tie with a gold clip that featured the American flag.

More importantly, a hard copy of Alicia's report on the deaths of Bill Sands and the unidentified man in the desert lay open on the commander's desk.

Mott reached for an unopened bottle of iced coffee from his minifridge and tossed it to Alicia.

Alicia caught it with her left hand.

"Have a cold cappuccino on me, Alicia," Lieutenant Mott said. "A caffeine fix will do you good."

"Thanks," Alicia said.

She opened it with one hand, avoiding the use of her bad arm and shoulder. Mott watched the dexterity of Alicia's right thumb and forefinger.

Alicia sipped the chilled coffee.

Mott opened a can of Pepsi for himself.

"You wanted to talk to me?" she asked.

"I did," Mott said. "I read your report to date. And I'm not sure where you're going with this case, Alicia," Mott said.

"I can only tell you what I've observed."

"Strange case, huh?" Mott asked. "Space chemicals. Sun tattoos." He paused. "Homoerotic art. Welcome to fucking Los Angeles." He paused. "And you've got it tied to this elusive little homicidal maniac whom you've seen in this area, whom you've actually questioned, but whom you've been unable to bring in?"

"Yes, sir."

"That's more than a little weird, wouldn't you say?"

"Yes, sir."

A beat, then, "Sure you don't want to talk about it over dinner sometime?" he asked. "It would be more informal."

"I'm fine right here, sir," Alicia answered. "I like to keep it professional."

She saw, or thought she saw, Mott run his gaze up and down her. She adjusted her skirt.

He sighed.

"I know we got two sun-tattoo deaths in the same area in the same month," he said, "but I'll be fucked if I can see a connection to Amos Joy. And the connection is not in your report. No evidence, anyway. Just theory. As if you're dreaming this up."

"It's all in there, Lieutenant," Alicia answered. "I think Amos Joy is involved. Call it instinct."

"The DA can't indict on instinct. And you can't make an arrest on it, either. Where's any piece of evidence that points in the direction of your conclusions?"

"I don't have anything yet."

"I know. That's what bothers me most."

Mott's eyes shifted from Alicia back down to the written report. "Do you have anything that's moving you in that direction?" Mott asked. "Other than theory?"

A montage of images blew through Alicia's mind.

Events in San Bernardino. Her conversations with Madame Olga. The dreams. The silvery images that Amos formed before her eyes. The vision of Amos across from her home. The disappearance of her niece.

She quickly constructed a dam in her mind and held back the flood of images. Time seemed to stand on its nose again for a moment. In her mind a vision of a silvery figure appeared, silhouetted against bright reddish light.

I'm back.

"Alicia?" Mott asked. *"Alicia?"* He was looking at her strangely.

Alicia was abruptly aware that she hadn't answered her commander's inquiry.

"What?"

"I asked a question."

"I know."

You know everything. But actually you know very little.

"You okay? Are you sure you're up to this case?"

"I'm fine," she said.

"You don't seem fine. You seem like you're a candidate for psych."

"I'm okay," she said.

He grimaced. "I'm thinking of assigning two more detectives to the case. Could you use them?"

"I don't want them," Alicia answered.

"It's not your decision."

"Yeah, but I don't want them. It would take things in the wrong direction," Alicia said. "It's a very intuitive case. Very mental."

"Mental, huh?"

"I need to think and make some sense out of this, myself."

Mott clasped his hands behind his head. He continued to study Alicia up and down. He sighed again. He was getting to be an expert on the accusatory sigh.

"I'll be honest with you, Alicia. I gave you this assignment because I thought it would ease you back into active duty after your injury. Now I can't tell what's going on, I can't tell if you're going tutti-frutti on me, and I can't tell whether I need to take you back off active duty."

"Why?"

"Your reports border on the incoherent. You seem completely flummoxed, your attention isn't even here in this room right now, and I have questions about you physically."

That's what they always say when they don't understand.

"What questions?"

Mott clenched his teeth. A tight, impatient scowl.

"I want the truth about your mental state," he said.

"It's fine."

Better than his. And completely wacko also.

"You're feeling okay. Not traumatized? Not feeling a little goofy. A little 'off'?"

"No."

The most brilliant of Earth thinkers are always locked up, as are those who have shared a vision of the spatial dimension.

"Everything that happens make sense to you?"

"As much as it ever did."

"You depressed?"

"No."

"Drinking?"

"A beer or two after work."

"One or two glasses or one or two pitchers?"

"Very funny."

"Okay, then why the fuck are you writing me reports mentioning extraterrestrial forces?" Lieutenant Mott inquired with more than a hint of frustration.

"Did I say that?"

"You typed this into your computer and signed off on it, didn't you?" Mott asked, holding it up.

"Bill Sands was a member of the Ammon Society, which believes in such things."

As well he should have.

"Is that right?"

"That's correct, sir. And I'm trying to address the situation as I see it, as I understand it, and accept any possible explanation."

Mott considered Alicia's assertion. He simmered.

"Well, don't put stuff like that in writing!" he barked. "These reports get reviewed! I can't control where they go. There's no way I can let this cross my desk without talking to you about it."

"Sorry."

"Now tell me about your arm and shoulder."

"Fine, too."

"Don't lie to me."

"I'm not lying, sir," Alicia lied.

Mott studied Alicia again for another second.

Then his right hand moved quickly and he opened the side drawer of his desk. He pulled out a deck of cards. It was a fresh deck, still in cellophane.

"What's this?" Alicia asked.

"Looks like a deck of cards, Alicia." The commander leaned back and steepled his fingers.

"I know that, Lieutenant."

"I want to see you open it and deal me a hand."

Mott waited. Alicia reached for the deck with her left hand. Then she realized what Mott was up to.

"I'd prefer not to," Alicia said.

"Of course not. And that's why you didn't care to open the bottle of coffee in the normal two-handed way, either. Right?"

Alicia said nothing.

Mott sighed.

"Come on, Alicia. Don't bullshit me. That shoulder is killing you, isn't it?"

What will kill you, sweet woman, is not the shoulder.

"There's some pain. Big deal."

"Pain you can work with, if you choose to," Mott said. "Paralysis is something else, isn't it?"

He paused.

"Can you deal those cards? If your job depended on it, could you deal those cards?"

"Maybe."

"Let's see."

Mott waited.

Alicia picked the cards up with her right hand.

With numb fingers, she clumsily removed the cellophane from the pack. Then she retained the deck in her left hand and dealt with the right. Two slick cards started to slide off the bottom of the deck. She had no sensation in her palm, couldn't grip and couldn't feel the movement of the cards. A second later, the deck fell and four dozen cards scattered on the floor. Four kings lay face up in the center, mocking her.

"That's enough to get you put back on disability," Mott said.

"The shoulder is getting better," Alicia insisted. "Give me some time. I'm fine on duty."

"Sure you don't want to have dinner? Maybe at my place?"

"Sure you don't want me to file a harassment suit?"

Mott sighed. Long and loud.

"I can overlook a little, Alicia, because I like you. But I can't overlook a lot. Not for very long. I'd like to give you more time off with pay, but I don't want to pull you off this case if you're close to something."

"I'm close."

"Something rational, I hope."

"I'm very close."

Yes, you are. A pause. Then, *Close to Mount Baldy, too. You must come visit soon.*

"Then show me some movement on this case within another three days, okay? I need it."

"And if there isn't any?"

"As I said, I'd have to talk to headquarters in Sacramento. And I think the best I would be able to pull for you is desk duty. And that's if you started being nicer to me."

Alicia thought about it.

"That stinks," she said in conclusion. "And so do you."

"I know it does. And that's why women don't make it

on jobs like these. They don't understand the proper give-and-take with a commanding officer."

She seethed. She wished she had recorded the meeting.

"So I'm doing you a favor," Mott said in conclusion. "I'm giving you three days. That's all, Alicia. Thank you."

Alicia stared furiously at Lieutenant Mott, then rose.

Want me to kill him for you?

"No, don't bother," Alicia whispered.

"What?"

"Nothing, sir," she retorted angrily.

She turned and left the room, his gaze boring heavily upon her back.

She went first to her desk, then to her car. She passed two CHP officers in the parking lot. They stopped talking when she approached them and, like Mott, watched her go by.

When Alicia arrived at her car she looked at them again. She froze.

They had turned to silvery humanoid beings, also. Just like Amos. Then, before her eyes, they morphed back into human form. They continued to stare at her and laughed.

A deep fear gripped her. A revulsion mixed with terror. The world was no longer a familiar secure place and neither was her own mind.

To the west, above the ocean, the sun floated above the horizon like a huge copper plate.

CHAPTER 31

Midnight arrived. Same day.

Alicia found it impossible to go home.

She sat in the parking lot at the edge of the beach in Venice, a solitary figure in a Jeep. The vehicle's engine was off. Her mind was a clutter of doubts, uncertainties, and suspicions.

She sipped from a freshly opened forty-ounce bottle of Budweiser. Meanwhile, through the haze of suds, her past and future alternated before her. She tried to put her thoughts in perspective.

She leaned back in the driver's seat of her Jeep. The top was off, and she stared upward into the night sky.

Stars. Billions of them. Glowing like little flames.

She stared for several minutes, then gradually closed her eyes.

At one moment she was a girl again, walking with her father on a warm afternoon by the Colorado River, not far from their vacation home. The next moment—her eyes still closed—she had traveled through time until she had punched a hole in the sky and was somewhere in space, a location that she didn't recognize.

She wondered if this was how Amos did it. Traveling from place to place on the power and velocity of his own brain. And did he also have the faculties to transform his thoughts into reality?

Or a sort of reality?

Alicia sailed again. Through time, through her mind.

So *this* is how he does it, she thought to herself. Pressing one's own mind to travel faster and faster in every direction.

She kept going. Kept sailing.

Then she arrived at the moment a few days ago when Amos Joy had disappeared before her open eyes. She blinked twice.

Hard.

Next, her mind was probing into the future, the resolution of the case before her and her potential forced retirement from the California Highway Patrol.

Retirement.

She pictured the scene. She hated the word.

A silvery whisper from the firmament: *Retirement.*

Yet suddenly she could see all the pieces of retirement moving into place.

Her arm was killing her.

It spasmed sharply every time she bent it.

Her shoulder ached.

How long could she hide the residual damage? Eventually, she would have to see the doctor again and the doctor would tell the department that she was physically unfit for duty.

Never mind mentally fit.

How could she go to the department shrinks and tell them what she had witnessed in Amos Joy?

"Amos is not really a human being. He's from another dimension. Or at least another planet. Therein lies the honest resolution to this case. But who would believe it, Doc?"

What a great opening statement.

It was exactly what she felt. And she had seen how well the explanation had played out with Lieutenant Mott.

"I saw a man disappear right before my eyes. Fade in, fade out. Now you see him, now you don't. Happens all the time. Then I met him in space. And by the way, that's where my niece has already gone."

She shuddered.

The arm would land her on the surgeon's table and the statements about Amos Joy would land her on the shrink's couch. The latter would be fine except for one thing: Alicia was *certain* of what she had witnessed.

By all that was holy, there *was* something extraterrestrial about Amos Joy.

Alicia had picked up on it the first time she had confronted Amos. She had seen it in her night visions.

A moment passed.

She sighed and opened her eyes. She swigged some more brew. What was there to do on this case? Where was there to go from here? Why, she wondered, had fate dropped a case like this at her feet?

Fate. Feet.

She suppressed a laugh.

Words pulled themselves apart in her head and then took shape again like little subversive telegrams.

Fait accompli. Feet accompli.

Fait. Feet.

Feet. Flight.

Flight. Fly.

Fly. An old tune came back from her youth. "Fly Me

to the Moon." She played with the words while music
from an unseen source played in her mind.

Fly Me to the Sun.

Her mind bounced from one freewheeling association
to another. Moon. Sun.

Sun Young Moon.

She sipped again. She wished some damned Moonie
would accost her right here with some literature. She
would have been happy to punch someone out just
about now.

Funny.

Rhymes with "sunny."

Moonie. Sunny. The world was upside down, inside
out.

Alicia hadn't felt like getting drunk until she was confronted with Amos and his disappearing act. Or had she
gotten drunk and *then* encountered the little guy's silver
fade-in fade-out freak show?

Was he a spaceman or a sociopath? Or were all so-
ciopaths spacemen? *There* was a notion.

Maybe, Alicia wondered, she should just shoot Amos
and see if he bled. Then she could tell the department
shrinks that she shot him because he was a space alien.

Would he bleed silver blood?

She laughed out loud.

Maybe she should shoot him with a silver bullet. Or
was that a fate, she guffawed again, reserved for would-
be werewolves?

She pondered it, turning serious again, thinking
about Amos Extra-T Joy, searching for an answer.

None came. As usual.

Well, one thing was for sure. She was starting to get
one hell of a Budweiser buzz again right now.

She thought of the frogs croaking the name of the beer
and nearly swallowed wrong. It was that sort of night.

But Alicia was sober enough to know where else she was.

She was on an edge that she never had known to exist. She knew that if she asked anyone for psychiatric help it would probably cost her her job. So she had to depend on herself to make her way through this case. Her own ingenuity.

"Goddamn Amos Joy," she cursed to herself in her Jeep. "Fucking no-good bastard."

Her eyes narrowed. She looked at the ocean from a hundred feet away. She thought of how she and Ed Van Allen would sit near the ocean and talk. There was a ripple of water coming toward the shore, emanating from somewhere out in the darkness.

Waves?

Sure. That's what most people would have thought. That would have been the most rational explanation. The moon was yellow and waning and that usually created great surf in Venice as well as down the coast.

But Alicia had a different hunch. A spaceman walking on the water or arising from the depths? Who knew what in hell else was in the Pacific Ocean? It was clear that no one really knew what was in the sky.

On impulse, she moved the spotlight at the window of her Jeep. She threw a beam out over the water, seeking the origin of the ripple.

She saw nothing.

Was Bill Sands's tormented spirit rising?

Whatever had caused the waves was invisible . . . at least for right now.

She turned the light off and returned to her immediate problems. How to proceed?

A bunch of bad ideas danced before her, one after another.

Get some bootleg painkillers. That would snuff the pain.

Don't tell anyone else what you know about Amos. Then no one will know you've gone crackers.

Have more booze. It makes the arm and the head feel better.

And still that confusion remained within her. A local earthbound bully boy had shot her down in Irvine. And now she was facing an adversary whom she thought was from another planet. One of the first principles of police work was, don't get emotionally involved.

Don't take a case personally.

She was taking both of these cases personally. And then there was the disappearance of Janet, which had half of southern California atwitter.

Alicia asked herself the important questions.

Was she still a good cop?

Had she endured her shooting with her sanity intact?

These things were at issue here in this suddenly breezy spot by the ocean, as she sat sipping a Budweiser and looking at the dark surface of the Pacific. And her mental journey forward and backward in time and space seemed like a single unfinished voyage.

Images from her meeting with Madame Olga came at her like acid flashes, the flashes she'd been trying to dismiss: the all-metal building, the deft execution of the trout, the photograph of Yuri Gagarin's death-ride jet sheering off the tops of trees.

The image of violent death rose from that final vision and embraced her, like a giant squid extending its tentacles.

Outside the Jeep, the night had turned colder. Alicia's internal thoughts dispersed. She again became aware of the radio playing in her vehicle.

No music. Pop-chat bullshit, instead.

She closed the bottle of beer, screwing the top back on with a third of the liquid left. She poked the buttons on the radio, surfing from one channel to another.

Somehow she kept coming back to the strongest signal, which was a Jesus station from Pasadena.

The man on the radio dropped all pretensions and was talking flat-out about Christ and salvation. The pitch was soft. The sell was hard. So was hellfire and damnation.

Stealth conversion. Rock evangelism. Guerrilla Christianity.

". . . gonna take you up to the spirit in the sky."

Alicia scoffed at both the message and the medium. She wondered why she hadn't seen God when she had been shot. Pondering the point further, she wished she had.

Oh, *how* she wished she had!

Her father had been a religious man. Where had he lost it? *How* had he lost it?

She wondered: How would God have explained an extraterrestrial?

"In the beginning, God created Heaven and Earth . . ."

Her thoughts jumped back to music. Abruptly, Alicia punched another button on the radio and brought up something from San Diego.

Some hard rock from the far reaches of FM reception. Something more atheistic. Where was Metallica when she needed it?

Classic rock. Much better. Her Christian God had failed her, so why not rock and roll instead?

The music brought back memories of summer romances in high school and college. She wondered—thanks to Amos Joy—about the nature of time, and if these events in the past were still going on over and over in some incomprehensible place.

Alicia pushed the notion away.

She started her engine.

She pulled her Jeep out of the parking place and turned away from the ocean.

"Got to break this mood," she told herself. "Got to get more positive."

In some ways she was embarrassed and ashamed of her own cynicism. Why couldn't she have a traditional religious orthodoxy like every other member of every police force she had ever served on. Was it the fact that she was a free thinker and *open* to new ideas that allowed alien ideas—*and aliens themselves*—into her head?

Why had she even survived her shooting? One bullet a little to another direction would have gone through her heart or through her brain.

Why was she still on this planet?

"I'm here," she reasoned aloud in the car, "because there is some bit of unfinished business for me, something I have yet to do, yet to accomplish, yet to be."

She meant all this in a fatalistic, nonreligious way. It was just the natural order of things, how they were meant to be and how they would be. Like the dream of getting shot that recurred over and over, the words, these thoughts, repeated themselves to Alicia.

. . . events can happen over and over, too, or they can reverse themselves; time bends, like a laser shot straight into space. It bends . . .

She spoke boldly. "There is a reason why I am here. That's it. There is a reason why I am here."

The deduction reminded her again of her late father. He used to say there was a reason Alicia became a cop and a further reason that his son didn't.

"Yeah. But we never knew what those reasons were," she answered her old man in absentia.

She managed a laugh after that one.

No response from the late Mr. Aldrich, however.

She ran through many images and memories of her father as she was alone again in the car. And on the radio, Arrowsmith blasted. Steve Tyler telling her which way to walk.

She sighed. Deep in her heart, Alicia knew that the extraterrestrial explanations for Amos were the only ones that made sense.

So why did she decide upon the extraterrestrial truth one minute and then challenge it again the next?

Then it happened! In tandem with her thoughts as she drove on Washington Avenue away from the ocean—

Holy Jesus!

"What's the old expression?" she demanded suddenly of herself. "Speak of the devil and the devil appears."

Think of Amos Joy and—

I've been waiting for you.

Washington Boulevard in Venice. Of all places.

Alicia hit her brake like a crazy woman to avoid the man standing in the middle of the avenue. She veered her Jeep to the side of the road and stepped out.

First Amos was there.

Then the silvery figure was there. Flashing like neon. The color of a new dime.

Then he was gone.

A few pedestrians stared at Alicia as she stood on the sidewalk. Stunned, she surveyed the place where she had seen Amos.

She *knew* she had seen him! But he had dissipated like ocean mist.

Then just as quickly he popped up safely farther up on the sidewalk.

He beckoned to her.

In human form.

Grinning.

The same grin he must have borne when he slashed the throats of the psychiatrist and child in Arizona.

She glanced at two men, with Central American faces, looking at her.

"He's a spaceman," she said. "Amos Joy. Got extra

mental powers. Comes from a planet we can only dream about."

She looked back and Amos beckoned again. Then she saw him step into a car.

A Saturn.

Same as what Madame Karmalakova drove.

The car started to move. Alicia stepped back into her Jeep. He led her to the nearest expressway.

The 10.

She followed through evening traffic. Then he led her north on 101. Then, over the course of forty minutes, past 104 and north of Pasadena.

She followed patiently, sinking into a mood of complacency as she drove.

She knew that the wiser move would probably be to use the police radio in her car. Summon backups. This was Amos Joy she was following, after all. Wanted in several states for murder.

But she also knew that a one-on-one rendezvous was in order between the two of them. There were personal matters to settle.

And she knew their destination that evening: Amos was leading her to Mount Baldy.

Sometimes, on the highway, his car traveled so far in front of her Jeep that she lost sight of it. But it barely mattered.

Alicia was confident of her destination.

And keeping the sunroof open, with a nod to Madame Karmalakova, she was able to drive and navigate by the stars above.

CHAPTER 32

The road snaked up the side of the rocky mountain. The sky above her loomed brighter because she was drawing closer to it. She was in one of the most remote and highest stretches of the San Gabriels north of Los Angeles.

She was operating on her own radar now. Her own instinct. Her own sense of what this was about. She was thirty-five hundred feet above sea level, climbing, thanking fate that she owned a Jeep, passing through low clouds. She hadn't seen Amos's taillights for several minutes, but the road only snaked in one direction.

Upward.

Even the coyotes and mountain antelope were scarce up here. Only boulders and jack pines to set the landscape in the yellowish moonlight.

Then she came to the place where the road ended.

Amos's car was sitting there. Empty.

Alicia's Jeep rolled to a halt. She stopped for a moment. She was in a little gully where the rocks and pines had turned the road into a dead end. Beyond a bunch of small scruffy trees there was a foot path that led to the summit.

She stepped out of her Jeep. Out of instinct and training, she unholstered her weapon. In one sense, she was still dealing with a madman. If he threatened her, she would have every right to shoot him on sight. There were fugitive bulletins out for him. She had a "free shoot" if she wanted one.

Who would ever question what took place here if she felt threatened and used deadly force?

But then there was the other sense of what she was dealing with. A sense of the supernatural or the extraterrestrial. She knew her gun would be useless.

She used her floodlight from the Jeep to scan the surroundings. She saw nothing. No Amos. It occurred to her to use the police radio in her car to leave her location with headquarters, or even to call for backup. Just someone to retrieve her body in case this was another ambush, in case she was to be found dead hours from now.

She reached in and pulled out the handset of the radio. The whole communications system was down. Dead. She tossed it back into the front seat of the Jeep. From the car door, she took a flash lantern and hooked it to her belt.

Then she raised her eyes again to where the path before her led past an assemblage of rocky boulders, and up into the uppermost plateau of Mount Baldy.

Her heart jumped. She saw the outline of a small man against the sky before he turned away and walked from view. Alicia turned off the engine of her Jeep, pocketed the keys, and kept her weapon drawn. She followed the path upward toward the stars.

The path upward was arduous, littered with jagged rocks, stones that moved and tumbled, broken pine branches that tripped her and slashed at her ankles.

The air was thin. Her breath and endurance quickly escaped her. She frequently needed to advance by leaning far forward and almost pulling herself by her hands.

But then she was there. An eerie stony plain.

A vacant plateau stretching out in every direction, maybe an acre wide.

The moonlight brightened.

She was overcome with the same sense of subdued panic that had pervaded her dream of spatial captivity. This was an odd, inexplicable alien place, not like anywhere in the world she had ever been.

The sky lit the plateau.

Cautiously, Alicia wandered out toward its center. The kooks from the Ammon Society claimed this place had been charged with energy by extraterrestrials, and at this point Alicia was disinclined to doubt it.

She felt something. *Something.*

She wandered further and made a turn or two. But there was no path to follow, nothing to use as a point of reference except the sky itself. Looking over the perimeters of the cliff, Alicia felt as if she were looking down onto a sea.

But the surface below was a cloud. She wondered if she were the only human being in this place at this time.

Amos was there. But she didn't consider him human.

She heard a faint noise and turned to find its source.

She saw the figure of Amos not too far away from her. Maybe fifty feet. He was motionless and upright, as still as one of those boulders.

"Amos?" she asked.

She was aware of the weapon in her hand, and the sweat pouring from her palm to its handle. Resolutely, bravely, she walked toward him.

Amos Joy waited for her.

"Amos!" she yelled.

The little man smiled and turned. Then Alicia was met by a blast of wet and cold. There was also a fetid stench in the air, one that reminded Alicia of decomposing flesh.

She called again to her suspect. "Amos! Hey, Amos! Let's just talk!"

The starry plateau gave no answer.

Nor did Amos.

"Come on, Amos. Come out here!"

No answer again. She tried to steady her grip on her weapon, but the cold had aggravated her spreading paralysis. She suddenly couldn't feel her fingers. The weapon dropped from her hand.

Amos remained twenty, thirty feet away from her, crossing the plateau toward its center. Like a tune on one's mind that one just can't place, Amos was there, but just out of reach.

Alicia noted the position of the moon and stars. It was easy to get lost in this sort of place. Unless she wished to die out here, she would have to find her way back. But she already knew how disoriented she was. She already knew she might have to wait for the light of morning.

Yes, the light of the sun.

Then there came an overwhelming conclusion.

The thing that is before me, she thought, the creature I am following, is not human in any way. She had come to this theoretical conclusion a long time ago. But now she knew that the terror was real, that she wasn't imagining it, that it was something she would have to live with for every remaining day of her life.

Then another image came back to her. That of the manitou, the mythical beast which lured hunters higher and higher up a mountain, then metamorphosed into something supernatural, against which human weapons were useless.

Immediately the manitou would turn upon its pursuer, ripping off limbs and ears as a prelude to eating the pursuer alive. The Xinticali Indians, the inhabitants of this region three hundred years ago, had shared the manitou in their folklore.

Had their manitou come from the sky? Had this area around the clouds been used for landings for thousands of years? she wondered.

In a few minutes, Alicia found herself in a small clear area in the center of the plateau. Large sturdy white stones were scattered around. She blinked. She felt as if she had entered a mystical domain.

"Not from this world," Alicia repeated to herself.

The words were in her mind, however. Not spoken.

Not audible to normal ears.

A heavy moment passed.

Then, "That's a bad thought," said a voice inches away from Alicia's ear. "I'm not a beast."

Alicia whirled.

Her heart walloped her ribs with two tremendous beats, so aberrant and forceful that Alicia thought her heart would take a final kick and stop. Amos had materialized immediately to the left side of her, just out of view until he wanted to be seen.

In his human form. Homicidal-maniac form.

Alicia stepped back.

She attempted to gather herself. She raised her lantern and turned it on. The yellow beam came upward under Amos's face, transforming the little man's features into a grotesque skeletal mask. It was like a Halloween party gone berserk, a monstrous fantasy vision suddenly turned real.

Amos raised a hand to the lantern.

"No lights," he said. "No lights in this place at night."

"I need a light," Alicia said.

"No lights," Amos said again.

He lowered his gaze to the lantern. The beam waned as he looked at it. It quickly dimmed, like a fire doused. Then it was out with a tiny sorrowful poof, like batteries draining before Alicia's eyes.

Alicia lowered the light. The beam was dead.

"Thank you," Amos said.

It dropped from her hand.

Beneath her jacket, Alicia's clothes were soaked with sweat. Her blouse was sticking to her ribs.

"How did you get so close to me? How do you do what you do?" Alicia asked insistently.

She was struck again by the eerie echo of the ambush that had left her on a tenement floor with a bullet in her chest. Once again, she had walked right by the man, if this *was* a man, that she was chasing.

"I can do a lot of things," Amos said simply.

And I can't believe this is happening. Alicia thought. I can't believe it, but it is.

Amos's eyes glowed a little. Like little yellow moons. "That's another bad thought," Amos said.

"What's a bad thought?"

"That you don't believe in me," Amos said.

Alicia flinched at Amos's words, startled beyond belief or explanation.

"How can you read my thoughts?" Alicia asked, realizing that Amos had just done it twice.

"You wouldn't understand."

There were times when Amos's low voice seemed to come up out of the ground. This was one of them.

Alicia could see only what the moonlight and starlight allowed her to see. The place seemed empty. The big white stones came into focus, a whole little army. Some were tall and narrow. Some short and flat. Probably visible from high in the air.

Then it came to her with horror. This *was* a makeshift

landing field. Shrouded by clouds. Protected from human eyes.

"I'm over here." Amos's voice came from directly behind Alicia.

She turned and saw Amos sitting on a long stone that seemed to be worn with age. Alicia took it to be one of the oldest markers on the mountain.

"For hundreds of Eoots," Amos said. "We've used this place for that long. A stopping-off point. A departure point for Earth colonization. A stepping stone to other planets and stars."

"As I thought . . ." she said.

"You're beginning to understand," he said. "Just beginning."

Amos seemed comfortable upon the stone. The little man smiled. For some reason, Alicia could see Amos very well.

"Now you're my guest," Amos said. "So you sit there."

Amos poked a finger outward. He indicated another stone. Alicia understood that she was being asked to sit on it.

Alicia turned but did not yet sit. She was about six feet from Amos, facing him directly, when he morphed back into his silvery alien form. By now, it all seemed so real and natural. What once had terrified her now seemed perfectly ordinary.

Impressive, huh? Amos asked.

It was.

"You're going to take me away, aren't you?" Alicia asked. "My niece and I. You're going to abduct us to another world. Your place?"

Yes.

"Tonight?"

Yes.

Alicia cringed.

"Is Janet there already?"

Janet is beside you.

"What?"

Use your eyes.

Alicia blinked.

Something came into focus a few feet away from her. It was first an unrecognizable human form, then it was Janet. She was standing fully upright, but not breathing. Not budging. A zombie of a girl. Her soul and spirit were somewhere else.

"Oh, God."

This is the past, the present, and the future. All time is static, but also moves. Time can also pass laterally and in reverse. As you've seen.

"I don't understand."

Soon you will. But no one will believe you. That will be your special torment until we come to take you away.

When Alicia finally tore her eyes away from the awful image of Janet, she was startled again. The alien had moved without making a sound. He was now near the base of a larger stone. His almond eyes were upraised toward the sky, searching.

Tonight I depart. But when I return, it will be for you.

"I don't want to go."

The alien turned toward her and for the first time his mouth moved in something akin to an expression, a warped smile.

You already have.

There was a brightness spreading across the plateau. At first Alicia thought that the sensation was only her eyes growing used to the starlight and moonlight. Then she realized it was more. She didn't know the source, but she knew it was coming from somewhere. Yet she had long ceased asking questions that could be answered by Earth physics.

She blinked.

Another shape took form next to Amos. A shape larger than his. From somewhere a truth came upon Alicia. She realized that the form was that of Amos's superior.

Then the shape became human and Madame Karmalakova stood beside the Amos-alien.

Alicia felt as if she had been kicked in the gut. The large woman morphed again, assuming her alien form. Large and silvery, an even more dominating presence than the first alien.

Beside her, two other forms appeared next, shimmering into being.

These forms were humanoid, too, but appeared drowsy and shuffling, like captives. They stood to the side, not far from Madame Olga.

The larger alien, the one that had been Madame Olga, looked to the sky. The plateau on Mount Baldy brightened again until it seemed as if the sun had broken the horizon.

Light everywhere.

But Alicia could see her shadow and knew that the light came from a single source.

She looked to the sky.

Slowly, small at first, a disc took shape, as if slipping through a hole in the firmament. She thought back to the research she had done on flying saucers and realized she was at one with the German travelers in the Himalayas, those who had written biblical text, and Alexander the Great himself.

She knew what she was seeing.

Once she would have doubted.

Not now!

The spaceship grew larger overhead until it was the size of a dinner plate held aloft. Then it came closer and closer and closer. There was no noise. No sensation. Rather, a remarkable smoothness and serenity gripped the entire plateau.

Then the ship was directly over Alicia, hovering maybe two hundred feet above. Yellow—burning canary-yellow—like a massive sun.

She was aware of the ship lowering itself, and a portal opening. She waited for her abduction, wondering if her heart would stop first.

She stared at the four aliens. Amos, Olga, and their captives.

Their almond eyes simmered at her.

Their gazes reflected no friendship. No warmth. Nothing earthly at all.

Then a beam of light absorbed the four voyagers from another place. They faded and were gone.

Alicia, her heart pounding like a kettle drum, waited to be next. She wasn't.

Janet rustled beside her.

Alicia blinked.

The light started to fade ever so slightly. Alicia looked to the ground and saw two human bodies.

John Doe in the Desert.

Billy Sands.

Their human remains.

Above her, the spacecraft began to move. It receded upward very rapidly and the light beam disappeared also. Alicia glanced at her watch and saw that it had stopped again. She wanted to whack her watch and force it to start, but couldn't.

She heard a voice suddenly. Human.

A girl's.

"Aunt Alicia?"

The voice kept speaking . . .

"Aunt Alicia . . . ? Aunt Alicia . . . ? Aunt Alicia . . . ?"

The policewoman felt something very cold run through her. She felt deeply chilled. As chilled as she would be, and maybe even more, if from somewhere out of the darkness of the night at her back, a pair of silvery cold hands had materialized and landed on her shoulders.

She turned slightly to check to see if anything was going to materialize from behind her.

Nothing did.

But the zombielike Janet was trying to move. Alicia wondered if Janet was dead or alive. Then Janet rolled her eyes upward in their sockets, exposing only the whites, which seemed to glow with a bright yellowish gleam.

The vision jolted Alicia once again. Her mouth felt very dry. She felt herself tumbling through time and space, all rational bearings gone.

"Help me," she whispered.

But no one could.

Janet's voice again. "Here. Aunt Alicia, here!"

Alicia squinted, her head throbbing and aching. Involuntarily she extended her arm. Janet placed a telescope in her aunt's hand.

"People come from the sky," the little girl said. "Honest. I know they're there."

Alicia accepted the telescope. She closed one eye and squinted with the other. She drew a breath and stood up straight. She raised the scope to her eye and pointed it toward the heavens. Toward the stars.

She tried to find the spacecraft. She tried hard.

Then she found a part of the sky that was brighter than the rest and knew she was close.

Then, with a flash, she found it.

Yes. I'm here. And I'll be back for you.

The flash was stunningly bright. Like a little minisun, punching its beams through the telescope and into Alicia's brain.

Déjà vu. An overwhelming sense . . . she had traveled a long, long journey and was somehow back in the place where she had begun.

The light in the sky was—

So stunningly bright that it made Alicia's eye blink shut and stay shut. Her head snapped back and her brain throbbed.

It was like being punched. Or poked in the eye.

A brilliant yellow flash. A minisun. A brilliant yellow glowing disc embedded in her brain.

Almost a strobe-light effect from a strange hole in the sky.

"Wow," she said.

"Auntie…? Janet asked.

Alicia still reeled. Her eyes blinked but couldn't remain open. They hurt too badly.

She settled onto the ground.

"Auntie…Auntie…Auntie…?"

The girlish, childish voice persisted. "What was it?" Janet asked. "What happened?"

Alicia braced herself, a bare knee to the grassy surface of the back lawn of her sister's home. "Something in the sky," she said, as if talking through a haze. "I don't know what it was. I don't know what I saw."

But she knew how bright it had been. And it had jangled something very deeply in her brain. As Alicia blinked and took her niece's hand, she knew something strange had happened. Something that defied reasonable explanation.

Her eyes returned to normal, little blue dots dancing everywhere, bizarre visions in her mind. A nearly comprehensible vision of a humanlike form stepping out of sunlight.

Maybe. She wasn't sure.

"Auntie…?"

"I'm all right," Alicia said softly. "I don't know what happened, but I'm all right."

Janet stared at her. Soft childish eyes asking her questions.

"Hey," Alicia said. She looked around.

A hole in time and space had opened and Alicia had tumbled back through.

It was a Sunday afternoon. She was in the backyard of her sister's house and the birthday party for Janet was still in progress.

Linda emerged from the house.

The little girl forced a smile.

Alicia stood on the lawn stunned. A whole vision, an entire scenario of events, had cascaded into her head in a second and she could not rightly dismiss them.

Linda speaking: "Ali? You okay?"

"I'm fine."

"You don't seem fine."

"Auntie saw something in the sky," said Janet.

"What did you see?" Linda asked. "Ali?"

For another instant time seemed to stop again. Then the policewoman shook her head. Nothing in her training had ever prepared her for this. Not even a near-death experience.

"I don't know," she said. "I couldn't even begin to tell you."

Silence for a moment.

"You better get moving," Linda said. "What was the call about? A body out in the high desert?"

Alicia shuddered involuntarily, a silent scream for help that only she could hear.

"Yeah," she said. "Who knows where that's going to lead?"

"Who *ever* knows?" Linda agreed.

The little girl giggled. Her birthday party was still in progress and the May afternoon was dying.

CHAPTER 33

Two months later, Alicia sat on a bench in Santa Monica, overlooking the Pacific Ocean, trying to put the proper spin on her life and, to a lesser degree, the images that continued to unravel within her head.

A bag of her personal belongings sat by her feet.

She was on psychiatric sick leave from the California Highway Patrol. And likely to stay there. Once again, Alicia was looking at contradictions, contradictions as vast as the ocean in front of her.

There were no answers.

Only speculation and haunting suspicions, theories of the extraterrestrial that found no receptive ears other than her fellow members of the Ammon Society. So she could mention these to no one who didn't, well "understand."

Then there were the frequent reawakenings each night from an uneasy sleep, when she would scan her surroundings to reassure herself that she was alone.

That she had seen a space alien and had witnessed the arrival of a flying saucer, complete with alien beings, she had no question. That the King of the Sun, as he had called himself, would return for her and take her away, was a given also.

She had told the psychiatrists with the police department about that. They hadn't much cared for her account of things.

She had driven Ed Van Allen out to Malibu to find Madame Olga's aluminum palace, but it had been reduced to rubble by an earthquake—or something—and Madame Olga had moved on.

No forwarding address.

"That's because she's somewhere up in the sky," Alicia had said. "I saw her leave one night from Mount Baldy. She left in her extraterrestrial form."

Even Van Allen had rolled his eyes over that one, suggesting instead that Madame Karmalakova may have simply returned to San Francisco, where she would fit right in, ET-form or no.

It had been Van Allen, her best friend, in fact, who had gently led her to the psychiatric case worker. A few strings were pulled and Alicia was allowed to leave her employment on full disability. Not bad, since she wasn't paying rent anymore, either.

"Mental stress over a near-fatal injury," said the State of California report.

Alicia tried to explain it differently, but Ed, at the final hearing with her, hushed her.

Exactly what explanation lay beneath Alicia's encounter with the King of the Sun, she had no way of knowing. Her previous life experience had no way of interpreting it, nor did her religion. Christianity and spiritualism were at loggerheads with the extraterrestrial, though perhaps they shouldn't have been.

She watched the water before her.

Seeing Amos Joy, being yanked out of her previous reality by an alien, was both the best thing that could have happened to her as well as the worst.

On one hand, the existence of the alien suggested the euphoric notion of a vast and spectacular universe. And yet on the other hand, it called into question everything she and everyone else on earth had ever believed.

She sighed. More contradiction. That's all life was: contradiction.

In her mind, events spiraled.

The effect of all the past months' events settled upon her as a melancholy haze. Through it, she tried to find some light, some illumination to guide the rest of her life. She figured it might take years, if ever, before she could make that discovery.

A gentle breeze from the Pacific caressed Alicia's forehead as she sat in perfect physical comfort on the bench.

A woman's voice intruded, jostling her slightly from her reverie.

"Is this seat free?" a stranger asked in heavily accented English, indicating the spot near Alicia.

"Make yourself comfortable," Alicia said.

The woman, a sturdy foreign-born female in overalls and a checked shirt, sat down and opened a paper bag, preparing to eat her lunch.

Alicia smelled fish. The woman had smoked trout.

Alicia began to laugh.

The woman looked to Alicia. They exchanged a smile.

Very vaguely, the visitor looked like the missing Madame Olga. Then, the more Alicia studied her, the more the woman's features shifted into place. The more she fell into the image of the brilliant Madame Olga.

Alicia laughed again.

"Share the joke with me, honey," the big woman said gruffly.

Alicia shielded her eyes from the sun.

"You remind me of someone I knew once," Alicia said. "A big lady who took off into the night in a spaceship."

The woman in overalls didn't miss a chew. She wasn't happy, either. "Is that right?"

"That's right."

Alicia pondered the point.

"Went off into the sky with a little homicidal maniac. Hey, diddle diddle, a bull dyke with a fiddle went off to do a fruit on the moon."

"Yeah?"

Long pause. Alicia continued. "They're coming back someday. I know it."

"That right," the woman said, eating faster now.

"That's right."

A longer pause.

"I used to be a cop," Alicia said. "I'm on disability now."

"Still got your gun?"

"No," Alicia said. "They took it."

"That's a good thing," the big woman said.

"No, it's not. You just never know what's going to appear in the middle of the night."

"Uh-huh."

"Ever traveled in space yourself?" Alicia asked.

The second woman assembled her lunch back into its bag.

"No, but I can see you have," the woman answered. "Damned homeless crazies," she muttered to herself. "They ought to throw all of you into the ocean."

"Jesus Christ may have been a space traveler, too," Alicia added. "Think about it. Jesus Christ as Luke Skywalker."

The woman heaved a sigh and gave Alicia a final look before turning and departing for another bench farther down the beach. Alicia watched as she fell into conversation with a man on the next bench. A moment later, following some words from the woman, they both looked at Alicia and laughed.

Alicia looked back out to the ocean and to the horizon above.

She sat and calmly waited, knowing that her wait could take years, and that few people would speak to her with any seriousness in the interim.

She knew the inner truth of what she had seen and experienced. She knew what reality was and that earth physics did not apply to the universe.

She knew everything that most people didn't.

She had bathed in a public shelter two days earlier. In the shower, she had found a small tattoo on her thigh . . . She had seen the tattoo before but it had never made sense. Now it was readily comprehensible.

Several small dots indicating planets and a big yellow circle, standing for the sun.

A personal map of the solar system, right there on the flesh.

She could not remember whether she had stumbled into a tattoo parlor and asked for such a thing, or if it had appeared by itself.

Illusion, reality.

Where did one end and the other begin?

And at her final medical tests leaving the police force, the doctors had found that funny space chemical—chrolystron—in her lungs.

How to explain that? Alicia had tried to explain, but the docs wouldn't listen.

The day died.

Alicia had nowhere to go. She lived on the street, talking to strangers at random, carrying her bag, all her money in a wallet.

She alone knew the truth. And she kept the truth with

her as she sat on a bench alone, watching the sun sink into the ocean and then watching the stars emerge.

Waiting . . . and hearing a familiar silvery voice.

Waiting . . . but not forever.

She knew he, "the King of the Sun," would return.

And when he did, Alicia would be ready for her great journey into the stars.

About the Author

A.A. McFedries is a pseudonym. The author resides in California.